Talio

To my daughter
Anne
with love from
Dad.

6-8-2020

Talio

JOHN NELSON DAINES

ISBN:	Softcover	978-1-6641-1218-6
	eBook	978-1-6641-1217-9

Print information available on the last page.

Rev. date: 07/27/2020

To order additional copies of this book, contact:
Xlibris
UK TFN: 0800 0148620 (Toll Free inside the UK)
UK Local: 02036 956328 (+44 20 3695 6328 from outside the UK)
www.Xlibrispublishing.co.uk
Orders@Xlibrispublishing.co.uk
816672

Chapter 1

The sun was setting in the West as Harold walked the battlements at Wymondham. He had not wanted to leave his family at Vent. He missed his fathers firm hand and wisdom even though he also felt the sharpness of his tongue, this was tempered by his mothers gentle and loving kindness to him. What would his sister be doing now? There was a void that could be filled only by her tinkling laugh. As a dutiful son he had obeyed his father and with his brother, Edmund, he had returned to take care of the family estates. Edmund was excited as he always yearned for travel and to be active. As he walked the idea came to him that his father might have been preparing them for their future.

Looking out over the parapet he spotted a rider approaching the castle. The man was in a hurry as he pushed his mount on towards the drawbridge. Harold descended to the bailey where he met the man who gave him despatches from London and said he was to open them as soon as possible.

Harold went up to his room and quickly unsealed the first. This was a letter from the Lady Ann informing him that Queen Isabella, with Roger Mortimer, had landed and was collecting an army from her friends and supporters. He opened the other two dispatches and found one was from the king calling him to arms to protect him from the invading force and the other was from a family friend at court.

This message had the latest date and had the news that the Dispensers had been captured and killed and Edward was a prisoner.

The young man sat in his father's study and penned a message to Sir John. He suggested that it might be a good idea to sell the house in London and keep to themselves in East Anglia.

Calling a messenger to him, he gave him the missive and sent him on his way to the French Chateaux Vent, where Sir John and the rest of the family, apart from Edmund, were staying. The latest events in London could alter all their lives. With a new king in London who knows what changes would take place. Harold called for a page to have his horse saddled at first light so he would ride to Dunston to discuss the situation with Edmund.

The following morning Harold rode at a steady trot, eating up the miles to Dunston. The weather was fine and he could see workers in the fields, some of whom waved. His fathers plans to encourage the tenants to work together for the common good was successful in most areas. The Earl wanted all his tenants to treat their workers fairly, he wanted them to work for a common good so that each man shared equal work for equal return and live in harmony. Some of the tenants however preferred to work for their own interests and retain the old serf system where workers had no rights and just did their lord's bidding. It was the fear that some tenants would return to the old ways that had prompted Sir John to send Harold home and report back.

Harold came out of the wood and could see activity around the moat of Dunston castle. The drawbridge was down and he rode into the bailey and found Edmund practicing with his sword against one of the guards. Harold could use sword and bow efficiently but Edmund excelled with both. Harold was more of a thinker and organiser, attributes that would stand him well in the future.

'Greetings, brother,' said Edmund as Harold dismounted. 'What news do you bring?' Harold explained the news from London while they walked into the castle.'I have passed this on to father,' Harold explained. Sitting in the castle they discussed the messages that had been sent to him. Reports from France had also brought news of a spreading sickness there.

'It is time that Father brought the rest of the family home,' said Edmund. 'I have pleaded with him in my report to do just that,' replied Harold. They decided to start the tour of the tenants in the morning.

The following day started with clear skies. They gathered together their escort and rode out to the farms. On their way east, towards the Fens and the coast, they found most of the tenants were pleased to see them and had been managing the farms well. Harold noticed that Edmund's mind wandered, he was more interested in reaching the coast to find smugglers than discussing improvement for their lands.

In Yarmouth they stayed with the mayor, he brought them up to date with the details of their shipments of wool. Harold studied the papers, finding no fault and complimented the mayor on looking after their interests. Edmund fidgeted through dinner and was obviously keen to take a walk down to the harbour.

'Take care down there, and stay away from French boats as they say there is a pestilence in France,' warned the mayor. Edmund agreed he would be careful.

'Take two men with you,' said Harold. 'It is a rough area.' Edmund nodded, calling to the men as he buckled on his sword.

There was a mist settling over the docks as they wound their way down to the moored ships. Passing a noisy public house they were accosted by a couple of girls inviting them to join them but Edmund strode on towards the harbour. Skirting the French ships he found one that had arrived from Flanders.

'Is your captain on board?' he asked a sailor. 'No Sir, he is down at the Anchor Inn, just through that passageway there,' answered the sailor.

Edmund and his companions followed his directions and found a dirty looking building with an old sign telling them it was indeed the Anchor Inn. Pushing open the door they entered a smoke filled room that was bursting at the seams with carousing sailors. Seated in a corner they spotted a man slightly better dressed than most. Pushing their way though the throng they introduced themselves and found it was indeed the captain they were looking for. After his initial surprise the captain said he was chartered by the Kortrijt family and had loaded bales of wool from Sir John Ivanson's estate. Edmund introduced himself and the captain said he was pleased to meet him as the shipment was not as large as he had expected. Edmund explained that he had only recently returned to Norfolk and assured him that he would investigate the smaller cargoes. After talking with the captain a little longer he left the tavern with his two companions. The mist was quite thick as they stood outside the Anchor Inn. 'We will find the warehouse to see how much is stored there,' said Edmund. They turned to go further along the alleyway when Edmund remembered it was the way to the back door of the warehouse. Two men stepped out from a side alley and even in the gloom Edmund could see the glint of steel in their hands. Turning, to make their way back to the Inn, they encountered three more men had stepped out of the Anchor and blocked their retreat. 'Watch your backs men,' said Edmund as all five ruffians approached them. Edmund turned toward the two and drew his sword, while his two companions faced the three from the Inn. A loud clash of steel on steel resounded in the passage as the men slashed and stabbed at each other. The ruffians soon realised they were outclassed especially when one of them went down from a thrust of Edmund's sword. The remaining four tried to run but Edmund was too quick for one of them and he fell mortally wounded. People were starting to come out of the Inn as two of the mayor's guards arrived. One of the men slipped through the crowd but the other two were cornered and held by the guards. Edmund was recognised as the mayor's guest by the guards and suggested he went back to the mayor and a report would be given later.

When they returned Harold fussed over them like a mother hen. Edmund calmed him and said he was more interested in what the captain had said about smaller shipments. Harold said an inspection of the warehouse would be made in the morning.

They rose early the next day and were soon on their way to the warehouse. On checking the records Harold realised there was less wool coming from the tenants than there should be. They decided to go on to Lowestoft to find out if the same problem was there. Fortunately Harold found that in that port, the wool from the tenants was similar to the previous year.

Edmund rode down to the docks. Seeing the ships moored there he felt an urge to travel, to go onto any ship and see where it landed. One of the ships had arrived from Spain, a country unknown to Edmund. He listened to the strange language of the sailors. Some words he could understand as they sounded a little like Latin. Arriving back at the Inn where they were staying, he asked Harold if he knew anything about Spain. 'Only what I have read and been taught by the monks,' replied his brother. 'It is very hot there they say.'

The two young men returned to Dunston where Harold called the reeve and questioned him about who might be sending less wool to Yarmouth.

Chapter 2

Harold was deep in thought as he gazed out of the window in the great hall. A few minutes passed before his eyes focussed on a large cart, drawn by two horses, approaching the castle. Six outriders accompanied the vehicle, they were well armed and continuously glanced around. What was in the cart that required such close guarding, thought Harold?

As he descended the stairs to the bailey the men were dismounting from their horses. One of them turned towards Harold and introduced himself as Andre Trouville. The Trouville family looked after the Vent estate when Sir John was in England. 'You are welcome, come inside and tell me news of my family,' said Harold. The Frenchman sat down opposite Harold and said, 'I am sorry to bring you sad news. Sir John and Lady Tania with their daughter Ceolwen had succumbed to the plague that has been sweeping France. My friends and I were away fighting in the North. When we returned only Sir John was still alive, he asked us to bring his possessions home to you. He passed peacefully away just before we left. I have this message he sent to you.' The man handed Harold a parchment. Harold was struck dumb for a moment, then rose and walked to the window. Opening the message he read his father's last letter to him. 'Thank you for bringing these to me. Please follow my Steward who will find accommodation for you.'

Harold gazed at the boxes that had been brought into the Hall. It was known that a pestilence had been moving across France, there was fear that it would reach the English shores before long. Harold approached a long box and undid the fastenings. Lifting the lid he exposed three long bundles. He opened one to disclose his father's long bow, another revealed the sword in its scabbard. Harold gently lifted out the weapon and drew the blade. It shone as though it had just been made. He read the inscriptions on the blade, felt the balance in his hand then returned it to the scabbard. Searching further he uncovered a fine dagger and a small purse. Inside the purse was a gold ring which he had seen on his fathers hand.

'I must get this news to Edmund,' he said to himself. Calling for a guard Harold sent him post haste to his brother with the message to come as quickly as he could. Searching through the rest of the boxes he uncovered his father's armour, shield, but no lance. There were very little of his mothers possessions, some pieces of jewellery and shoes. Harold picked up the sword again and withdrew it from the scabbard. He did a practice swing and felt nothing special. Going down to the Bailey he called a guard over and said he would like to spar with him for a few minutes. He soon called a halt as he felt no difference than sparing with his own sword. Placing the ring on his finger they started again but there was no difference. Father must just have been a very good swordsman he thought.

There was talk that the sword was magical and had a power of its own. Sir John had become a swordsman of renown and many men had died from this blade in his hands. His reason for going to France was to search for information about the weapon the sword was made from, and its previous owner. Was there a connection between the ring and the sword? Inside the ring there were strange writings in a language that looked like some Arabic writing that Harold had seen. The sword had been made by his grandfather, his father had told him the old smith had made it from a strange shaped sword brought back from the Holy Land when he returned from a crusade. Harold returned the weapon to its scabbard and placed it back in the box.

No doubt these tales were told to create a mystery around the blade and strike fear into an opponent.

Edmund arrived the following day and Harold explained all the news. Edmund went up to the battlements to try to come to terms with the loss of his family, especially his father. Over the last few days they were together in France he had fenced with his father and had borrowed his sword. He had felt the superb balance of the blade and wanted to wear the ring as well but his father had refused and said he would have to wait. Would Harold let him have the weapon? Edmund longed for adventure, looking after Dunston and its estates was stifling him. If he left who would take care of Dunston? Something I need to put my mind to, he thought. He left the battlements to find Harold, it was time for serious talking.

After dinner the two brothers sat in front of the fire, both quiet as neither of them had the words to start the conversation. At last Harold spoke. 'You are the better fighter, I am probably the more organised,' which brought a smile to Edmund's face. 'I am sure father would want you to have his fighting equipment.' Edmund sat still waiting for the next pronouncement. 'I will take over the running of our estates,' continued Harold. 'This will leave you free to organise and train our fighting men. This will give us a formidable force should the king need us and also better protection for ourselves. As the eldest son I will become the Earl so it all fits. What are your thoughts?' Edmund pondered for a moment and then said, 'The money created from the estates and our wool contracts would provide for all that our military would need?' 'Yes,' said Harold. 'Will you want me to live at Dunston or here?' asked Edmund. 'I think it would be better if you were here. Most of the fighting men are in this Castle or in the Villages near here and we have the better training facilities.' 'That makes sense, but who will be in charge at Dunston?' asked Edmund. 'That is something we must resolve and quickly,' said Harold. 'There is Stephen, now he is a Knight it would be good to give him more responsibilities,' volunteered Edmund. 'That is the answer. He can move over there and we can see how he takes to the job. He will need help for a while but I am sure you would be able to do that,' said Harold. 'We will talk to him tomorrow.'

Harold felt pleased with the situation as it had evolved and started to plan for the future. His main disappointment was that he could not retrieve his father's body from France and have it buried here in Wymondham. The deaths in that country were mounting Harold was concerned that no-one brought it over on one of the ships. Yarmouth and Lowestoft had tightened their watch for anyone showing signs of sickness.

Harold spoke to Edmund of his concern regarding his position as Earl. He assumed he automatically became the new Earl as he was the eldest son and Edmund agreed. This would have to be ratified by the countries ruler, whoever that might be in these troubled times, and the Lord Chancellor.

Riding back to Dunston the following morning Edmund thought about his new role. He did prefer fighting to organising the farms and he always appeared to get himself in knots when he was dealing with the accounts. Still a young man his body was developing fast. He was already taller than his brother and more muscular. His loves were his horses and practicing with the various weapons he had.

Dismounting in the bailey Edmund asked the whereabouts of Sir Stephen. 'He is on the battlements, lord,' replied a groom. On his way up to the top of the castle he thought how all the men in the family used the battlements to think. Stephen turned as Edmund approached. 'Did you have a good visit with your brother?' Edmund told him of his families deaths in France. Stephen was saddened as he liked Sir John who had treated him as a family member. 'Yes, we discussed many things and one of them concerns you,' said Edmund. 'We would like you to take on the responsibility of Dunston Castle and it's tenants.' Stephen was quiet for a moment and then said, 'I am honoured that you think me capable and I will do my best to continue the work that your father started.'

Edmund breathed a sigh of relief and they both went into the Castle and celebrated at the evening meal. The next days were spent in going over the accounts of the Castle and making plans to visit the farms.

Chapter 3

Edmund was sad in some ways to leave Dunston, he visited the smithy and his grandparents home. The village had changed under his fathers time as the lord. Tenant cottages had been improved, field hands were happier as they knew that they were working for a better life for all of them.

He hoped that Harold had the same ideas as their father and continued to improve the lives of all who dwelt in their estates.

Edmund implemented a tough training schedule for his men, and himself. One of his men, a villager called Gareth, was proving to be the best swordsman, he was also more intelligent than most. Edmund strapped on his fathers sword and slid the ring onto his finger. He said to Gareth. 'Spar with me but hold nothing back, I need a good workout.' Edmund drew his sword and Gareth made the first moves. Edmund found the sword easy to use, he felt the balance allowing him to move freely. Gareth became bolder and advanced on Edmund using all his skill to finish the fight. Edmund was driven back and had to defend himself, he began to feel a little annoyed that he was under threat from a man he had trained. With a determined parry he moved aggressively out of a corner and suddenly in a blur of strokes Gareth found himself without his weapon which had been neatly whipped out of his hand. Edmund's sword point was near Gareth's throat before he could stop. Edmund stood back shaking,

Gareth had gone white and leant against the wall, the rest of the men who were watching went completely quiet. 'Are you all right?' said Edmund. Gareth said he was as the sword had not actually touched him. Edmund sheathed his sword and felt heat from the ring on his finger. 'I am sorry if I scared you,' he said to Gareth. 'I am not quite sure what happened, everything went so fast.' 'So did your swordplay Sir,' said one of the men. 'It is my fathers sword,' explained Edmund. 'The one they say has magic?' said Gareth. 'I shall have to be more careful when I use it,' answered Edmund. They crowded round him and asked to see the weapon, which he drew from its scabbard. 'What does the writing say?' asked Gareth. Edmund sat on step and told them how his grandfather had forged the blade and engraved the inscriptions on it. 'I hope I never have to fight against you in battle,' said Gareth. 'Stay with us and you won't have to worry,' replied Edmund.

Going back into the castle, Edmund went up to his room and tried on the armour. He was tall enough but lacked some of the bulk that was needed. I can wear an extra tunic, he thought. With the extra padding he felt like a stuffed dummy but it worked and he clumped around his room making thrusts at imaginary foe.

Later, in his favourite place, the battlements, he thought about how he would organise his fighting men. Gareth was good enough to lead a group of horsemen, he now needed someone to lead the archers. This group were most important as they have the ability to reduce the number of enemy the rest must face. Tomorrow they would have a day at the butts where he could see how his men performed. This responsibility had made Edmund a more thoughtful and conscientious man and Harold had noticed this and was pleased at his brother's growth. He hoped that this would make Edmund settle down to working with him and building up their fiefdom. He knew Edmund liked adventure and often talked of other countries.

Harold made contact with some of his fathers old friends in London and York. In a lot of cases it was their sons who answered and Harold started to build his own network of informants. His main concern was the effect Queen Isabella was having on some of his fathers friends. There was certainly an undercurrent of unrest against the queen's rule. From his contacts Harold knew that the queen and her lover, Mortimer, were coming to Northampton.

Edmund practiced every day with his sword and became unbeatable against his guards. The weapon appeared part of him as he danced around his opponents and his men were relieved when he decided to practice with his bow.

'The sword should have a name,' said Edmund to Harold. 'Call it what you like,' replied his brother. Edmund went up to the battlements to think, he wanted a name that would be respectful to his father and take into account the inscriptions on the blade. He knew that St Dustan was a fighter against evil and the castle took its name from him. Naming a killing weapon after a saint would not be right. He thought about the purpose of the sword. To right wrongs, to bring retribution to evil men. 'I have it,' he said to himself, 'Talio' I shall call it. (Latin for retribution) He swung the blade and fought imaginary foes on the battlements still marvelling at the balance and the way the weapon fitted into his hand. Holding the sword to the sky he called out. 'From henceforth you are Talio, my protector and retribution to all who are evil!'

Edmund collected twenty of his men and departed for a patrol of the boundaries, complete with baggage cart as he did not want to stay with tenants. They headed west towards Swaffham and camped for the night outside the town.

Edmund, with Gareth as companion, rode into the town. It was a quiet night and not many townspeople were abroad. 'We will visit that Inn,' said Edmund. They could hear the noise of the barroom as they approached this stopped immediately as they entered.

'What can I serve you with, good sirs?' Enquired the landlord. 'Two jugs of your ale, please,' said Edmund. They found a seat in a corner of the room as the conversations started up again. The main topic was the treaty that had been signed in Northampton, the general view was that it was unpopular. The bar tender came over to them and said. 'Can I bring you more ale sirs? I can see you are gentlemen and I have a special barrel that I am sure you will enjoy.' 'No thank you,' said Edmund. 'We shall be on our way.' He stood and made his way to the door. Several pairs of eyes followed them and they heard someone remark that they were too well dressed for a place like this.

'Keep your wits about you,' said Edmund as he tested that his sword was free. They reached camp without incident and Edmund posted guards as a precaution, which proved to be the right decision as a group of riders were spotted approaching the camp.

When they arrived Edmund found himself confronted by the lord of the manor. 'Who are you, and why are you camped with your armed men near my town?'

Edmund explained that they were on a ride around the fiefdom and that he was the Earl's son. 'Then you should have come openly to me. Swaffham is my town and I have not seen the Earl for many months, rumour has it he is not in this country.' Edmund realised his error and tried to explain that they did not want to cause any fuss as they made their journey. 'I also have to tell you that my father died of the plague in France. My brother Harold will inherit the title and is preparing to visit all the land owners and tenants very soon.'

'I am sorry to hear of Sir John's death, he was a fair man with progressive plans for the shire.' continued Sir Walter. 'Please come back with me and stay with us. Your men may shelter in my barn.'

'Thank you sir,' said Edmund. 'It will certainly better than sleeping rough. I apologise for not making myself known to you. I was attempting to gain an unbiased view of the shire.' Sir Walter smiled and thought Edmund was spying on him.

Sir Walter led them to his Manor House, Edmund and Gareth were invited inside and his men were taken to the barn. Gareth was a little nervous being in the company of nobility, Edmund realised this and kept him close.

Sir Walter introduced Edmund to his wife and daughter, a comely girl slightly younger than Edmund. They all sat at the table as food was brought, Edmund soon relaxed. He found Sir Walter an interesting man who had followed his father's method of cooperative farming.

'Not all the land owners have agreed to your fathers methods, they will learn in time that it reaps dividends. Will you work with your brother improving the shire?'

Edmund, a little taken aback said he had taken the role of improving the fighting men, Harold was much better at organisation and he would soon take responsibility for the shire as the Earl.

'There are some that will oppose that,' said Sir Walter. 'Until we have a king on the throne again there will be turmoil in the country.'

'We shall need a strong force of fighting men if we are to protect our lands, the work I am doing with the help of men like Gareth, will be useful,' commented Edmund.

'Men are always thinking of fighting,' said Mary, the lord's daughter.

'It is necessary at times to keep you safe, my dear,' said her father. 'I must away to my bed as I am to go to Nottingham tomorrow and attend our king.'

The following morning Edmund and his group said farewell to Sir Walter and left for Wymondham. Edmund began to query Sir Walters statement that he was going to attend the king, as far as he had been informed on their return Queen Isabella and Mortimer were still ruling the country. One of the outriders came back to report that a large group of horsemen were coming towards them. Edmund went up to the nearest vantage point and could just make out the colours on the pennants.

'I think it is the mark of William of Holt,' he said. 'We will meet him in that meadow.' Sir William's group arrived to find Edmund across the road blocking their path.

'Who is this who stops a lord of this shire?' 'Edmund of Wyndham, what is your hurry?'

Sir William rode up to Edmund 'I remember, you are Sir John's son. I heard all the family had gone to France.'

Edmund explained his fathers death and that Harold was now the new Earl.

Sir William told Edmund that Edward and his supporters had captured Isabella and Mortimer and pronounced himself king

Chapter 4

At home in Wymondham, over a meal that night, Edmund told Harold all that had happened to him. 'You should have discussed your plans with me before you went,' said Harold.

'You are always too busy,' replied Edmund. 'The men needed to get out and ride the countryside.'

'I am to go to Nottingham at the kings order. Get together enough men that would escort an Earl, a show of strength would be in order. I mean to have my position ratified as soon as possible. There may be some opposition.'

They departed the following morning with a large entourage, banners flying with Harold and Edmund in armour. People came out and cheered as they progressed through the villages. After several days march they reached the city of Nottingham.

The streets were crowded and Edmund could feel an excitement in the air. Keeping his men together they reached the castle. Marshals directed them to ground where they could make camp. After refreshing themselves the two brothers, accompanied by their squires went up to the castle. Knights and nobles were milling about in the ante rooms adding to the general confusion. Harold pushed his way into the anteroom to the kings quarters with Edmund following.

A steward came out of the king's room and called 'Sir John Ivanson.' Harold stepped forward and said. 'That is my father sir, unfortunately he cannot be here, I come to represent him.'

'I know the young man, I am Sir William de Bohun, Earl of Northampton. Where is your father young man?' Harold replied. 'Sadly our father is no longer with us sire, he died in France from the plague.' There was a murmur from those present and exchange of looks. 'I am saddened by this news, if I can be of any assistance just ask,' said Sir William. The fussy little Steward ushered Harold into the room with Edmund close behind. The found themselves in front of a young man, no older than Edmund, sitting in a large chair wearing a crown. The brothers bowed low and waited for the king to speak.

'Where is your father, we wished to speak with him?' Harold explained the circumstances of his fathers death and that he, as the eldest son, had inherited his fathers position, subject his majesties agreement.

'Yes, yes. It saddens me to loose a good friend of the crown, we assume we can now rely on your support,' said the king. 'We look to the new Earl to be like his father was. We will visit you soon, as we are interested in the farming methods you have developed.'

Harold bowed and said he would be most welcome.

'We shall be calling on you to assist us very soon,' continued the king.

The audience being finished the brothers withdrew. Back in the antechamber Harold noticed two or three men were scowling at him whereas most wanted to know what had happened to Sir John. Sir William de Bohun asked Harold if he might visit him to which Harold agreed.

'I am glad to be out of there,' said Edmund when they were on their journey home.

'Too much intrigue and trying to be in the favour of the king,' agreed Harold. 'It will be interesting to talk to Sir William when he comes.'

One night sitting around the fire Harold asked how the men were performing. "Are they ready for battle?'

'Ready and wanting to try out our new manoeuvres,' said Edmund `he started to explain some of his tactics to Harold, the Earl, however soon lost interest and Edmund fell silent.

'They may not have to wait for long. The king is marching on Scotland very soon and has asked us to be ready to join him.'

'A long trek before we fight, when are we to be ready?'

Harold replied that there would be a meeting of the shires in this area, the date to be sometime in the next two months. In fact it was only six weeks and they received the order to join the army at Grantham.

Edmund assembled his group, he had1000 fighting men and a further 700 who came in from the villages. There was a lot of excited chatter as they set off Edmund guessed this was due to nerves as only a few of them had seen battle before, himself included.

The army had spread itself over the fields outside the town, the mayor had imposed a strict curfew within the walls which did not go down too well with the men. Edmund settled his contingent and then reported to the camp commander.

Their march north was uneventful until they reached Bamburgh Castle where Edward left Queen Philippa. Marching on to Berwick they met stiff resistance from the town and eventually put it under siege. A large Scottish army was approaching from the north and Edward positioned himself on a hill where he could see the town and the surrounding countryside. The Scots had to advance to the English over boggy ground and then climb the hill. They struggled in the mire and the English archers let loose. Some made it to the English front but were in no condition to fight and the English pressed forward. Edmund and his men were soon fighting. Edmund drew Talio and with the ring warm on his finger struck out at the foe. This was the first time Talio had been used in battle, the blade was a blinding whirlwind of steel and no-one could stand against him. Edmund felt that the blade was in control of him rather than the other way round. They chased the Scots down the hill as they ran for Scotland. Edmund stood gasping for breath, a mounted knight pulled his horse to a stop and leaned down. 'A dozen more like you sir and we won't need an army.'

Later in the camp many men passed Edmund and complemented him on his fighting. He sat and tried to understand what had happened. Gareth said he had never seen anything like it and it proved the sword had magic in it. Edmund wondered why his father had not explained this to him in more detail.

The next day Edmund gathered his troops together, fortunately they had only lost three men in the battle. 'We are going home, there is no more fighting here. Our homes and families need us.' He went to the king's marshall and explained he and the men were required at home urgently for the harvest and sheering or there would be no money for the taxes. They set off on the their trek back to Wymondham.

Nearing home the men were in good spirits making up songs about their young leader. They were full of praise of his fighting skills and Gareth remarked that this had bonded the men together. Edmund had grown up fast on this trip he had learnt a lot from the older men who had seen battles before, even so they responded to his leadership.

When Edmund returned to the castle Harold met him and was eager to know the news. He had to wait until their meal before Edmund could relax and recount all that had happened.

'The king will be pleased the Scots have been sent back,' said Harold.

'I don't think he will stop there. Once he has fortified the borders he will go on north until he has defeated them once and for all,' replied Edmund.

'It is time we got the estate back to where it was when father left it,' said Harold. 'We need to know how much wool is going to Flanders, are the cattle in good health and are the crops growing and being cultivated well? Tomorrow pick out some men to accompany you. I will stay here as there is still much to do.'

Edmund rode out in the morning with three hundred men and the Reeve, he wanted a show of strength to the villagers. Reaching the fens he searched for Aelfraed. When he reached Aelfraed's village the leader was sitting with his back to a hut quietly smoking a pipe. "Good morrow sir,' said Edmund. 'I hope I am not intruding, I would like to talk to you.'

'Step down, young man and tell me news of your father. Has he returned from his travels?' Edmund sadly related the news of his fathers death. Aelfraed was shocked at the news he immediately offered Edmund any help he needed, although their part of the fens had suffered badly from the plague and he was short of men. The young man explained they were trying to find out why the wool going from Yarmouth was less than it used to be.

'It might be a good idea to check the beach between Yarmouth and Lowestoft. It used to be a favourite place for smugglers to land their contraband. If it is a good spot to bring goods in then it is a good spot to send goods out, without being seen.'

Edmund thanked him and made plans to visit the area the following night. With the men bedded down Edmund walked around the village. He noticed Aelfraed had posted guards and wondered if this was his usual procedure? The men acknowledged him as he walked by and he could see they were well armed. They would be a useful addition to his force if the need arose.

He made his way back to his quarters to plan his strategy for the coming encounter. He was deep in thought when Aelfraed asked if he might speak with him.

'I shall be glad of your company,' said the knight.

'I know there is some unrest with some tenants in the south of your estates, it is being stirred up by some peasants from Essex. They say they are not getting a fair share of the wealth of the farms,' explained Aelfraed

'That is not true as you know,' protested Edmund. 'If I find any lord of the manor defying my fathers way of sharing the wealth among his workers he will be brought to a reckoning.'

They discussed the situation for a time and Edmund told Aelfraed his plan. Parting Edmund tried to rest.

Chapter 5

The morning dawned bright and with clear skies. Edmund assembled his men and they moved off towards Yarmouth. Aelfraed sent one of his sons as a guide and he led them out of the sight of Yarmouth towards the village of Hopton. They camped at the old Roman fort and waited for nightfall.

In the twilight just before the total darkness of night Edmund split his forces sending some towards Yarmouth to approach the beach from the north and a group towards Lowestoft to come up from the south. He retained a third of his force to accompany him to the cliff edge and survey the beach. The men secreted themselves in the long grasses and bushes while Edmund, Gareth and Edgar (Aelfraed's son) crawled to the edge of the cliff.

Sure enough there were men loading bales on to a small boat secured in the shallows.

Looking to his left he could see a small light that signalled the men from the north side had arrived and were hiding behind some rocks. Looking right he thought he could see the same from the men from the south.

The men on the beach were obviously not expecting to be discovered as they laughed and joked among themselves. Edmund could see a path descending to the beach. Signalling to the men with him they rose and quickly started to run down the slope. There was a shout from the shore, the smugglers turned and stood, not knowing who was coming. 'Stand and surrender!' shouted Edmund. The men from both sides also appeared and the smugglers stood still. Edmund shouted for some to secure the boat while the remainder disarmed the smugglers. One man was trying to hide amongst the rest.

'Hold that man and bring him to me,' called Edmund. He was grabbed and brought before Edmund. 'Who are you. What is your name?'

The man muttered his name was Philip and he was from Saxlingham and all the men came from the same place.

'Why are you stealing my wool? Have you no respect for your Lord?' 'We are kept in poverty while you are rich,' replied the man.

Edmund had them tied and marched to the top of the cliff while his men unloaded the boat.

They marched into Yarmouth and deposited the men in the prison. They would be brought before the magistrate the next day. Edmund found the mayor and told him what had transpired. He senced the man had knowledge of what was happening.

'I am leaving you in charge here,' said Edmund to Gareth. 'I will go on to Saxlingham and try to find out what is afoot there.'

Early the next day Edmund set off with just a seven man escort. They travelled quickly and arrived at the Saxlingham farm in the late afternoon. The tenant farmer told him a story of men arriving from the south trying to spread discord among his workers. He suspected his wool was being stolen but had done nothing.

Edmund told him that his tenancy could be under threat. He would report to Harold and he would make the decision. The tenant tried to justify what had happened by saying that they had no leadership with Sir John away. Edmund said, 'I am here and my brother is the new Earl. We will be watching you carefully to see that you improve things here.' They left and made for Dunston.

Stephen greeted them, pleased to have some company. 'Will you stay the night?' 'I must get back to Wymondham,' said Edmund. 'Harold must have this news as soon as possible. A meal and short rest and we will be on our way.' His men did not look too pleased, riding at night was slow and dangerous.

There was a bright moon as they set out for Wymondham and they were going at a fast trot. Early morning they could see the Castle and they were soon dismounting in the bailey. Edmund went immediately to find Harold and tell him the details of what had happened.

'Why did you not stay in Yarmouth and talk to the magistrate? Why did you not deal with the Saxlingham tenant?' asked Harold. 'You have a responsibility to the fiefdom just as much as I have. Do I have to do everything?'

Edmund was taken aback by Harold's outburst and tried to say that as Harold was in charge of the tenants he did not want to do something that would not be right.

'It's not good enough Edmund. We share in the riches of our estates so we must share in the problems that sometimes arise!'

The younger brother turned on his heel and stomped out of the room. He climbed up to the battlements and walked round fuming. The guards got no response when they wished him good morning and kept out of his way. Gradually he calmed himself and realised that his brother must also be under considerable pressure trying to govern their estates after their fathers death. An idea began to form in his mind, by the fourth circuit of the walls he had the possible answer.

Edmund found Harold in his chambers and as soon as he walked in Harold rose and extended his arms and embraced Edmund.

'I am sorry I was so bad tempered with you. There have been many problems to sort out over fathers death and the inheritance. I have received confirmation from the king and also a message from parliament that my position is ratified. This will make it a little easier to implement my plans.'

'I have also given thought to my position and have a suggestion that will make life easier for both of us,' said Edmund. 'I want to travel and see more of our world. I do not have the skill or the desire to be the lord of the land. You would be free to employ who you wanted to help you. I would ask that you release Gareth to me as my squire and young Cuthbert as page. With father's sword and equipment I am sure I can make my way. How say you brother?'

Harold looked at his younger brother and walked over to the window. He was quiet for a few moments then turned and looked at Edmund.

'It will be sad for us to part. I know you are restless but this will pass. Remember that this is your home and you will be welcome on your return. Why not start your adventure in France at the old house in Vent. You could visit our parents grave. If you want further travel go to Flanders and visit our friends who take our wool.'

Edmund thought this was not the adventure he craved but it would be good to see fathers grave and France is not a bad place to start.

'The two men you ask for,' continued Harold. 'That is their decision but I will not hold them.'

Edmund grasped his brother and thanked him. 'Wymondham will always be my home. I shall honour it and you, in my travels.' He left and went to find Gareth and Cuthbert.

He found both men in the stables looking after Edmund's horses. 'Come and sit with me I have something to suggest to you. I am departing for France as soon as I can be ready and I want you, Gareth to accompany me as my squire and you Cuthbert, as our page. Will you come?' Both men smiled broadly and agreed immediately. Edmund pointed out the horses they would take, a destrier and charger, horses for themselves and two pack horses.

'Come and help me to start packing, the sooner we are ready the better. We will make for Lowestoft and look for passage.' The three men left the stables and made for Edmund's room.

Two days later they were packed and ready to leave. Harold came to the bailey to see them off. 'Send letters when you are able and come back soon. I am going to miss you.'

'I will do my best,' said Edmund.

'God be with you and keep you safe,' was Harold's last call as they moved off.

Chapter 6

There was an excitement in the air as the three of them rode to Lowestoft. He had some pangs of regret in leaving his brother but he knew Harold would soon settle into being the lord of Wymondham and Earl of the shire.

Edmund felt free for the first time and the mood of the group was excitement as they looked forward to the adventures ahead. They made good time to the port, Edmund made for the mayors house to enquire about the ships. The mayor insisted they stay with him while he found them a berth. A ship was sailing to Cherbourg the next day and could take them and their horses.

The crossing was calm and Edmond walked the deck looking for the coast of Normandy to come into view. They had planned to sleep rough and not enter any Inns until they knew if there was still pestilence in the area. Talking with the captain and crew he discovered that the sickness had moved north.

Disembarking they set off for Vent. They arrived outside the chataux on the second day. Edmund sat his horse looking at the house and remembering the happy times they had there as a family. He missed his father especially at this time. He needed his council to guide him. Gareth and Cuthbert hung back as they could see their young knight was upset. Opening the gates they rode up to the house.

The main door opened and a servant asked who they wished to see.

'Tell your master that Sir Edmund Ivanson would like to see him.' Suddenly from behind the servant a man descended the steps. Edmund dismounted and was soon enveloped in the arms of monsieur Trouville.

'I am so sorry that your family died here. I too lost my wife at the same time. The sickness was everywhere. Come inside and I will tell you all I can.'

Edmund listened intently to all monsieur Trouville told him and knew there was nothing more the Frenchman could have done.

'I will visit my families grave tomorrow,' said Edmund. 'Tonight we will rest. May we stay here?'

'Naturally, this is your house as much as mine. Please make yourself comfortable. Join us for dinner this evening.' It was a quiet meal and Edmund soon excused himself and went to bed.

A somber group stood round the graves the next morning. Edmund decided to walk to the village, Gareth joined him while Cuthbert stayed to look after the horses. Many of the villager remembered him and expressed their sympathy. They stopped at an Inn to refresh themselves. Inside not everyone was so friendly, many were against the English and Edward's claim to the throne of France. They finished their drinks and returned to the chateaux.

Loud banging on the front door woke them the next morning. monsieur Trouville entered and urgently told them to get up. A messenger had arrived to tell him that the English had landed and there was fierce fighting in the north.

'I am fearful that local militia will come here for you. I have a place for you to hide and I am always buying horses so yours should be safe.'

Edmund thanked him and hastily dressed. They hid until evening, listening to men moving around the house, fortunately they were not discovered.

'We will leave tonight and try to join up with Edwards army.' Edmund felt excited at the thought of fighting again with the English army.

As darkness fell they dressed in their fighting gear and saddled the horses.

'I remember your father in that armour,' said Trouville. 'How like him you look. I am pleased everything of your fathers reached you. Do you have his special sword?'

'Talio is always at my side, we thank you again for sending everything to us.' With these words the trio rode out into the night.

Moving quickly across country they met up with the English army on its way to Caen. Edmund found William de Bohun, Earl of Northampton, who recognised him and called him over.

'I did not know you had been summoned. You could have joined us in England.' Edmund explained he wanted to visit his fathers grave. 'I understand,' said Sir William. 'You are welcome to join us now if you wish.' Edmund accepted and rode with Sir William until they camped for the night.

The noise of the camp preparing for battle woke Edmund in the morning. Gareth came to help him dress while Cuthbert saddled his destrier. He joined Sir William and they were soon advancing on the town. The first attack was on the Abbey and then onto the town. There was no control over the army and they rushed the bridges into the town. Edmund found himself facing a small group of men surrounding a French knight. He went to work with Talio and men started to die around him. With Gareth at his back he faced the knight, the ring was hot on his finger and he could almost feel a vibration from the sword. Edmund saluted his opponent and urged his horse forward. There was a clash of steel on steel and then a flashing blur as Edmund drove at his enemy. He pulled up as he realised there was only a headless body astride the horse facing him. The main army were now in the town, looting raping and setting fire to the buildings. Edmund was sickened at the way the army were pillaging the town, turning and seeing another French nobleman guided his horse toward him.

'I yield, I yield! I would stand no chance against you.' Called the Frenchman. 'I am the Count of Eu and I surrender.' 'I accept your surrender sir, I am Sir Edmund Ivanson of Wymondham.' He accepted the Count's sword and passed it to Gareth who had joined him then led him to a knot of men around Sir William.

'Who have you got there lad? He looks wealthy enough to raise a good ransom.' Edmund looked him in the eye and said 'I am a man, not a lad, strong enough to kill our enemies and bring in prisoners worth capturing.'

Sir William sat back in his saddle, stunned by Edmund's outburst. 'Well said Sir Edmund, my apologies.' Edmund smiled and felt better, the news of how he fought was gradually being circulated round the camp.

When the army finally moved off towards the river Seine they left behind a ruined city. Edmund rode on his own with Gareth and Cuthbert and thought to himself, was this his future? To be part of this mass of men who had done so much damage to innocent people? He halted and turned to Gareth. 'Tonight we leave quietly and make for Bayeux. I met a sailor in Lowestoft from a Spanish ship and it appears to be a country where men like us could make our fortune. Will you come with me?'

Gareth looked at Cuthbert and answered. 'Wherever you go we follow.'

As soon as the camp had settled for the night Edmund and his companions slipped away back to the Normandy coast. They camped several miles away from the army in a wood. Eating a cold meal they talked of what might happen on their journey. Rising early they packed and moved on to the port.

Edmund rode into Bayeux and went immediately to the dock. There were several ships at the quayside. Talking to the sailors he found there were none from Spain but there was a vessel going to the port of Biarritz. With money as the persuader he managed to secure a place for them and the horses. Edmund mentally thanked his brother for the generous purse he had given him.

They loaded the animals and the ship set sail. The journey was not as smooth as crossing the English Chanel. Cuthbert was soon hanging over the side loosing what food he had. The horses were very restless too and Gareth spent time calming them which did not help his stomach eitherEdmund spent most of the voyage time talking to the captain and learning as much as he could about southern France and northern Spain. The further south they sailed the warmer it became and Edmund thought to himself that it would be uncomfortable to wear armour.

Chapter 7

They docked early one morning before the temperature had risen. Saying farewell to the captain and crew they started out for the Spanish border. They were stared at whenever they entered a village as there had not been many Englishmen this far south.

'French is probably spoken both sides of the border so we should be all right for a while. We must try and learn some basic words before we go deeper into the country,' said Edmund. Gareth and Cuthbert looked a little nervous. 'How far are we to go into this land?' asked Gareth. 'Where fortune takes us,'answered Edmund.

The land gradually changed to the foothills of the mountains they could see in the distance. They kept to the shore line and passed through pretty villages with the people giving them suspicious looks. One day as they were stopping for a noonday rest a group of men appeared on the road before them. Their leader called, in a form of french, to dismount. Edmund called back that they were peaceful travellers and would stay where they were. The leader rode towards Edmund.

'I am the chief of these parts and you will pay me before you can pass,' he said.

Edmund dismounted and said, 'Come down from your horse and make me pay. If I win we pass free.' The chief dismounted and walked towards Edmund.

'You are not French, who are you and what are you doing here?' As he spoke he unsheathed a curved scimitar.

'I am Sir Edmund of Wymondham and England. We are on a peaceful journey to discover Spain.' Suddenly the chief sprang forward, slashing at Edmund whom he missed as Edmund jumped sideways and drew Talio. The basque recovered and sliced at Edmund again. Several times he attacked and Edmund parried until suddenly there was a clash of steel and the scimitar flew through the air, Talio was at the chiefs throat in an instant. There was movement from the Basques towards them, Gerald and Cuthbert unsheathed their swords.

'Hold, Stop, Arrete.' Called Edmund. Looking at the man on the ground he said. 'A free passage I think that was the agreement.' 'All right you have won. My men will not attack you, you are free to go. There are many more bands along your way, you will not win them all.'

'Will you eat with us?' asked Edmund. 'We were just going to stop for our midday meal?' Surprised the leader looked steadily at Edmund and said, 'Yes we will eat with you. My name is Garaile' He called to his men and they walked over to where Cuthbert was spreading out food they had bought in the village.

'Why are you here in Basque land. We do not see men from your country?' 'Adventure and a desire to learn more of the world,' answered Edmund.

'You will have great difficulty, not speaking the language. Our Basque language is different to other parts. When you climb over these mountains you will be in Castile and another language.'

Finishing their meal the men rose, they all smiled at each other and shook hands with the Basques moving off towards San Sebastian.

They had not been gone long when Edmund heard the sounds of battle a short distance ahead. Charging towards the noise they found the Basques being set upon by a lager group of men, some of whom were well armoured. 'Stay back,' said Edmund to Cuthbert. 'Come Gareth we will help them.' They charged into the fighting men. Edmund looked for what could be the leader and with Talio throbbing in his hand he scythed his way to the man. His opponent was armoured and he smiled at Edmund as he raised his sword. That was his last action before he died as Talio bit down across his neck and his head fell. There was a shout from the attackers and gradually the fighting ceased. Edmund rode back to Garaile and asked if he was all right.

'Thank you for coming to our aide. We were in trouble, but not as much trouble as we will be now. You have killed a nobleman of this region and his family will be after your blood. We must hide in the mountains until things quieten down.'

Garaile's band had been securing the defeated men and robbing them of all they carried. Swords, money, armour, horses and anything they liked. They all quickly made for the mountains and rode at a brisk pace until darkness slowed them and they made camp. Garaile posted lookouts as he said he did not want to be taken by surprise. He told Edmund that they would be near their village tomorrow and there he would leave them.

There was quite a chill as they stirred in the morning. The mountain air was clear and Edmund walked to a small outcrop and gazed at the resplendent view.

'This is the place to live,' said Garaile as he came to stand next to Edmund. 'Good air, fine food and an excellent wine.'

'And lots of people to fight,' said Edmund with a smile.

'Even more now after the fracas down below. They will certainly try to hunt us down so we must move now.'

They rode on through a valley and up into the next mountain. Gradually Garaile's men began to slip away. 'They have places they can hide for a while so it is best they disappear.'

'Are you going to disappear to a hiding place?' asked Edmund.

'No, I think I will stay with you for now. You fight like I have never seen before and you need someone to look after you. You don't speak the language so you need an interrupter.' 'You mean an interpreter.' Edmund said. 'You know what I mean, I will be very useful to you. No?'

'Put like that I guess you will,' said Edmund. 'Where did you get your scimitar from?'

'I met a Moor who should not have been here and he lost it. You could have lost your weapon except I lost my footing.'

Edmund threw back his head and laughed and was joined by Garaile and the others.

That night they found a large cave which gave them shelter. They were able to light a good fire that was not seen outside and cooked a hot meal from rabbits that Garaile trapped. As they relaxed Garaile told them tales of the mountain men and the fights they had been in to keep their independence.

In the next days they descended from the mountains through the foothills and reached the plains of Angora. Edmund noticed the different breeds of sheep, some having a fine wool. There were healthy cattle and occasionally large black bulls with huge horns. 'How would you like to fight one of those?' said Garaile. 'They put them into a ring and fight them with just a sword and a cloak.'

Edmund smiled and thought that it was another of Garaile's tall tales.

They stopped for their midday break under some trees as the temperature was rising. Cuthbert was tending to the horses when he called. 'There are some men approaching.'

Edmund stood as they arrived. "Who are you, and what are you doing travelling on my land?' asked the leader of them.

'We three are English travellers and this is our guide. We mean no harm and are just exploring this country,' explained Edmund.

The leader dismounted and came up to Edmund. 'I am Count Ramirez and my home is nearby in Tarazona. We have to be on the alert for we have lost many cattle to rustlers from the hills,' he said looking at Garaile.

'Will you share our meal? asked Edmund. 'I would like to know more about this area.' 'Thank you,' said Ramirez, and signalled his men to dismount.

'I am Edmund of Wymondham, England,' said Edmund and held out his hand. The visitor grasped his arm as one knight to another.

'What are you doing in this part of Angora? We do not see Englishmen this far inland. Sailors sometimes get as far as Zaragoza, but not many.'

Edmund explained that they were looking to find work as personal guards or any purpose a lord might have for their skills.

'There is a tournament in Tarazona in four days time, why don't you come and display your skills there?' said Ramirez. 'Come to my Castle tomorrow and I will show you where it will be held.' Edmund thanked him as they mounted and rode away.

The sun was shining and the temperature was beginning to climb as they rode to the castle in the morning. Arriving in Tarazona they found the castle was more of a large fortified house than what they knew as a castle. Garaile said he had friends in the town and would stay with them to get the latest news of the area, he would see them at the Tournament. Reaching the castle they found Ramirez waiting to greet them and escort them into a large ornate room where an older man rose from his chair.

'Allow me to present my father Señor Domingo Ramirez. This is Sir Edmund of Wymondham from England, father.' The old man smiled and bid them welcome. 'I will take you to your rooms,' continued Ramirez. 'Your horses will be taken care of.

They climbed a grand staircase and were taken to a large room for Edmund and a smaller one for Gareth and Cuthbert. 'There are servants here to do your bidding and when you are ready, come down and meet the rest of my family. My given name is Raoul.' Edmund thanked him and said they would be as quick as possible.

When Raoul had gone Edmund sent Cuthbert down to see to the horses. He said to Gareth. 'This is obviously a wealthy family. Get ready and dress in the best you have.' Cuthbert returned to tell them that all the horses had been cared for and he had been invited to join the staff for a meal.

Edmund and Gareth joined Raoul in another ornate room where he offered a glass of wine. 'How do you defend a place like this?' asked Edmund.

'From the perimeter walls outside and the roof,' replied Raoul. 'I also keep a cavalry unit that can charge out when necessary. I hope you are not thinking of attacking me.' Edmund laughed as he said that he was not that foolish.

'You have a strange fellow in your company, a Basque. They are mostly bandits and fighters. I hope your questions were not for his information.'

Edmund explained how they had met Garaile and how they had helped each other. He was also wary of his intentions but so far they had been friendly and genuine.

The rest of Raoul's family arrived, his wife and two daughters. Edmund found that he could hold a conversation now without too much trouble. The daughters were very beautiful, he thought, but a little out of reach. They moved to another room and sat down to the best food Edmund had eaten for a long time. After the meal they sat and talked for a while. Everyone relaxed the girls started to chat and Teresa the youngest tried to improve Gareth's Spanish much to the hilarity of the rest. Caterina, the eldest, wanted to know about England and how it was different from Spain. 'Do they fight the bulls in England?' asked Catrina. 'No, we use them for breeding and eating,' said Edmund. 'So what do you fight?' persisted the young lady. 'We have tournaments as you do and sometimes we fight our neighbours as all countries do. It is better I think, to not fight at all.' 'To make love not war,' said Raoul. The young ladies giggled and blushed.

'After all their travelling I think our guests will be tired,' said Raoul which was a signal for them all to retire.

Chapter 8

Edmund learnt that the Tournament was to last four days. On the first day they accompanied the family to the magnificent cathedral for High Mass. Edmund had noticed that the region was devoutly Catholic. Raoul told him that the most of Spain was Catholic apart from some small regions that were inhabited by Moors. The king's ambition was to drive all the Moors out. There were lots of introductions to dignitaries of the town, so numerous that Edmund could not remember them all. After the service Edmund suggested to Raoul that he must look for lodgings. The Spaniard said he would like them all to stay as his guests for the length of the Tournament and then decide what they wanted to do.

There were some attractive gardens nearby and Caterina asked if he would escort her, as she wished for some fresh air before they returned home. Edmund noticed a young man had been waiting as if to speak to Caterina, he glowered at Edmund as they walked away. The gardens were very pretty and there were many couples meandering around paths. Caterina chatted merrily away and Edmund felt relaxed and at ease.

Returning to the house Edmund decided to go for a ride, Gareth said he would join him. Cuthbert saddled the destrier and a stallion and they rode out into the country. Edmund had a feeling they were being followed. The weather was warm and the country roads made easy going, seeing a small wood they stopped and sat in the shade of the trees.

'Riders coming,' said Gareth. A small group of men were heading towards them. They stood up and when the riders reached them Edmund recognised the man who had been staring at them outside the Cathedral.

'Here is the Englishman, who thinks he can steal our women. We will teach him not to do so in future.' As the man said this he moved towards Edmund who grasped the horse's bridle and foreleg, while pulling the head round and pushing his shoulder into the animal, it went down dumping its rider onto the ground. Gareth and Cuthbert drew their swords to deter the others from taking part. The fallen man rose, cursing and drawing his weapon. He rushed at Edmund who stepped aside and drew Talio. Edmund parried attack after attack and then went forward. With a few lightening strokes his opponents sword flew into some bushes and Talio's point was pressing against his chest just over his heart.

The incident was over in a few minutes and Edmund said to the man. 'If you wish to fight me as equals on foot or horse, then name the place and time.'

'You will regret this. My father is a powerful man in this city.'

After the group had left Edmund and his two compatriots rode back. Edmund found Raoul and told him what had happened.

'His father is a powerful man in the city, south but it is his son who has attacked my guest. I will go to see him in the morning to tell him what actually happened.'

'I do not wish to cause trouble here, perhaps it is time for us to move on,' said Edmund. 'Let us see what the outcome is tomorrow,' said Raoul.

That night Edmund called Gareth and Cuthbert and decided that when the house was asleep they would quietly leave. 'Raoul has ben very good to us and it will be better if we just disappear, we would have moved on soon, anyway. I would not want that man's death on my conscience as I am sure next time we met he would have felt Talio enter his heart.'

The night was moonless as they quietly slipped away. 'What about Garaile?' asked Gareth. 'We haven't seen him since we arrived.' 'We don't need him now,' said Edmund.

They headed west and were soon into woodland.

For several days they travelled through country villages where they were welcomed. At one village they encountered, the people frightened off a band of ruffians who were doing as they pleased. Stealing anything of value, raping women and demanding to be fed. Edmund offered his services to the headman, who readily accepted. Talio was soon in action and the offenders left with the loss of five of their band. The villager were overjoyed and persuaded Edmund to stay in the village for a while until they felt the pull of their adventure again.

Packing their bags and saying goodbye to the villagers felt like leaving home again. Many of the girls had hoped the English band would have stayed but the men were glad to see them go.

They headed south again hoping to find the city of Segovia. They caught up with a caravan of Romanies who had stopped for their midday break. The leader invited them to join in their food. Edmund accepted and they sat on the ground near to the leader. He told them they were on their way to Segovia as there was to be a gathering of Gitanos there, they were welcome to travel with them.

They appeared to be a very happy group, the women did all the work while the men sat and smoked. In the evening some of the men disappeared and returned later with food for the pot. As night fell and the children were put to bed a guitar was produced and singing began. The tempo increased and a woman came into the firelight and began to dance. Edmund had never seen anything like it and was mesmerised by the twirling figure. He found himself joining in the clapping to the beat of the exciting rhythm. The leader turned to him with a grin. 'That is flamenco and how it should be danced. Do you like it?' 'Yes, very much,' said Edmund with Gareth nodding enthusiastically. The three Englishmen went to their shelters talking of how good it was and wondering if this happened every night.

The camp was soon up and underway the following morning. Milosh, the leader explained it would take several days to reach the city especially as they were a large number. Edmund and his friends, for that is what Gareth and Cuthbert had become, talked to their travelling companions as much as possible. Sometimes the romanies spoke together in a language that they did not understand.

Milosh came from an ancient Gitanos family, his father had been a lord of the region. When his father died Milosh took over the mantle of leader but the hills where they roamed were full of Basque fighters and after several battles between them, Milosh decide to take a smaller band travelling. They were on their way south when Edmund fell in with them. They were a happy band and had a comfortable life, working for various farms, land owners or anyone who needed their skills. Edmund enjoyed being with them and learnt many new things!

Suddenly from out of the trees that bordered the road, a group of men on horseback attacked them. The Romanies fought back while the women and children ran to the caravans. Edmund and Gareth were soon in the thick of the fighting and Edmund felt the heat from the ring. Talio was a blinding blur as Edmund attacked and killed. Those of the attackers who were left ran back into the trees with the Romanies chasing them. Edmund looked down at some of the bodies and found they had darker skins and a strange dress. Milosh came up to him. 'Thank you for your help. You are obviously a fighting man.' Edmund asked him who the men were who attacked them? 'They are band of Moors that have been roaming the countryside. Most were driven out of Spain but there are some still about. Not so many now, you will find many buildings still have their influence.'

They continued on their way and that night there was indeed another dancer. She danced a slower dance then a very fast twirling one. There was also a man who sang a love song, so they were told. Edmund thought it sounded more like he had a stomach ache.

The camp was quiet, apart from the sound of snoring. Edmund lay thinking of England and his brother, it was not that he was pining for home just wondering what was happening there. There was a sound outside his shelter, the door flap was drawn back and a woman stood there wrapped in a cloak. She entered and letting the cloak drop slipped into the bed beside him. As the cloak dropped he could see her naked form. She placed a finger over his mouth and whispered in his ear that she had come to thank him for saving them and to teach him some of the Romany ways. Edmund learnt that night how much he didn't know about love making.

When he awoke the woman was gone and he wondered if it had been a dream. After he had bathed in the stream he went to one of the cook fires and was handed food by one of the women. He looked around to see if he could recognise his nighttime visiter but several of the women looked alike and they all smiled at him. When they started on the road again, Milosh came up to him. 'We are going hunting, into the forest you can see to your right. The local Count gave our family permission after we worked for him and saved his son's life. I see you have a bow so come with us.' Towards evening when the caravan had stopped, Edmund and Gareth joined the men and they rode off. When they reached the forest they left their horses and went into the trees on foot. A couple of the men were very good trackers and soon picked up the trail of a herd of deer.

They spread out in a long line and moved as quietly as they could. They arrived at a clearing and there stood an old stag, two young ones and four hinds. Gareth drew his bow and the old stag fell, the others took down one of the younger stags. Milosh held up his hand as a signal to stop. 'That is enough for this visit, it will feed us all for a few days,' he said as the deer bounded away. They gutted the animals and then carried them back to the camp. It was a sumptuous meal that night, there was no dancing only some country songs that Edmund did not understand.

Edmund retired to his bed and waited expectantly. It had been a tiring day and he was soon asleep and nobody came to keep him company. They journeyed on the next day and came to a large village where Milosh was known. 'We have work here for three days, a barn needs repairing, a stream unblocking and several other tasks. We will camp in that field,' he said pointing to a large field near to the village. Once they had set camp and the men had gone to their work Edmund was at a loose end. He wandered into the village and found an Inn where he could sit outside and sample the local wine. This is a very agreeable land, he thought, better weather than home, happy people and an easier life all round. He missed home a little but the adventure was still uppermost in his mind.

Gareth joined him and they wandered to the edge of the village. They could see a dust cloud approaching on the road. 'Someone in a hurry,' said Gareth. They watched the rider gallop into the village and stop in front of the largest house, he left his horse and ran into the property. Two men then ran out and went to the little church. Suddenly the church bell rang out and people began to run towards the church. Edmund and Gareth ran to the church too, they saw Milosh in the crowd and asked him what was wrong. 'We shall hear from the alcalde soon enough.' A man stood on the steps leading to the church door and spoke to the crowd. 'Friends, our brothers in Caltera are in trouble. We must help them, assemble in the square with your weapons.'

Very quickly a hundred armed men were assembled some of the Gitanos were among them. Edmund made his entry in full armour with Gareth at his side. There were gasps of astonishment at Edmund up on his destrier. Milosh spoke to the alcalde. 'Here is your leader, a valiant knight, whom we have fought with.' A cheer went up and the cavalcade moved of. They made good time to the village and as they entered many of the raiders were trying to leave. Edmund directed men to cut them off, the main body stood their ground in the square and Edmund led the charge into them. Talio was slashing left and right and soon there were only four of the marauding gang left standing. These quickly surrendered and begged for mercy. A group of women flung themselves on them and in very quick order they joined the others in death. Edmund was shocked at this but understood when he was told how these women had been treated.

The dead were taken out of the square and people began to come out of hiding The rescued villagers surrounded the men and a feast was prepared. The alcalde came to Edmund and thanked him for his part in the fight. 'You are like El Cid, fighter for the poor and downtrodden. Why is it you travel with the Gitanos? You could have your own castle.' 'They have been good friends to me and I enjoy their company. They are also helping me to find my way around Spain,' replied Edmund. Milosh came up to him and said, 'I cannot believe the speed of your blade. You can kill three men to our one, how is this possible?' Edmund told him he would tell him a tale when they returned to camp. When the meal and celebrations had ended they rode back to their own village. Milosh went to Edmund and said, 'Come and sit with by the fire and tell me this story of your sword.' Edmund related what his father had told him and how the sword had a mind of its own in battle.

'There are many strange things in this world, young man. You are a "favoured one" as they say amongst our people. Take care of your blade and it will protect you.' Edmund thanked him and made his way to his bed.

He lay there, thinking of the battle at the village and could hardly remember any detail. There was no doubt that the sword had a mind of its own when it was in his hand. So far it only felt like that when he was fighting enemy, what if it should start to kill his friends? Should I put it away and fight with an ordinary sword and rely on my skill? The protection it gave him and the way men looked up to him made his mind up for him.

There was movement outside his tent and a woman walked in. As before she was wearing only a shawl which she dropped, again he could see the outline of a beautiful figure as it slid in beside him. He tried to see her face but her black hair soon covered his face as her lips met his. This time he was more responsive as he remembered what he had learnt the time before. They sank into that wonderful world of love making.

Chapter 9

Edmund awoke to the sound of the camp preparing breakfast. He rose and washed in the stream. Returning to the cooking fire he looked hard at the women who were busy there. Four of them turned and smiled at him, two were sisters who had been widowed at the previous fight. One of them said, 'Would you like to eat señor? You will need your strength today as we shall be moving on.' They all giggled and looked at one another. Edmund could feel his face colouring and he quickly turned away. Milosh called him over. 'We should see Segovia by nightfall. We are making for the city to take part in their annual fair. You will enjoy it.' 'What do you do there? Is there a Tournament?' queried Edmund. 'It is a very colourful fair with stalls and singing but I have never seen a tournament, it could have changed. We want to sell our wares and take part in the flamenco and singing competitions. You should ride into the city on your big horse wearing your armour showing you are a knight and see what happens. There will be good prizes for the competitions and we want them.' Edmund went back to Gareth to make sure all their belongings had been packed. He was a little uneasy about the comment that Milosh made 'see what happens'.

They made good progress that day and everyone was in high spirits. They came to the top of a rise and suddenly there before them was the city of Segovia bathed in the glow of the setting sun. Edmund was stunned by the beauty of the scene, he could see the castle clearly standing out higher than all other buildings The turrets had cones on the top which made them look like fairy castles. Positioned on a promontory with the river at the base, it is impregnable. They chose a site to camp for the night still in sight of the City.

Edmund stood for awhile looking at the view as the sun went down, he could feel a strong emotion that somehow he was meant to be in this fascinating country. Gareth came to him. 'Your tent is ready for you,' Edmund thanked him and they both walked over to the fires that the Gitanos had made and where the women were cooking. Cuthbert joined them. 'I've never seen a Castle with points on the towers like that. Will we be going there?' Edmund looked at him and replied. 'I very much hope so, who knows what will happen in the next days.'

That evening there was more flamenco dancing as a practice for the forthcoming competitions. All the friends sat and watched and Gareth remarked that the older women danced better than the young girls. Edmund smiled. 'They have a lot more experience and practice. It is true that applies to most things they do.' The hour was late when at last they all retired to bed, Edmund lay thinking what was the purpose of wearing his armour tomorrow, what did Milosh know and was not telling him? He did not see his visitor come in but only felt her warm body as she nestled in beside him. He quickly reached for her and they were soon coupled together. This was a different woman, some of her moves left Edmund gasping, perhaps they were taking it in turns. Enjoy what you have, he thought, tomorrow is another day.

Gareth finished fastening the last strap on his armour and stood back. 'You look fine sir, a true knight of the realm.' Edmund grunted and stomped out to his horse. He could already feel the heat of the sun and it was still early. A round of applause accompanied him as he reached his horse, it seemed as though half the camp had come to watch him. Milosh came over to him and said. 'You will honour us as we go into the city with you at our head.' Was this his reason, thought Edmund, to make it look like a knight and his retainers visiting the fair and therefore demanding the better sites for their wares? The whole company moved off with Edmund and Milosh at the head, Gareth followed with Edmund's shield and helm. They headed for the main gate, under the aqueduct and into the city. Edmund was impressed by the buildings and the great cathedral.

Crowds were lining the streets and they cheered and threw flowers, Edmund wondered who they thought he was. They entered the square in front of the castle entrance where there sat four fully armoured knights on horses. Edmund stopped and waited for them to speak. One of them moved forward and said. 'Who comes to challenge the kings champions?'

'I am Sir Edmund Ivanson of Wymondham in England and I do not challenge anyone, I come in peace.' The knight moved back and spoke to his companions. 'Are you the knight that saved the village of Caltera?'

'I am, sir.'

'His Majesty the king wishes to see you. He is at present visiting Segovia and has heard of your fighting skill, come with me.' Edmund followed the knight into the castle and dismounted with Gareth's help. They went into the main part of the castle and to the throne room. A beautiful room with a highly decorated ceiling.

King Alfonso sat in one of two thrones that were on a platform. Edmund bowed low, well, as low as his armour would let him. 'We have heard that you saved one of our villages, and that you are a great warrior. What are you doing in our lands so far from your home?'

'I am looking for adventure, your majesty, and to explore more of the world. I am finding Spain very interesting, and warm.'

'We welcome our visitor from across the seas and invite him to dine with us this evening.'

'Thank you your majesty, a great honour.' Edmund bowed again and left. A page came to him and asked him to follow him. He guided him to a large bedroom and said he could use it for his stay. Edmund sent Gareth to find Cuthbert and find stabling for their horses and bring their belongings to the room. 'Get me out of this armour before I am cooked like a deer.' Edmund found another door and when opened it revealed another smaller bedroom with two beds. Just right for his friends. There was a knock at the door and servants entered with water for washing and wine for drinking. Edmund chose the later and sat to think of the past events.

Gareth came in from the next room ready to accompany Edmund to the kings table. They decended the grand staircase to a large finely decorated room where a large table had been set for the banquet. One of the knights called to him and offered a glass of wine. 'Greetings Englishman, I am Alberto Menzies and this is my brother Emilio, the other two are Gianni and Ignacio. We serve our king and keep his foes at bay.' Edmund replied with his name and they stood talking.

'You made a grand entrance into our city,' said Alberto. 'We thought you had come to seize the castle.' This was said with a smile.

The dinner was a grand affaire with many dishes Edmund had not seen before. There were singers and mummers, acrobats, dancers and at the end a wonderful display of flamenco. Edmund could see the Gitanos women there.

The meal finished with flowery speeches from an unsteady King Alfonso and a welcome to the Englishman. Eventually they all staggered off to their homes or rooms.

Edmund was woken by the strong light of the sun streaming through his window. A tap on his door announced a servant with water for washing and breakfast. Edmund thought that he could get used to this type of living after the journey with the Gitanos, although they did seem to wash a lot. He wondered where the gypsies were, had they set themselves up at the fair? Calling Gareth he decided to take a walk around the city and attempt to find them. Hiding Talio under the bed he left the castle with just his daggers. As they left the castle the next large building was the city church. They entered and Edmund sat for a moment to collect his thoughts. His mind settled on Wymondham and his brother. He had been a long time away from home. What was happening there, was Harold able to manage on his own? He missed the time he had spent at Dunston. People began to fill up the pews and Edmund realised mass was about to start. They stayed for the service and as they left

Edmund felt easier in his mind, his adventure had not finished yet, who knows what lay before them.

Their steps led them to a large square where the fair had been set up. Edmund found Milosh busy organising his people in setting out their stalls. He looked for the four women and found the two sisters setting out jewellery they had made from beads and coloured glass. They looked up and smiled at him. 'Señor it is good to see you, we have missed you. Are you keeping warm at night? This is a wonderful city and we will make much money here these next days.' They said, while giving him large smiles.

Edmund felt his face beginning to turn red. 'The sun is warm already,' he said, while the women giggled. He turned away and found himself confronted by the other two. 'I must find my squire he has wandered off.' Amidst laughter, he quickly sort refuge amongst the other stalls. Gareth had been watching and asked him what was causing all the fun. Edmund walked away not answering. 'Will we come back here when the competitions start?' asked Gareth. 'Yes,' answered Edmund. 'I would like to see the flamenco.' They continued on around the fair stopping at a stall that was selling flat pancakes, they then put various fillings on them and rolled them up. 'These are very tasty,' said Gareth with his mouth full and juice dripping down his chin. 'I agree,' said Edmund. 'We need to sit and finish them or we will look filthy.' They sat alongside the wall looking out over the valley.

As the midday sun reached its zenith most of the locals made for shade and somewhere to recline. Edmund and Gareth found a patch of grass and stretched out under a tree. It was not long before they were both fast asleep. Edmund was awakened by an urgent shaking. He opened his eyes and saw a young pageboy shaking him and calling him to wake up. 'What's the matter boy, are we under attack?' 'No sir, you are wanted at the castle. My lord Alberto has news for you, you must come now.' Edmund dug his toe into Gareth and they both followed the pageboy. Alberto met them in the castle keep and gave Edmund a parchment. It instructed him to ride to Salamanca and inform the count there that the king would be visiting in ten days time. 'You will take an escort of twenty men, which I will arrange, as there are still pockets of Moors and brigands in the area. I suggest you leave early tomorrow. One of the men will be your guide.'

Edmund thanked him and found Cuthbert to tell him to have the horses ready. On his way to his room he bumped into a young lady going the other way. 'A thousand pardons miss, my mind was occupied and I did not see you,' said Edmund. The young lady curtsied and carried on. Edmund thought to himself how comely she was, who was she? Edmund and Gareth prepared themselves for the journey the next day then decended to the dining room where a dinner had been prepared, it was not like the feast of the previous evening but still more than they could manage. Edmund thought if they eat like this every night he would not fit into his armour.

Chapter 10

Edmund met his escort in the morning, one of the men stepped forward and said his name was Rodrigo and he would be his guide. He was born in Salamanca and knew the region well. Edmund gave the order to mount and the cavalcade moved off. Cuthbert accompanied the baggage carts which contained Edmund's armour and some extra pieces for the men. Edmund supposed that he was now in the kings army.

They rode at a comfortable pace and Edmund was able to move through the group making himself known to them. The first night they camped at the edge of a small wood and some of the men went hunting. Returning with a small deer and some wild fowl they prepared them for the pot, one of the number was a good cook. Sitting around the fire after they had eaten Rodrigo produced a guitar and they sang country songs until it was time to turn in. It was a very warm night and Edmund was restless. He rose and walked to the dying embers of the fire. He looked into the glowing wood and thought of home again. Was it time to turn back and join his brother in running the estate? This was an interesting country but in truth, life here was very much the same as anywhere. He returned to his bed and eventually fell asleep.

The warm night developed into a very wet morning and the fire had gone out. They decided on a cold breakfast to enable them to move on. Edmund wanted to push on as quickly as possible and deliver his message. They were descending from the mountains when the skies began to clear and the sun came out. The pace Edmund set eat up the miles and the group were making good time, resting the horses every few miles. Stopping in a small village for a midday break they found a taverna where the landlord was able to feed them. He complained that his business was being affected by a band of Moors who were pillaging the countryside and robbing travellers.

'I thought they had all been driven out,' said Edmund. 'There are still bands about who have turned to guerrilla tactics on villages, with murder and robbery on the highway,' replied the landlord. 'You had best be prepared on your journey.'

After their rest they mounted up and started out again, Edmund sent two rider ahead to spy out the land. A short time into the afternoon they came back to report that they had seen the sun glinting off steel in a small wood, and heard the snorts of horses. The scouts could not tell how many there were. Edmund decided to send ten of his men to the edge of the wood away from where the attack might come, the rest of them carried on. As they neared the wood a group of men rode out and called on them to stop and surrender or be killed. Edmund's men all drew their swords and the Moors put spurs to their horses and charged at them. They had their attention focussed on their prey and did not see the rest of Edmunds men come up behind them. The leading Moors crashed into Edmunds group and the fighting started. The second group were now joining the fray from the rear and adding to the Moors confusion. The fighting was fierce, Edmund felt Talio alive in his hand and he began to lay about the Infidels. The fight did not last long soon the Moors lost too many men to continue, those that were left threw down their swords. They were quickly bound and tied to trees. Edmund counted the cost, two of his men dead, one would not fight again, eight Moors dead, six severely wounded and the remaining eight tied up.

'Gather their horses and arms,' said Edmund. 'We will bury our dead but then we must move on.'

They were soon on their way again, Edmund's men fell silent as they rode. 'Gareth what is the problem with the men, they are very quiet?' asked Edmund.

'They are wondering what manner of man you are,' replied Gareth. 'They saw Talio in action and believe you, or the sword, or maybe both, are bewitched. When we stop again it would be wise to tell them the story of the blade.'

'Do you think that will ease their minds or cause more doubts?'

'At least you could show them the blade sir.'

Edmund rode on deep in thought, it was good council from Gareth and he decided he would tell the story of the blade. They made camp for the night and after all had eaten Edmund sat by the fire and unsheathed Talio. He passed it round but two of the men would not touch it.

'You can see it is just a fine blade and any of you could wield it,' said Edmund. 'My grandfather made it so to honour him I learnt to use it well.' What Edmund did not tell them was the connection with the ring. 'I am just a man like you, I bleed when I am cut and one day I will die, as do all men. I am just fortunate to have this beautiful sword and I wield it in memory of my father. Sleep now, tomorrow we arrive at Salamanca.'

They crossed the old Roman bridge into the City just as people were rousing themselves from a siesta. Edmund marvelled at the buildings and the large square in the centre of the City. He asked for the house of the alcalde and was directed to a fine looking building on the edge of the square. Edmund introduced himself and passed on the message, he was invited to stay at the house where there was room for his men and the wounded man was taken to the convent nearby where they could be tended to. At dinner that evening Edmund told them of his meeting with the Moors.

'They are a nuisance in this area,' said the alcalde. 'We must try to clear them out before the king comes. The city is well protected but the countryside offers too many opportunities for ambush.'

'I will suggest his majesty increases his guard for the journey,' said Edmund.

'Are you to return to Segovia before his majesty arrives here? If not I would be pleased to have you help us in removing these brigands.'

'I was not instructed to return immediately so if you wish we will be happy to assist you in cleaning them out.' Gareth looked at him and thought that is what Edmund enjoyed, fighting.

They made several sorties out in the region where the King would travel. They met two bands of Moors which they quickly despatched, there were no prisoners this time.

The day before the King was due to arrive Edmund and a strong guard rode out to meet him at his overnight camp. On arrival he was taken to the king.

'How fare you, my English warrior?' Asked the king. 'We hear you are becoming a slayer of Moors. The less we see of them the better we like it. We must see that you are rewarded, we shall think on it.'

'Thank you, your majesty. I am pleased to serve you in any way I can.'

Edmund joined Alberto at the fire. 'Is your brother with you, I did not see him,' said Edmund.

'He is organising the guards and sending out scouts,' replied the knight. 'Come sit with me and tell me of your adventures here.'

Edmund plied Alberto with questions about what lay further south. He was also told of the great city of Madrid. This fired his enthusiasm to see more of this land.

'You should visit Avila,' said Alberto. 'My home is there. It is a walled city and has some beautiful architecture. It has never been taken and is a very safe place to live. 'Do you visit your family often?' queried Edmund

'I am due to go as soon as the his majesty can release me. I think he will stay here for some time.'

Emilio returned and joined them at their evening meal. The king was in good humour and started telling, what he thought, were humorous stories. Edmund joined in the polite laughter!

There was great activity in the morning as they prepared for the king's entrance into the City. Fortunately the weather was fine and sunny and Edmund rued the fact that he would be in armour. The procession set off and was soon in sight of the city.

The battlements were full of people and so were the streets, decorations hung everywhere. They arrived at the castle where the king decended from his carriage and waved to the crowd who cheered as he walked into the castle.

Edmund dismounted aided by Gareth and his horse was taken by Cuthbert. The young page looked like a native with his black hair and sun browned features. He had taken to the language well and was the most proficient of the three. Edmund went up to his room to get rid of his armour. The rest of the day was uneventful for Edmund he was not needed until the evening banquet and even then he would not have been missed.

Early next morning he was awoken with knocking on his door. Alberto came in to tell him he had to go to Avila with despatches and Edmund was to accompany him. 'We may be staying there so pack all your belongings,' said Alberto. Edmund called Gareth and sent him down to tell Cuthbert to prepare the horses. When they were packed and ready Alberto joined them and they set off for Avila.

They made quite a caravan as they journeyed on towards the city. Edmund, Gareth and Cuthbert with their horses, Alberto with his squire Ahmed, a Moor who had converted to christianity, and Philip his page the oldest page Edmund had ever seen, also their horses and baggage. They rode at a comfortable pace with stops at midday and the evening. Edmund listened as Alberto talked of the countryside and his home in Avila. One clear sunlight day, as they surmounted a hill they saw in the distance the towers and walls of Avila.

'It looks very well fortified,' said Edmund. 'You would need many troops to man those towers and walls.'

'My father has enough, you only man the towers that face the enemy. If a large force came against us we can call in many more men.'

'Is your father the alcalde?' queried Edmund. Alberto smiled and said, 'he is much more than that. He is lord of the city and the surrounding countryside. That is similar to your Earl, yes?'

They entered the city and Edmund was impressed with the beautiful houses and buildings. Reaching a large square Alberto made for a magnificent house standing on one of the corners. Riding round to the rear they found a large courtyard with groom waiting to take their horses. A footman approached them and spoke to Alberto. 'My father will meet us when we have sorted ourselves out, follow this man and he will take you to your rooms.'

The rooms were large and they were attended by maids and footmen. Dressed and groomed Edmund and Gareth went downstairs and were directed to a comfortable sitting room. Alberto was there and introduced them to his father and mother. 'May I also introduce you to my two sisters, Jolentia and Rhyannon.' Edmund found himself looking at two beautiful women. He recovered his composure and bowed to both. When they went into dinner he found himself opposite Rhyannon, the younger of the two. The meal progressed well and Edmund found he was able to join in the conversation with not too many mistakes. Rhyannon was full of girlish chatter and wanted to know all about England and where he lived. Relaxing back in the sitting room Alberto's father had many questions too for Edmund about England and their estates there, he was most interested in the method of farming that his father had started.

The next day being Sunday all the family attended mass in the cathedral. Edmund noticed how many of the townspeople paid deference to the count. Walking back to the house Edmund found himself accompanying Rhyannon. 'Will you stay long in Avila?' she asked. 'It depends if the King calls for me, the little that I have seen I like very much.'

'You must let me show you more, shall we arrange a tour tomorrow?' Edmund agreed and the arrangement was made to meet after breakfast. They arrived back at the house and Alberto said that his father wanted to meet with him tomorrow regarding their affairs. Edmund told him of his arrangements with Rhyannon.

Alberto smiled and said that it was a good idea. That night as he lay waiting for sleep Edmund's mind turned to Wymondham and his own family, that had been tragically reduced. Was it time to return?

Chapter 11

Edmund woke with a certain excitement, today he was to be with Rhyannon all day. She was beautiful and a pleasant person to be with she also appeared to like him a little, or was that wishful thinking. He dressed carefully and calling Gareth went down to the dining room. Rhyannon was just leaving, she smiled at him and said. 'I will be back soon and meet you in the hallway.'

They toured the city with Rhyannon explaining this building and that statue. Gareth joined her maid and they were soon in conversation. After about the sixth church Edmund suggested they stop at one of the tavernas for refreshment. Sitting in the sunshine drinking a cool wine and talking to this beautiful young woman, Edmund was in seventh heaven. When they continued Rhyannon turned for home and Edmund asked why. 'This is the time for our siesta, to escape the heat of the day. Have you not done this before?' Rhyannon asked. 'As a guard for the king we have to be on duty all the time,' said Edmund.

'Well, today you will rest and be ready for the evening.' Edmund thought he would be ready for the evening rest or not. When they reached the house Rhyannon and her maid quickly left them. 'Off to our rest then,' said Edmund.

That evening there were more guests for dinner, friends of De La Cruz. Among these friends were two young men who were obviously keen on the two daughters. Rhyannon introduced him but there was an obvious coolness in their response. After dinner a group of musicians and dancers came to entertain them, Edmund thought about the women of the Gitanos who had danced the real flamenco. He missed them for many other reasons too. The evening drew to a close and everyone left leaving Edmund talking to Rhyannon. 'Shall we continue with our tour tomorrow?' she asked. 'I would like that very much,' said Edmund.

The next morning the sky was overcast and they had not been walking long when they felt spots of rain. Sheltering in a nearby church the subject turned to Edmunds travels. 'How long will you stay here?' asked Rhyannon. 'I do not know, I like it here very much. I must find something to do soon as I cannot impose on your family too long. Would you like me to stay?' Rhyannon lowered her head to hide her blushes. 'I would like to know more about you and your family,' she answered. Edmund told her all about their estates in England and of his fathers death in France and why he had decided to travel. The rain stopped and they continued their tour until it was time to return to the house.

That evening Senior De La Cruz asked Edmund if he would be willing to escort him to Madrid. 'I have some business there and to be accompanied by two knights would deter anyone who wanted to attack me. Alberto has agreed, how do you feel?'

'I would be honoured sir. I would like my squire to accompany me.'

'That is no problem,' said the Count. 'My name is Gilberto and we will leave in two days time.'

Alberto found him the next day and said they would be a party of twenty with his father, mother, retainers and themselves. Edmund and Rhyannon managed to meet again and she was again full of questions about England and his family. Edmund also learnt more of how powerful the De La Cruz family were in this part of Spain.

Came the day of their departure, goodbyes were said and the cavalcade moved out of the walled city. Edmund felt a loss of security, as the walls disappeared from view. 'A well fortified city,' he remarked to Alberto.

'Defence is very good,' agreed the Spaniard. 'Also it is easy to attack from the walls and towers. Parties can be sent out to harass the enemy and return quickly. The city has stood for many years without being taken.'

They entered a country of valleys and hills some very steep. Edmund kept a sharp lookout as it was prime country for an ambush. The count was in a jovial mood and even started to sing, Edmund thought he was in pain at first, Alberto explained it was an old shepherd's song.

They found a sheltered draw at the side of one of the valleys and made camp for the night. While they were sitting around the fire someone hailed them from the darkness, into the light came three men, the leader spoke. 'Good evening señor, if you look around you will see it would not be wise to go against our demands.' Moving into the firelight came enough crossbowmen to surround the camp, with their bolts loaded for firing they realised it would be suicide to resist. De La Cruz stood and said. 'Who are you and what do you want?' 'We just want you to quietly pack up and come with us, without your arms of course.' As he said this men moved in among them and began to collect swords and bows. Edmund tried to hide Talio but he was spotted and the sword joined the others. When everything was packed they were forced to have their hands tied and to follow the leader towards the hills.

After several miles of twisting and turning the road brought them to a deserted village where the robbers had set up home. Gilberto, Alberto, Edmund, Gareth and Ahmed were shut in a room near the old prison, the rest of the party were confined in another. After about an hour a man entered with a basket of bread and a jug of water. There was plenty of straw on the floor which they used to make beds.

'What do you think they are after?' asked Edmund.

'Depends if they know who we are,' said Alberto. 'My father is a rich man and if he has been recognised then we will be up for ransom.'

'I would like to get my hands free,' said Edmund wriggling about.

The door suddenly opened and one of their captors came in followed by the man they assumed was their chief.

'I hope you are all comfortable,' said the chief with a grin. 'We have sent a message to the De La Cruz family and as soon as we have the money in our hands you will be freed.' While he was talking the other man was cutting their bonds. Edmund could see other men just outside the door watching them so no chance of freedom yet.

'Let me introduce myself, I am the terror of the countryside 'El Zorro!' you have no doubt heard of me,' announced the chief. 'Another little man full of self importance' thought Edmund. No one answered him so he turned and strode out. When they were alone again Edmund searched the room they were in. The one window was too high and too small to be of use. The room was quite large and had at one time, been used by animals possibly horses for the guards of the prison. There were several rings set into the wall on one side and as Edmund casually pulled on one he felt it move. When he looked it was the stone in the wall that had moved. He tried it again and could see the stone was very loose, also the ones adjacent had lost their mortar. Was there a way out? The door was flung open and the guards brought in more water, luckily they had just finished their supper before being ambushed. When the guards had gone Edmund spoke softly to Alberto and told him what he had found.

'I think it is a single stone wall as there is no second floor above us,' said Edmund. 'We need to know what is on the other side. If you stand on my shoulders you should be able to see out of that window.

Alberto climbed up and said there was a road passing the wall but it was too dark to see anything else. 'That means their fire must be somewhere the other side. Let's see if we can move just one slab out of this wall without bringing the whole lot down on our heads.' As he said this Edmund went back to the ring. He was just going to grab hold of it when the door opened again and a guard came in with a bucket which he dropped on the floor and said, 'use it if you have to.' Edmund grabbed the ring again as Alberto joined him. Gradually they worked the stone until they were able to pull it free.

The wall was thick but only of single stones, Edmund tried the next stone and it began to move. 'If we can make a big enough opening, Gareth and I can squeeze out find the others and where the horses are, said Edmund. Alberto agreed and added, 'I will stay and put the stones back, we will make two beds up with straw dummies in case we have visitors. I do not think we will see them again tonight.' They carefully removed enough stones for Edmund and Gareth to get out and then replaced them.

The two of them stood for a moment to get used to the dark. The sound of footsteps made them hide in a dark corner as a guard strolled bye. Moving quietly along the wall they came to the old prison. From the noise that came from this building they gathered this was where the bandits were gathered. Moving further along brought them to another barn. 'I wonder if this is where the others are?' whispered Edmund. 'There's a window boarded up see if you can see between the cracks.' Gareth peered in and managed to see Cuthbert sitting on a bale of hay, he could also hear the murmurings of the others. Still moving along the wall they came the ruins of a house. Climbing over the rubble they could see the front of the prison, a fire burned in the street and two guards stood talking close to it. Edmund and Gareth crouched down and quickly crossed the street, one of the guards looked in their direction but the light from the fire affected his vision and they managed to cross without incident. They stopped behind another ruined house and Edmund whispered to Gareth. 'We need to find the horses.' Moving on they came to another partially demolished barn and immediately could smell that this was what they were looking for. The problem was that the door was very near the prison and their captors. Edmund led the way further up the street, keeping to the backs of the houses. Crossing back to the other side they moved as quietly as possible to arrive at their building and Edmund pushed on one of the stones. A whispered voice said. 'Is that you?' Edmund smiled and answered, 'Yes it is me, Edmund. Pull out the stones so that we can get in.'

Easing themselves through the gap the two men brushed themselves down as best as they could. They all sat down as Edmund described what he had found. Making a drawing in the dust on the floor Edmund outlined a plan he had. They would create a diversion and then release the others. Alberto and the rest agreed and De La Cruz volunteered to organise the diversion that was needed. They all settled down to get to sleep in what was left of the night with one of them, taking it in turns, to keep awake and waken them before dawn. This would be when the guards were not expecting any trouble. Edmund's main concern was that they had no weapons and this must be a priority in his plan.

Chapter 12

Edmund felt a hand on his shoulder and he awoke with a start. 'It is time,' said Gareth. The others were rousing themselves and looking around for any sort of weapon. Edmund found an old rusty bar under some straw and Gareth had a piece of wood. They removed the stones in the wall and De La Cruz led Ahmed to the place they had agreed for the diversion. Edmund with Gareth and Alberto made their way to where the rest of their party were imprisoned. They went to the back of the building and found the boarded up window. Edmund called softly to Cuthbert and they began to work on one of the boards that looked the weakest. They soon had a gap wide enough for them all to escape. Edmund sent three of the group to De La Cruz to support him. Now came the moment of truth, would their plan work?

Suddenly, from the bottom of the street, came shouting and the noise of what sounded like a fight. Edmund smiled as De La Cruz made the most of his men. One guard dashed into the prison calling for them to wake as they were being attacked the other looked down the street but it was not light enough to see anything. The bandits came pouring out of the prison and set off down the street towards the noise. As they disappeared in the morning gloom Edmund led his band across the street and into the prison. There were only four men left inside and Edmunds men soon despatched them. They quickly found their confiscated weapons and Edmund spirits rose when he had Talio in his hands. From an inside pocket he withdrew the ring and with it on his finger he called them all to follow him outside. They could hear the bandits returning and Edmund told them to hide in the shadows. The bandits were talking among themselves wondering what had caused all the noise as when they arrived at the end of the street there was nobody in sight.

Edmund stepped out and called for the chief to surrender, instead of which the man led his men in a charge towards them. From both sides of the street came the count's men and battle was joined. Edmund made for the chief and soon Talio was wreaking havoc. The chief went down, minus his head, and then Edmund was among the rest. The fighting was ferocious and the noise of screaming men rang through the village. Without their chief the brigands were in disarray and threw down their swords and surrendered, that is the ones who were left alive. Alberto rounded them up and this time they used the prison as it was intended. De La Cruz came to Edmund and said, 'I congratulate you, young man, on a well executed plan. Due to my age I was a little slow in reaching the fight but what I saw I can hardly believe. There can be no one who could stand against you. Alberto told me of what he knew of your story and now I have seen it with my own eyes. You must be careful how you use the blade, it will be a great temptation to do exactly what you want with it in your hand.'

'I know sir, and so does the blade, as it will only fight like that against evil. In normal times it responds as would any blade. I can train and joust with my friends as anyone else and they are safe. Sometimes I feel like getting rid of it but it was my fathers and made by my grandfather so I am bound to use it for good where I can.'

The count nodded and Edmund went to Gareth to find out their losses. Surprisingly there were only two of the count's men lightly wounded. Alberto had set a couple of the bandits to digging graves and burying the dead. They recovered the horses and now had twice as many. Ahmed found the bandits food store and soon had a breakfast prepared. They were all hungry and as they ate the aggression they had felt calmed down. The sun had risen and the day began to warm as they loaded their belongings onto the horses. The count said they would travel until the midday and then rest before entering Madrid the next morning.

The party set off having given the prisoners water and bread enough for three days. They would send guards to collect them later.

The midday stop was in a beautiful valley where they could rest in the afternoon sun. Edmund noticed that the men were a little nervous of him and most kept their distance. This was always the result when he had been fighting with Talio. One of the guards called out that there was rider approaching. When he arrived he went to De La Cruz and handed him a message. 'We are not going to Madrid after all,' said the Count. 'My friend has moved to Toledo and will meet us there. We will camp here for the night and continue in the morning.'

Laying in his tent that night Edmund thought over the days events. He was now convinced that the ring sensed his feelings and transmitted them to the sword, hence the difference between fighting an enemy or just practicing with a friend. How could he ever find out what really possessed the sword. Where could he go to look, perhaps he should try and find where the ring originated from. He fell asleep with these thoughts spinning in his head.

In the morning they began their journey to Toledo. Alberto told Edmund what a grand city Toledo was and that it was the most important city in Castile. He told him of the wonderful sword makers there, Toledo steel was the finest in all Spain, if not the world. He had a friend who was a sword maker and he would be most interested in Talio.

They entered Toledo through one of the fine gates and Edmund could see that again the City had protection by being built on a hill with river on 60% of its sides. These Spaniards pick their sites he thought. They arrived at a large house with a square in front and were welcomed by a portly man who ushered them inside. 'My men will see to your horses and baggage,' he said. De La Cruz introduced him as Señor Rafael Berchello a great friend and also his cousin.

They were all taken to their rooms and asked to meet in the drawing room when they were ready.

There was quite a gathering when they all finally met. There were glasses of a fizzy wine that Edmund did not like and lots of bread with cheeses and meats. Eventually most of them retired to bed leaving Edmund, Alberto, De La Cruz and their host sitting at a table. The door opened and into the room walked a young man accompanying a beautiful dark haired woman. Edmund wondered how there were so many beautiful women in Spain.

Berchello rose and introduced his daughter, Maria, and his son, Stephan. Edmund jumped up kissed the hand that she offered and shook the young man's. Alberto continued telling the story of their capture and Edmund's part in their escape. Edmund could feel his face reddening and said he was just lucky.

The following morning Edmund met Alberto and asked him what they should be doing? Alberto replied that the day was his to do what he wanted. He would, however, like him to visit his friend, the sword maker, and show him Talio. Edmund agreed and so it was arranged.

The streets of the city were very steep and Edmund found it quite hard going in the little back alleys. Eventually they came across the sword-smith's shop and Edmund was introduced. The smith examined Talio and was amazed at the quality of the steel. He told Edmund he had nothing to match it and asked where it came from. Edmund told him the story of how his grandfather made it but left out any mention of the ring. 'Your grandfather was a very clever smith and has included something else into the firing but I know not what,' he said. Edmund thanked him and they continued to look around the city.

When they returned to the house everyone was preparing for the evening meal. Edmund was seated opposite Maria, an enchanting woman who also appeared well educated, he enjoyed the conversation. He found that they had only recently moved into the house and she had not had time to form many friends yet. Edmund asked her if she would join him in visiting the cathedral tomorrow, to which she agreedA glorious day greeted them as they set off for the cathedral. Maria's maid followed accompanied by Gareth. The cathedral was cooler and dark. They strolled around the interior, Maria showing him the various chapels to Saints ending up in front of the high altar. They sat for a while in thought and prayer and Edmund began to feel at peace. Life had been hectic since he had come to this land and to sit calmly with a beautiful woman at his side gave him a feeling of contentment. She was not his woman however, he liked her company and maybe he could take a chance and get to know her better, he thought.

They left the cathedral and visited a colourful market where Maria enjoyed looking through the stalls. Edmund was fascinated by a stall selling Toledo daggers and knives where he purchased daggers for himself and Gareth. They stopped at a taverna and had a simple lunch of bread and stuffed eggs washed down with a white wine. The sun was near its zenith when they arrived back at the house where most had gone for their siesta. As they parted Maria whispered to Edmund, 'call for me.'

Edmund was taken aback by her invitation, he certainly felt a warm glow when he thought of her. Their time together had been so short how could it be love! She is beautiful and intelligent, does it hit you that quick?

When the heat began to lessen Edmund went to Maria' room and quietly knocked. A soft call bid him enter and he found Maria sitting by the window with the breeze gently blowing her hair. He went to her and she moved to let him sit beside her. 'Did you enjoy our walk today? She asked. 'I enjoy all the time I spend with you and I miss you when you are not with me,' said Edmund. He gently put his arm around her waist and she stiffened and said, 'No, do not spoil this moment and be patient. I do have feelings for you but I must be given time.'

They stayed together and spoke of their families and the differences between them. "Will you go back to England?' Edmund thought for a moment. 'I would like to see my home again, I also like this land very much and want to see more of it.' Maria turned to him and said, 'I have an uncle in Sevilla which is many days ride from here to the South. I have never been there, it is very beautiful they say.' Maria's maid, who had been sitting in a corner, coughed and startled Edmund. 'A lady is never without a chaperone,' said Maria and laughed. 'Do not be alarmed she is very discrete.' Edmund stood, took his leave and returned to his room. Gareth joined him and they went downstairs to the evening meal. Maria joined them and smiled at him.

That night as he lay in bed Edmund thought of Maria and imagined her beside him. He knew this would not be possible without marriage. Was he ready for that? Was he still too footloose to enter into a commitment like that? His feelings for Maria were very strong, he was still unsure that it was love? How could he know with such a short acquaintance. He tossed and turned and eventually fell into a fitful sleep.

'Are you not well?' asked Gareth in the morning. 'I did not sleep much,' answered Edmund. 'I think it must be the heat. I think I will ride today ask Cuthbert to prepare my horse.'

'Shall I accompany you?' asked Gareth.

'If you wish, we could ride along the river bank.'

They departed before the rest of the house had risen and after a some distance Edmund slowed and they rode together. 'Does the maid tell you much?' asked Edmund. 'About the family and their friends.'

'She is quite talkative,' said Gareth. 'The family is very wealthy and have connections throughout Spain. They have only recently moved here and Maria does not have any suitors yet but here father wants her to marry well. Are you interested, I have seen how you look at her.'

Edmund was quiet for a while and then said, 'I must write to Harold it is a long time since the last letter. I think we may be here for a while longer. How do you feel about that?' Gareth thought for a moment and then replied, 'I like the country and now we speak the language it is much more enjoyable. If I was in England I would have hoped to further my position however here there are different opportunities. I will stay with you willingly.'

They turned back to the house where Edmund decided to walk in the gardens. He was gazing at an orange tree when he heard someone approach. Señor Berchello spoke to him. 'They are not quite ripe yet, when they are you will find them very sweet. I am glad I have found you as I want to speak to you regarding my daughter. I see there is a friendship blossoming and before it goes any further I would like to know more about you.'

'I understand sir, and I will tell you everything you wish to know. My father was Earl John Ivanson of Wymondham and his fiefdom included the shires of Norfolk and Suffolk with part of Lincoln. My brother, Harold has inherited the title which has been upheld by the king. I am a knight and have a castle in Dunston, a village in Norfolk, the surrounding lands provide a good income. I have decided to travel for a while to broaden my knowledge and have explored France, the Basque country and now Spain. I intend to return to England one day.'

'Thank you for being honest with me and I have no objections to your friendship with Maria as long as it is just as friends for the moment.'

They walked back to the house together and could see Maria at one of the windows, watching.

Chapter 13

Alberto came to him the next day and said he had been summoned back to Salamanca by the king and that Edmund should accompany him. Edmund thought carefully of his response and wrote to the monarch asking to him to release him from his service. He gave the letter to Alberto and asked him to deliver it to the king. 'I will stay in Toledo until I receive his answer,' said Edmund. 'I shall find somewhere to live as I cannot impose on señor Berchello any longer.' 'I know someone who will miss you,' said Alberto. 'It is a wise decision in the circumstances.'

Edmund talked with señor Berchello and told him of his decision. 'I have a friend in the city who would be pleased to have you. I will take you to meet him.' Edmund thanked him and went back to his room to pack. When they arrived at the friend of Berchello, señor Alsheikh, the accommodation he offered was a small house with stables. The rent would be protection for him on his business journeys, Edmund did not know what that business was. They spent the rest of the day moving in. Cuthbert said the stables were very good, plenty of room and the horses were quite happy. Edmund toured the house and found four bedrooms, a large kitchen and another large sitting/dining room. All were well furnished, so now he had to think of staff and their cost.

Edmund went to see the owner of the house. 'We have moved in and can you help me in finding staff.' 'Do not worry about that, said Alsheikh. 'There are already staff and they will arrive tonight to prepare your meal. They are part of my staff and are included in our arrangement.'

Edmund asked, 'What exactly do you require us to do?' Alsheikh asked him to sit down while he explained. 'I am a trader in precious metals and jewels. I have to travel around Spain and I need protection. Señor Berchello told me of your prowess as a fighting man and as I do not wish to draw attention to myself with a large number of guards this is a good alternative. My colleagues and I are also bankers. Do you agree to my arrangement?' Edmund thought I have already agreed and cannot refuse now, I hope he is as wily as a banker as he has been with me. A thought came to Edmund that this would help with his transfer of funds from England, he would talk to the Jew later.

That evening Edmund called to see Maria. He was shown into a small sitting room where Maria and her maid joined him. 'I called to tell you where my new home is. I am staying in Toledo and have told the king this and asked him to release me from his service. You probably know your father has spoken to me. You probably are aware by now that I have fallen in love with you, I know we have only known each other for a short time but I want to call on you as a suitor, if you do not object.'

'I don't object at all,' said Maria. 'I shall look forward to you calling at any time.' She came towards him and held out her hand, he took it and kissed it. They looked into each others eyes and Edmund knew there was love for him there. He took his leave and went back to his house.

Isaac called the next day to tell them he was to go to Madrid tomorrow and would they be ready to set off at six o'clock. The air was quite cool as they departed and Edmund thought this is a good time to travel. Riding alongside Isaac Edmund learnt that the Jew was worried by a murmur against his race, in other countries there had been persecutions and he was concerned for his family and friends.

Edmund could not understand what people had against them. Isaac chatted on about his son and daughter, he hoped his son would take over his business one day. Madrid was a busy city fortunately Isaac knew his way to the house where his contact lived. Edmund was on his guard as the street was narrow and there were several unsavoury looking characters hanging about. 'Come in with me and meet my friend,' said Isaac. Edmund agreed and said to Gareth and Cuthbert. 'Stand guard at the door and keep an eye on those characters.'

Gareth looked back along the street and the group that had been looking at them began to move away.

Edmund followed Isaac into the house where a fussy little man asked them to follow him and led them to a large bare room where several men sat at desks writing. One of the men rose and smiling came to greet them. 'Isaac my friend, welcome to my house.' They embraced and the man led them to another room, this was dominated by a large desk, bookshelves lined the room. Isaac introduced the man as Jacob.

The two bankers got down to business and Edmund turned to the bookshelves, he had not seen so many books in one place. An hour passed and then Isaac called him over to where they sat at the desk.

'Jacob has suggested that he makes contact with his colleague in London and asks him to go and see your brother. They can arrange a way to provide you with money here, should you need it. Do you agree to this?'

'Thank you for your suggestion of help. I am not short of funds at the moment and the king still owes me my pay, which I understand his chancellor is sending. I would appreciate a way of getting capital, and your suggestion is appealing. This would have taken considerable time, all the travelling involved.' said Edmund.

Jacob smiled at him. 'Not so long as you think, young man. I have a network that has been built up over many years and methods of communication that are far better than that order of knights who offer a banking service. You will have my proposal very soon.'

The two men, having concluded their business, embraced and Isaac said he was ready to leave. They went to the street door and as Edmund opened it he turned and thrust Isaac back inside the house. 'Wait there,' he said as he joined Gareth and Cuthbert who were facing four men at the end of the street. Coming from the opposite end were three more. Edmund moved quickly to support his two friends and the strangers rushed at them. Edmund was soon into the fray and Talio was moving like lightening. Down went two of the men and a third slumped to the ground wounded, the other turned and ran. The three from the opposite end joined in the melee and the fight became ferocious. A big man came at Edmund swinging an axe, he parried the blow and the man swung again. This time Edmund brought Talio up in a powerful swing which resulted in the man loosing his axe and his arm. The three turned and fled helping the wounded man who was screaming loudly. Edmund counted the cost, two of the assailants dead, two severely wounded. Cuthbert had been wounded in the shoulder and Edmund had a nick in his leg. They went back to the house where Jacob was fussing about. He told them there had been a spate of robberies in the Jewish community and there was a growing mood against them in the city.

His wife and a maid came in to take care of their wounds, they were not serious so they were fit to travel. A loud knocking on the door made them start. Jacob came back with two men dressed in part armour and helmets. 'These are two of the Saint Hermandad patrol and want to know what happened,' said Jacob. The men questioned Edmund about the fight and told them there had been many robberies in the area. Fortunately several people had seen the episode from their windows and could support Edmund's account. Jacob offered them shelter for the night so they could rest and continue their journey home the next day, this they readily accepted.

They set off early the next morning so they could clear the City before many people had stirred. They set a fast pace as Isaac was nervous that they would be attacked again. He was not happy until they entered Toledo and reached his house. Sitting relaxed at last in his sitting room he said to Edmund, 'Thank you for what you did, without you and your men I could have been robbed and killed. Here is a small reward as it is clear the task that I asked you to do is more dangerous than I first thought. We are living in dangerous times. I will call on you when I have to make my next journey.' Isaac handed Edmund a fat purse which was quite heavy.

Edmund thanked him and they left to return to their house. Their wounds were not serious and after a good nights sleep they all felt much better. Edmund said that he hoped not all Isaac's visits were as hectic. Gareth suggested that they should train more between the three of them so as to hone their skills. Cuthbert was a little reticent after watching Edmund in the fight but soon entered into the training sessions when he realised Edmund could fence without Talio going berserk.

Chapter 14

Harold was in his usual place when he wanted to think, on the battlements. He wondered if it was a habit inherited from his father. His concern was how many tenants he had lost in the plague that had swept the country. His fiefdom had not suffered as much as some and he could still send wool to Flanders. Labour was hard to find and fields needed planting and cattle looking after. His attention was drawn to a rider approaching at a fast gallop. Descending to the keep he met the man who introduce himself as Julius Storm. Once ensconced in the hall he said he was from a London Merchant Company that had connections in Spain and one of his contacts knew his brother Edmund. Harold was keen to know any information that he had about his brother. Julius told him how he was now living with a friend of their Company and assisting him in his work.

'I have been asked to tell you that your brother would like you to use us for any financial transfers you might make to him. We are more secure and very much quicker than the system you have been using.' Harold looked at him and thought for a while. Julius continued, 'I am aware that you do not know us or me, and this will need some time for you to decide to trust us. To assist you I have a letter here from your brother.' Julius handed over the letter and walked to the other end of the hall and looked out of the window. Harold read the letter and joined Julius. 'I can see my brother trusts your company and I am willing to to do what he wants. This does seem similar to the knights, who I believe have now ceased their system.''We are not like the knights at all or like the way they did their business,' said Julius. 'We are more simple and easier to deal with.'

Julius stayed the night and departed in the morning with a letter from Harold to Edmund.

Harold thought about what he had agreed to as he rode over to Dunston. He hoped Edmund understood the undertaking they were making. Whatever Edmund needed in funds the company would advance them and they would be guaranteed from the profits that were made in England. Arriving at Dunston he was met by Stephen and they fell to discussing the wool that was to be shipped.

Stephen listened to the proposal that Harold had agreed with Julius. 'I have heard of similar ways of moving money, and this is the most secure. I hope it helps Edmund. I would like to see him come home soon. I have to concentrate on finding men that can work with the sheep and the land.'

'The whole shire has the same problem,' said Harold. 'We have not suffered as much as some.' He stayed for a while walking round the castle and thinking of when he was a boy and used to visit his grandfather. 'I wonder how Edmund is handling the sword, is there some magic in it or is it a rumour to frighten the foe?' He smiled to himself as he remembered it did nothing for him. When the country had settled down and returned to normal perhaps he would go to Spain and find Edmund, he missed him more and more.

He said goodbye to Stephen and set off for Wymondham. He spurred his horse on so that he and his squire would reach home before dark. There was also another reason for his haste, the new Earl of Nottingham was to visit this evening and stay for a deer hunt, he would be bringing his daughter with him. Harold needed to marry soon to ensure the family line carried on and he quite liked the girl. He only just made it in time to change his clothes when he heard the Earl's party arrive in the keep.

The evening meal helped to restore his spirits and the company of Elizabeth was certainly very pleasant. Harold had spoken to her father regarding a possible match and the Earl had said he was not against it providing his daughter agreed. The two houses would be brought closer and give strength in the region. When the evening had finished Harold was quite sure that Elizabeth would make a fine wife. They walked up to the battlements and in the moonlight Harold proposed and was accepted. Elizabeth's father was pleased, he and Harold fell to discussing the dowry. After numerous glasses of wine they agreed on the details and went to bed happy men.

Edmund received a message from Isaac to meet him at his house. When he arrived Isaac smiled at him and said. 'Good news Edmund, all has been agreed with your brother and so you may request funds and we can provide them in line with the agreement. Here is a letter from your brother which will explain what happens in England.'

Edmund read the letter which not only explained what he had done but brought him up to date with news of all that was happening at home. The letter also included the news that his brother was to marry. While reading Edmund felt quite homesick. One day he must return and that day should not be far away.

Isaac sent a message that asked Edmund to accompany him to Buitrago, near to Madrid. Edmund called to see Isaac and the dealer said he was to collect some valuable gem stones from a family who lived in this town. 'It is high in the hills so you will see some beautiful parts of the country. There are bands of robbers in the hills but I know you will look after me.' Edmund wondered if three would be enough to stave off an attack, Isaac still insisted that a larger force would attract too much notice.

The day started with bright sunshine and they were all in good humour. They reached a small village in the foothills and stopped at an Inn for lunch. Clouds were gathering as they set off again and spots of rain began to fall. They headed for some trees to shelter as the spots turned to a downpour. 'I shouldn't think we will see many bandits in this weather,' said Edmund. The rain stopped and the sun came out as they moved on. The rain had slowed them down making it later than expected to reach the next village where they were to spend the night. They topped a rise and could see the lights of the village through the evening gloom, they could also see a group of men blocking their progress. One of the men shouted to them to hand over their valuables. Edmund rode towards them. 'Get out of or way or face the consequence.' He drew Talio as he said this. A big man who was the leader shouted back, 'I am the undefeated champion of this region and your life is now in peril. Give us your money or you will die.' With that he charged and Edmund had to quickly parry his attack. The rest of the gang were beginning to move forward as Edmund began his attack and the big man demonstrated he was no beginner with a sword. Gareth and Cuthbert had also unsheathed their weapons and had spurred into the fray. Edmund was busy matching the leaders cut and thrust he could feel the heat from the ring, he suddenly feinted a move followed by a thrust and drove Talio through the man's heart. He joined the others and downed two more, with mortal wounds. The rest turned and fled. Isaac had moved his horse out of the way of the conflict and was staring at Edmund. 'Thank you, I had thought we were in deep trouble then. You are a master with that sword Edmund.' Gareth had received a small cut on his arm which they quickly bound and continued on their way to the village.

Edmund rode up to Señor Berchello's house and asked to see Maria. 'Will you walk with me Maria, it is a beautiful day?' Maria looked at him and said, 'I have been waiting for you to call.' During their walk Edmund told her of the letter from Harold, he said that at times he missed his brother. The sun shone down on them as they strolled and talked of everyday occurrences but not about themselves. They paused under a large oak tree, Edmund turned towards Maria. 'I have never met a woman like you, beautiful in body and mind, I do not think I will be able to live without you. What I am trying to say is that I have fallen deeply in love with you.' Maria lifted her hand and placed a finger on his lips. 'I too, am in love with you since we first met, it can happen that quickly. I am not sure my father would agree. What are we to do?' Edmund took her hand and looking directly into her eyes he said, 'Maria will you marry me?' 'Oh yes please,' said a beaming Maria. 'Then I shall speak to your father on our return.' Maria fell into his arms and Edmund felt and tasted the sweetness of her lips. Recovering themselves they realised that they were in full view of the people walking through the gardens. Most were smiling at them and some waved much to the embarrassment of Maria.

Arriving back at the Berchello house Edmund asked to see Señor Berchello. He was to meet him in his private quarters. Edmund gave a nervous knock on the door and a voice bid him to enter. Señor Berchello stood up and welcomed Edmond. 'Did you enjoy your walk, it is a splendid day is it not?' Edmund was tongue-tied for a moment. 'Has something happened, you look most uncomfortable. Sit down young man, is there anything I can do?'

'I wish to marry your daughter sir, and she wishes to marry me. I know I should have come to see you first but it all happened under that oak tree in the park, things came to a head and I could not help myself.' The words tumbled out of Edmund in a rush. Señor Berchello looked at him with a stern face. 'Yes, that is what you should have done and I am surprised that it has taken this long,' he said and then burst into a broad grin. 'Maria told me that it was you she wanted. That oak tree must be enchanted as many couples have plighted their troth there, including myself and my wife. May you two are as happy as we have been. Join us tonight, with your friends, when we can celebrate with our family.' Edmund thanked him and departed with a large grin on his face.

That evening Maria's mother, Señora Margararetta Berchello and brother Stephan joined them at dinner to celebrate the occasion. The discussion afterwards centred around wedding arrangements, Rafael, as he insisted Edmund now called him, signalled to Edmund to join him with Stephan, Gareth and Cuthbert, in his room. When they were comfortably seated with a drink in their hands Rafael spoke to Edmund. 'The only concern I have for you both is, what will you do for a living. Your method of income is a little precarious and also dangerous. Maria could be a widow any day. I have a solution, if you will accept it, Maria's grandfather left her some property that was to be part of her dowery. Tomorrow join me and we will ride out to see it.' Edmund again thanked him and felt as if he was in a whirlwind with all that was happening so fast. What did Maria's father want him to do, even she could not fathom out what her father wanted? Edmund wrote to Harold that evening with the news and begged him to visit.

The next morning Edmund thought over the events of the previous day. There was no turning back now, not that he wanted to. They joined Rafael at his house and then set off into the hills around Toledo. Within an hours ride they came to a large set of gates, going through they found themselves riding past rows of grape vines. They at last reached a rambling house surrounded by barns. A man greeted them and Rafael introduced him as his Gerante who ran the vineyard. They walked into the house which was quite large, certainly a family, home.

'This used to be part of her grandfather's estate, it is the only piece left that my father had not sold before he died. I have my own lands and business. You will find it needs some updating but the wine sells well and can provide a good income.' Edmund had the feeling that Rafael would like to have run the vineyard himself.

'I have no knowledge of wine production,' said Edmund. 'I can learn very quickly and I am sure that Gerante will help me.'

'He is a good man, and devoted to Maria. He runs it well now but, as I said, it needs some work done.'

They completed their tour of the buildings and sat down to lunch. Emile, the Gerante, said he had some problems with a band of Moors who wanted to destroy the vineyard as it produced alcohol. The local militia had chased them off and they had not been seen for some time. Edmund could see a chance to use his expertise. 'We will need to train our own guards,' he said. 'I will have to look at the accounts as soon as possible.' Rafael agreed and they would be available back at his home. On the homeward journey Edmund had lots of questions which Rafael answered most, those that he could not were promised when they arrived at his house.

Maria stood waiting for them when they arrived, wanting to know his reaction to the vineyard. 'I think it will make a good business and a good home,' said Edmund. Maria wanted to to talk about the wedding arrangements but Edmund needed to go to his own house and talk to Isaac. He also wanted to discuss the future with Gareth and Cuthbert. Gareth said he missed England but he liked the vineyard and the prospect of living there. Cuthbert asked a lot of questions but his overall decision was that he would not leave them, he had no ties with England as he was an orphan and had been brought up at the castle.

A loud knocking wakened them one night, Edmund grabbed his sword and joined Gareth who was already at the bottom of the stairs. Edmund called out and there was a muffled reply that they could not understand. 'Open it carefully,' said Edmund. Gareth moved it a little and then they heard a voice. 'This is a good welcome for your brother, I have travelled a long way and am tired.'

Edmund flung open the door and the two men hugged each other. When the party, for there were several people outside, had come into the house Harold introduced a young lady as his wife Elizabeth. Edmund stood back and smiled at Harold. 'You have beaten me again. I welcome you both and am anxious to hear all the news but you must rest first.' Gareth had roused the staff and they were busy trying to find beds for every one. When they had all come in and their belongs taken to the rooms. Harold and Edmund sat in the kitchen, the only room without people sleeping. 'We managed to find a ship bound for Lisbon and the captain was in a hurry,' explained Harold. 'We bought good horses in the city and had no delays. I needed to speak to you and as we deserved a break I decided to bring Elizabeth, and of course she needed a maid, our party just grew.'

Harold told Edmund all that had been happening at home. How the plague had affected their wool business. Edmund likewise brought his brother up to date with his adventures. They did not finish talking until early morning, Edmund suggested that they call on señor Berchello the following after noon after they had rested, when his brother and wife could meet Maria.

Harold was impressed with the Berchello house and liked Rafael immediately. Edmund listened to them talking about business and slipped away to find Maria who was busy talking to Elizabeth. 'It is a good opportunity to practice my English' she said. 'I will be with you soon, find Stephan he wanted to talk to you about the ceremony.' Edmund placed his finger to his lips telling her to be quiet as the ceremony was a secret. Rafael insisted they stay for a meal and they ended up staying the night.

It was a very pleasant ride back to the vineyard, Harold said he had found Maria a lovely girl and Edmund was marrying into a wealthy family. He asked who where the other two older knights who were accompanying them, Edmund said he would explain when they reached the vineyard. Harold complained that it was too hot and he would be grateful when they reached the shade of the house.

Chapter 15

Edmund asked Gareth to accompany him to the local church where they had been attending mass when they were at home. They sat for a moment feeling the coolness and peacefulness of the building. 'You mentioned some time ago about your advancement,' said Edmund. 'The time has now come for you to take that next step and I want you to prepare yourself for knighthood.' Gareth grabbed his hand and thanked him. 'When shall it be done?' he asked. 'Two nights from now you will prepare yourself and come to this church at dusk. You will be met by two other knights who will help you. They came with us to carry out the ceremony. You will spend the night here in prayer and the following morning the ceremony will take place. I am your sponsor so señor Berchello will officiate. I suggest that you take Cuthbert as your squire, he deserves it, and there is a young lad at the vineyard who you could consider as a page.' Gareth could not stop smiling and shaking Edmund's hand. Edmund would need a new squire, he had discussed this with Rafael who had suggested his son Stephan. Edmund liked Stephan so this was agreed.

Gareth spent the next night alone in the church preparing himself for his forthcoming ceremony. The following evening he was dressed in a white robe which was covered by a scarlet cloak he again went to the church and was met at the door by two knights in armour who led him silently towards the altar where a kneeler had been positioned. Gareth knelt and started his Vigil. Several times during the night he felt his eyes close and he wobbled which wakened him. At last the dim light of dawn seeped into the church, a priest entered and mass was said for the three of them. The two knights then dressed him in armour that they had brought with them and at last spoke to him. They were friends of señor Berchello and as Gareth stood in his armour they congratulated him warmly. The door of the church opened and señor Berchello, Edmund and all the family plus some friends, walked in. All the knights were in armour and they gathered round Gareth. Edmund told him to kneel and offered Rafael Talio. He took it and laid the blade on Gareth's shoulder. 'I dub thee Sir Gareth of Hopton, arise Sir Knight of England.' There was a shout of welcome from Edmund and they all congratulated Gareth. There was much celebrating at a feast that had been prepared that night. At last they all staggered off to bed, Gareth, still with a broad grin on his face.

At last the day of the month the wedding took place, as far as Edmund could remember, he had been there, everything happened in a blur. The people of Toledo certainly were aware that it had taken place as it was one of the grandest they had witnessed. The cathedral was full, mainly with family and friends of the Berchello's, Harold was impressed and wondered if Edmund would ever return home. When the revelry afterwards was in full swing Edmund and Maria slipped away to Edmund's house. They had planned to leave for the vineyard early in the morning.

The house was quiet now, Rafael had offered Harold, Elizabeth and their group, accommodation and Gareth had not yet returned. Edmund stood looking at Maria, both were slightly nervous as they undressed. They climbed into bed quickly and Edmund took her in his arms. Maria had not been with a man before, this did not stop her reacting to natural feelings. Edmund was very gentle he remembered what the Gypsy women had taught him. A night began that they would never forget.

Loud noises woke them as the house went about its morning activities. Edmund reached for Maria. 'Good morning wife, come, love your husband.' Maria giggled and slipped into his arms and their bodies reacted to their feelings. Later there came knocks at the door and Gareth's voice asking if they were still alive. The plans for leaving early for the vineyard had to be reorganised and they left just before noon. Maria, with her maid Chiquita, soon started organising the household staff while Edmund met with Gerante who brought him up to date on what was happening in the vineyard. Harold and Elizabeth with their entourage arrived as they had decided to stay with Edmund for a few more days before returning to Wymondham. Harold joined Edmund in the discussions and was surprised at how mature Edmund had become and able to take charge of the situation. The Moors had made another attempt to raid the barns but had been beaten off. Edmund put Gareth to the task of organising a strong guard and increasing the patrols of the perimeter.

Gerante told him there were men in the nearby village who would be suitable and would like to work for the vineyard. Edmund thought about a name for the vineyard and suggested Castillo Dunston, everyone agreed, Harold was pleased there was a connection to Norfolk. Maria thought it was a good marriage between England and Spain, just like theirs.

The next months were a hive of activity at Castillo Dunston as Edmund learnt all about wine growing and how to run the estate. Harold was able to help using his experience at Wymondham, he thought about how to improve some of the old fashioned methods without upsetting the men and women who worked for him.

Autumn was fast becoming winter, Edmund still could not get used to how warm it was. In England they would be preparing for snow where here it meant just putting on another garment. Harold had returned to England, the grapes had been gathered and the presses were in full use, he loved the smell as he walked through the barns. The big vats would soon be full. The sale of their wine was mostly to large estates within a days travelling distance. Edmund was walking around the rear of one of the barns when he came across a small building he had not been in before. Looking through the large bunch of keys Emile Gerante had given him he found one that opened the door. There was little light inside as there were no windows, lighting a torch he saw a staircase going down. He decended into a huge chamber with another leading off from it. The chambers were full of racks and in the second, half of these racks were full of bottles of wine. Edmund retrieved one from the lowest rack and came back out to the sunshine. He walked back to the barn where he knew Emile was working.

'Emile, what is this wine?' asked Edmund as he confronted him. 'Oh, I see you have found the cellars. I did mean to tell you about those. The wine is some that we had left over from previous harvests,' said an embarrassed Emile. 'Is it any good now? Let us open it and find out,' said Edmund and promptly withdrew the cork. They poured a cup each and sipped the wine. 'I think it is excellent,' pronounced Edmund. 'It does improve with age,' agreed Emile. 'Why is there so much there?' asked Edmund. 'We could certainly benefit from the money it would raise.' Emile told him they often made more wine than they could sell so some was saved and some was given to farmers for their pigs.

Edmund decided to approach the Bishop of Toledo to take his wine for communion. He would try to meet with him after mass on Sunday. The cathedral was full when they arrived and joined señor Berchello. After the service Edmund found the bishop and his secretary and spoke to him about using his wine. Edmund offered a bottle he had brought with him and they moved to a side room where they could sample the wine. The bishop was most impressed with the flavour and strength and instructed the secretary to purchase from Edmund enough for his own use, if Edmund had a lesser wine he would also use that in the diocesan churches as it was all bought centrally. Edmund thanked then bishop and invited him to visit and bless the vineyard.

While they were in Toledo Maria wanted to visit her father. Rafael was interested in their visit with the bishop and as he was one of the cathedral stewards he would make sure the bishop kept to his word. They discussed the changes that were being made at the vineyard, Rafael was concerned that the Moors were still around and causing problems. 'I hope that this situation does not escalate and we have trouble in Toledo,' he said. Edmund told him of his decision to increase his guards, this would make the Moors think twice about attacking him again. Edmund gathered his group together and they left De La Cruz and his family waving to them as they headed towards the gate. They reached the foothills and Edmund remembered the last time they were here. He had been surprised and captured by hill bandits, their leader, El Zorro, had intended to ransom them. Fortunately they had escaped and El Zorro had lost his head, in more ways than one. On their way home Edmund was deep in thought, Maria asked if there was anything wrong.

'I was thinking about Dunston and England. I would like to take you there for a visit so that you could see where I used to live.' Maria thought that would be a good idea but could they go in the summer when it was hot here and warm in England. Edmund agreed and said he would plan the trip to go in three months time.

When they returned to the vineyard they were surprised how many men were milling about in the yard. Gareth came out to tell them that the word had spread that he was looking for men and all these had come in from the villages.

'We will have plenty of choice then,' said Edmund. 'Be very selective and take only ones who have some experience.' Gareth agreed and carried on sorting out the men. Edmund pondered on the fact that now, so many people will depend on the vineyard being successful. He smiled to himself as he remembered leaving Wymondham because he did not want to be part of running the shire and here he was involved in commerce again.

Edmund was woken by the sun streaming through the bedroom window. He stretched and felt the body next to him stir. They came together naturally and Edmund marvelled at how their bodies fitted so well together. Making love at this time in the morning cleared his mind and relaxed him for the whole day. Today he must not be relaxed though, he must be alert as Gareth was showing how his guard were progressing. Edmund accompanied Gareth on one of the patrols and they found signs of an encampment. Edmund suggested double pickets at various points around the vineyard. Activity from the Moors quietened down and Edmund planned his trip to England. Gareth would stay in charge and take a break later. Edmund would take Stephan and Assad, a young Moor who wanted to become a christian, Edmund had taken him under his wing as a page.

Assad had been one of the men in the yard when they were recruiting guards, most of the men stood away from him as he was a Moor. He had withstood the insults up until one man insulted his mother. Assad had shown how well he handled himself until Gareth stepped in and halted the fight. Edmund liked his spirit and employed him as a page. Assad's real skill was in the way he could handle horses, Edmund thought he would be very useful when they were away from the vineyard. Two guards would also accompany them. Elizabeth would have her maid, Chiquita, and two other ladies. Their route to the coast would include a stop at Salamanca and then through Portugal to Oporto, embark on a ship for England.

They said their goodbyes and set off on their adventure. Edmund wondered if the king would be at Salamanca. An uneventful journey brought them to the City and Edmund sent Stephan to find them lodgings. That evening as he walked round the city with Maria, Edmund wondered if he was making the right decision in going home to England. Where was home anyway, now, it was with Maria in the vineyard.

They rested for two days in the city, Edmund used the time to discuss the journey with Maria. He was used to travelling and making instant decisions, this time he realised his responsibilities were at Castello Dunston and the people who worked for him. When the time came to journey on Edmund announced that they would be returning home. They would go back via Avila and visit Señor De La Cruz, from the Spaniards came a sigh of relief as they were all a little apprehensive about visiting a country so far away. With a light heart they set off for the walled city of Avila. Señor De La Cruz welcomed them all to his house. De La Cruz wanted to hear all the news since Edmund had left them, it was noticeable that Rhyannon disappeared to her room when Edmund spoke of Maria and their marriage. They stayed with the Count for a few days enjoying his hospitality. He said he could not repay Edmund enough for rescuing him from the bandits. When the day came that they were to leave, Rhyannon was seen chatting to Maria and the two women were smiling together as they glanced at Edmund.

Edmund turned to Stephan and said. 'Keep your eyes open, last time we were here we were attacked.'

They rode on with everyone alert and feeling nervous. Several times they thought they saw movement in the trees. When it came time to camp for the night Edmund chose a place that was very open with no trees near. He organised a guard and kept awake himself for most of the night. When the sun greeted them in the morning there had been no attack although Edmund had thought he had seen movement in the trees just before dawn. There were no further incidents and they reached Toledo safely.

They stayed with señor Berchello, who was pleased they had decided not to go to England. Edmund spent several hours discussing the ways to run the vineyard and found Rafael's experience very helpful. He promised to visit the vineyard soon as he also had a new customer for Edmund.

Arriving back at the vineyard there was rejoicing that they had come home. After they had all settled down Edmund spoke to Gareth. 'What has been happening whilst we were away?' Gareth told him that there had been further attacks on the vineyard, one night the Moors tried to attack the house but they drove them off. 'I think it is time we tried to find their headquarters, or where they are operating from. Tomorrow we will make some plans.'

That night as they climbed into bed Maria expressed her delight at being home. 'I would like to come with you and see your home in England when we are more settled here.' Edmund pulled her to him and thought how lucky he was to have such an understanding wife. Their lovemaking was passionate and long that night and it was difficult to wake in the morning.

After breaking their fast they assembled twenty of their best men and Edmund called Assad to him. 'I understand you are a good tracker. Do you think you can find which direction they went when they left?' 'I can sir,' replied the young man. 'Two of their horses have loose shoes and another is slightly lame, it shows clearly.'

They set off with Assad leading the way. The trail became clearer as they left the vineyard and lead them into a range of hills. They tracked the Moors all day without getting any closer. They called a halt for the night and Assad said to Edmund, 'There are plenty of sign to follow, they are heading for a village I know, near here.' Edmund was puzzled, if they are going to a village was it their hideout? Edmund settled down and thought of Maria, he would be glad to get back to her. In the morning they set off following the tracks and were soon in sight of the village. Edmund called a halt and sent Stephan and Assad to investigate. When they returned they reported there were no Moors there at all and no-one had seen them. They searched around the outskirts of the village and came upon a fresh trail that led away. 'Damn,' said Edmund. 'They have circled back, we must hurry to the vineyard.'

Setting a fast pace Edmund led them on as quick as he could. They did not stop, only for short intervals to rest the horses. Arriving at the edge of the vineyard they found the body of one of the guards with his throat cut. Edmund spurred his horse and raced for the house. There had been a fierce fight at the house which was evident by bodies and wounded in the front yard. Gareth was sitting against the wall holding a cloth to his head. Edmund leapt from his horse and ran into the house calling for Maria. He ran from room to room calling her name but with no response. Chiquita was not to be found either. He went outside and stood in front of Gareth. 'Where is my wife?' he asked. Gareth tried to answer but he was too groggy for his speech to make sense.

Chapter 16

A thorough search of the house found no sign of Maria or Chiquita. Some of the rooms showed the result of struggles, Edmund was relieved that there were no bodies. 'They have obviously been abducted, but why. Ransom do you think?' asked Edmund of Stephan. Assad came in to say he had found tracks heading south. 'We must sort out things here first and then I will decide what to do,' said Edmund as he went out to speak to Gareth.

Gareth was now on his feet but a little shaky. He had been knocked on the head in the attack. 'I must start to trail them as soon as I can and I need you to be fit to take charge here,' said Edmund. Gareth urged him to go after them. 'Don't worry Cuthbert is well and will carry out my orders. Chase them as quickly as you can. They were Moors, and I could not understand them but Sanchez has a little knowledge of their language and they talked about heading for home, wherever that is. They said the woman would be a valuable prize.' Edmund wondered if that meant ransom or selling in a market.

Stephan came to Edmund and said he and Assad wanted to accompany him, would he need more men? Edmund did not want to weaken the guards at home so he had intended to chase them alone, however the two extra men would be an asset and he knew he could trust them. Edmund learnt that the guards who had remained fought well but could not stop the abduction. He sent one of them to Toledo to inform Maria's father.

Edmund decided to rest at the house and set in pursuit within the hour. With Stephan's help they prepared their horses, including Edmunds charger. Assad had gone further along the route of the Moors and would meet them later. Cuthbert came to him to say the dead had been buried and the house and yard were now in good order. Edmund decided to take a quick walk round the house and barns before he rested. He saw the entrance to the cellars and noticed they were unlocked. He tried to open the door but it appeared to be bolted from the inside. He banged on the door and called out, 'Whoever is hiding, come out now.' After a few minutes he heard the bolts being drawn, he stepped back and unsheathed Talio. The door opened and out rushed Maria into his arms, closely followed by Chiquita. Disentangling himself from the two women an overjoyed Edmund walked them round to the front of the house. The men in the yard stood amazed for a moment, then there was applause and cheering. Chiquita went to Gareth worried about his wound, Gareth did not seem to mind this attention. They were entering the house when señor Berchello rode into the yard accompanied by his men. He was relieved to see Maria and to know that she was unharmed. Maria found all the staff and arranged a dinner for them in the house and sent Chiquita out to make sure the men were well catered for. Edmund posted guard and sent Cuthbert to find Assad and bring him home.

Señor Berchello stayed for the night, he discussed with Edmund the possibility of the Moors returning. Edmund said that he had already decided to increase his guards, coupled with better walls where needed, this should keep intruders out. He would also make access to the cellars through the rear of the house.

When Rafael had left the next morning Edmund put into action the plans he had made. Builders were soon erecting stronger walls, better doors and a secure way into the cellars. During this time he began to feel that this place was really his home. It should be the family home and that was the important part, raising a family. Edmund and

Maria had been hoping their lovemaking would produce a child, as yet there had been no success.

One afternoon they were roused out of their siesta by the arrival of a young man who demanded to see the Captain of the guard. Cuthbert stepped forward and the young man said he would prove his worth to be a guard by fencing with him as he was certain he would win. There was a lot of laughter from the guards who were there. Suddenly Edmund called out he would test the young man. He stepped out to meet him. 'What is your name?' asked Edmund. 'Why do you want to fight us?' 'I am Julio Cardozo and I have the best sword in Spain. Who is this man with a magic sword?'

Edmund drew Talio and said. 'It is not the sword but the man who wields it.'

He parried the first thrust of the young man. Circling him he advanced and lunged at him, this was easily parried and the youth attacked again. Edmund was calm as he used his guile and experience to unsettle his opponent. Cardozo was getting frustrated and tried to rush Edmund who side stepped and nicked his arm. This infuriated the youth who lost control and threw himself into vicious attack. Edmund felt the ring tremble and with a quick two strokes sent his opponents sword flying through the air.

Cardozo stood still with his head hung and the guards who had been watching applauded Edmund. 'Pick up your sword young man and come here. You will have to control your temper if you want to win. Having a fine sword does not bring success, you also have to have skill and calm nerves.' The young man retrieved his sword and presented it to Edmund. 'I usually win,' he said. 'You are too fast.' Edmund looked at the sword and recognised it as Toledo Steel, a fine blade. 'You will train under Cuthbert, a fine swordsman and tactician. Depending on what he reports will determine if you join us or not.' Edmund turned and walked into the house.

Over the next months they settled into a routine and life became easier. No matter how they tried there was still no sign of a baby. Maria was not as cheerful as she had been, some days Edmund was like a bear with a sore head. Everyone kept out of his way on those days. They decided to consult a doctor in Toledo who had been recommended by Maria's mother, after the consultation they visited the cathedral. Whilst they sat in a pew the bishop came and spoke to them for while, he said he would offer prayers for them.

Time went by and there was still no signs of a pregnancy Edmund began to think it was his fault and pondered on what he could do. Something the bishop had said turned his thoughts to the Holy Land. The crusades had finished but there was nothing to stop him going there on his own, perhaps a visit to Christ's birthplace would be the answer. The thought became stronger as the days and months passed, as sometimes happens with fixations.

Edmund thought about the way to get to the Holy Land. Taking the land route would take a long time and fraught with many dangers in foreign lands. By sea was just as dangerous from storms, castaway and drowning, it would also be expensive. Should he take anyone with him? There would have to be some one responsible left to take care of the vineyard. He could not subject Maria to that journey. The decision will have to wait a little longer.

The grapes grew and ripened, they were picked and turned into wine. The cycle turned relentlessly on and Edmund had given up on being a father. Maria was still attentive to his needs but he had no enthusiasm, he even turned to a village girl in desperation. The venture proved nothing as she remained childless too.

Edmund made his decision, he would go to Jerusalem. Stephan and Assad agreed to go with him. Maria pleaded to go too but Edmund said it was too dangerous. They made their plans to go overland so one sunny morning they said their goodbyes and set off for France.

Chapter 17

The journey along the coast to Marseille was uneventful. They rode at a leisurely pace, Edmund did not want to hurry for a reason he could not fathom. A knight with his squire, page and pack horses, had been a common sight. People assumed another crusade was taking place which was true except they were the only crusaders. Assad found an Inn that had room for them and their horses. The landlord greeted them warmly. 'I have not seen knights on a crusade for some time,' he said. 'Will there be more of you?'

'I fear not sir. We travel to the Holy Land for a specific personal purpose.' Sitting down, Edmund called for ale and wine. The landlord was quick to offer food, to which they agreed. 'There is another knight resting here who is going in your direction. I will tell him about you.' The landlord went to another room and returned with an older man whom he introduced as Sir William of Shrewsbury.

Edmund rose and invited the knight to join them. Sir William explained he was returning to the Holy Land on a personal pilgrimage as he had lost his brother there in the last crusade. Edmund invited him to join with them which he accepted. 'I am most grateful to be with a fellow Knight as Saladin is fortifying the Castles we left and is not too friendly to Europeans. I am waiting for my Squire to join me, he should be here in the next two days. Can you wait that long?'

Edmund thought for a moment. There was something that niggled in his mind, it had made him delay already and a further couple of days would help clear his head. The couple of days stretched into more and on the fifth afternoon they heard the arrival of a party in the Inn yard. The front door burst open and a woman rushed through and made straight for Edmund.

'Thank God you have rested here,' said a breathless Maria as she clung to Edmund. 'We travelled fast only stopping for the briefest rests. I missed you so much. I thought that if you were making this pilgrimage for us then I should be with you. You can't send me home as I have dismissed my escort and only Chiquita is here with me. Say you will let me come, PLEASE.' Edmund staggered back and still holding Maria looked into her eyes and saw love there. 'I knew there was something holding me back, now I know what it was. It will be an arduous journey, my love, and we will do it together.' At this point the Landlord announced that the food was ready. Edmund introduced her to Sir William who remarked it would be an arduous journey for a woman.

When Maria came down the next morning she found Edmund and Sir William in deep conversation. 'We are planning our route,' said Edmund. 'There is no Pope in Rome so we shall keep to the coast.' 'There is a Pope in Avignon,' said Maria. 'Not one I recognise,' said Edmund. 'He should be in Rome, where St Peter drew his last breath. I will go to the harbour and enquire if we can journey further by sea.'

Edmund and Sir William searched among all the ships for one that would take them and their horses onward. They found no captain who would oblige them and were returning to the Inn when a rough looking character asked them to follow him. He lead then to a large ship that at first glance had seen better days. A fat bearded man met them and introduced himself as captain Andreas Constanta.

'What is it you want?' he asked.

'We are making our way to the Holy Land and would take part of the journey by sea if you can take our horses,' said Edmund

'That is a long way,' said the Captain. 'There are many risks, pirates, storms and animals do not like sea voyaging. This will cost much money.''Where would you land first?'

'The island of Corsica and then to Sicily.' 'When will you sail?' asked Edmund.

'The tides and wind will be right in six days time,' answered Constanta.

William nodded and Edmund told the Constanta they would see him on the morrow to finalise the trip. Returning to the Inn they found that Sir William's Squire had arrived.

Henry, the squire to Sir William, was a thick set man, medium height and older than all of them. He had met Sir William at the battle of Halidon Hill where his original knight had been killed. He was devoted to Sir William after the knight had taken him under his wing when other knights were telling him he had to return to being a page.

They rode out each day to exercise the horses and on one of these excursions they were confronted by a gang of brigands. Edmund and Sir William automatically swung into action, their battle experience carrying them to the fight. This surprised the brigands and they turned and fled with many of them bearing cuts from the knights.

'Does everyone want to fight these days?' said Edmund.

Sir William replied, 'It is the same in any land, in my experience. They think it is easy money, but I warrant that group will change their mind after this.'

On the day before they were due to board the ship they were riding in the hills to exercise their horses prior to their confinement aboard. They came to a narrow valley and out of the trees came the brigands again. This time it was a much larger group.

'Guard the horses,' shouted Edmund. Assad gathered the loose horses while Edmund, Sir William, Stephan and Henry drew their swords and stood their ground. The brigands charged and they met the four men head on. Edmund felt the ring on his finger burning and Talio leapt into action. His arm was a blur as Talio sliced and stabbed at lightning speed. Men fell from their horses, others screamed as they lost a limb. Some of the brigands made a rush for the horses but Assad held them off until Henry turned to help. The brigands gradually retreated and then turned and fled leaving the dead and dying. Edmund dismounted and quickly despatched the dying, he was about to behead one of the attackers when Sr William shouted to spare him. 'Let us see what he can tell us before you send him to Hades.'

The man explained that they wanted revenge for being beaten previously and they had heard the knights were carrying money.

'Who told you this?' said Edmund. The man shook his head and suddenly groaned in pain, it was the last sound he made.

'The sooner we are away from this town the better,' said Sir William. "Where did you learn to fight like that. I have never seen swordsmanship like it before, it is though the sword has a life of its own.'

Edmund looked at him and then told him of how he came by the weapon that his grandfather had forged.

He told him how his father was also a champion and it must be an inherited skill. Edmund kept the part the ring played to himself. Sir William thought it was a good story but there must be more to it.

The day of their departure dawned and packing their belongings they made their way down to the docks. The captain was there to meet them with his hand held out for the money they had agreed. Edmund gave him a purse and told him it was only half of what was due, the other half would be given to him when they reached their destination. The Captain grunted and pocketed the purse and muttered something in a language that Edmund did not understand. The horses were loaded and the rest of the group boarded and were directed to their cabins. There were enough to accommodate them all if they shared. There was also a large cabin where they were to eat and could sit. Edmund found the crew sullen only responding to orders with the threat of the lash. The captain and his lieutenants patrolled the decks with whips and batons. They were all told to keep out of the way until the ship had left the docks and gained open sea. When they did at last come on deck they could see the French coast gradually receding. All the sails were being filled by the stiff breeze and the old ship was showing a fair turn of speed. Edmund moved up to the prow and as he stood getting used to the movement of the ship Maria came and stood beside him. They were on their way, what adventures lay before them?

Chapter 18

Several days into their journey Edmund was checking the horses when Sir William joined him. 'I think we must keep a careful eye on the captain and his officers. We upset their plans, I think, when they did not get all the money.'

'It would be prudent not to be alone on deck,' said Edmund. 'The crew look a mutinous bunch too, it would not take much for them to try and take the ship.'

'We shall arrive in Corsica soon. Constanta has not said where yet I assume it will be Bonifacio,' said Sir William. As they approached the coast the Captain kept the vessel in the centre of the channel and they sailed past the city and turned north towards Porto Vecchio. They sailed up a narrow channel towards the harbour and mored up to a wooden pontoon as the water was not deep enough at the quayside.

The captain came to the day cabin to talk to them. He explained that it was very expensive to dock at Bonifacio so that is why he had come to Porto. He needed the rest of his money so that he could pay his crew as they were a mutinous bunch and knew Edmund had money. Edmund asked what had he done with the money he had already given him? The captain muttered something about provisions and bills he had to settle. 'We have to take the horses off to exercise them and I will have to think about what you have said. We don't want an unsettled crew on the rest of our voyage so while we walk the horses I will talk with the rest of our party and if they are agreeable we will advance more money. Stephan will stay here as security for our return.' The captain grumbled but agreed and went away.

They sat round the table and looked at Edmund. 'I fear we will not see the rest of our journey alive,' said Sir William. Edmund sat thoughtful for moment and then said,'It is nearly dusk and night falls quickly here so I suggest we leave with the horses just as the sun is setting. Hide as much baggage as you can and the rest make into bundles. We will leave Stephan here as he is the best swimmer and can stay under water, which I have seen him do,' said Edmund. Stephan smiled and nodded.

As evening approached Edmund found the captain and told him they would be ready to go into the town. 'We are going fully dressed and armoured which will keep prying eyes away from your ship and show that we are nobility.' The captain thought for a moment then a large toothy smile spread across his face. 'I like it, you make like a baron and scare the town. After my men will visit and be like your soldiers. They will have a fine time in the town tonight.' Edmund looked at him and said. 'Leave us time to talk to the mayor and you will have no trouble.' The captain nodded still smiling.

Edmund and Sir William readied themselves, donning their armour and dressing the destrier with their trappers, which covered the bags hanging under the horses. They all came on deck and the crew applauded to see the knights in armour. They carefully negotiated the pontoon, walking the horses slowly until they found their land legs. Reaching the dock Edmund realised quite a crowd of townspeople had gathered to see the knights come ashore. A small important looking man stepped out of the throng and doffing his hat announced that he was the mayor. Edmund said he would like to talk to him immediately. They followed him to a large house and Edmund dismounted signalling to the others to stay mounted. The mayor and a large man waited for him, the mayor introduced his companion as his captain of guards, Edmund was surprised at the mayors command of English. 'The ship we have just left is full of cutthroats,' said Edmund. 'I overheard them talking of robbing people in the town.' 'Thank you for that information, my guards will be ready for them on the pontoon and they will not get off the ship.' There was a ripple of noise in the crowd and a wet Stephan appeared. A woman went to him and produced a cloth to help him dry, other young women went to help with much giggling and embarrassment for Stephan. Edmund, with the help of Assad, remounted and bid the mayor farewell. They moved off following a road to the north.

Edmund turned to Stephan and asked, 'did anyone see you leave?'

'No,' said Stephan. 'I managed to open the window in the stern cabin and lower myself down on a rope. The crew were busy sorting out swords and cutlasses for their attack on the town.'

'They are going to get a surprise when they try to get off the ship.' Edmund told him the mayors plan. 'I suggest we move on quickly and not get involved here.' They left the town behind and reaching a small wood where they stopped and divested themselves of their armour, repacked the horses moved off to the north.

The sun was setting as they approached a small village and Edmund sent Assad ahead to reconnoitre. He returned to tell them all was quiet and the people he had met spoke Spanish. They stopped at a country Inn and the landlord welcomed them, Edmund guessed he did not see many travellers. The landlord said he had a room for Edmund and Maria and another small one for Sir William the rest could sleep in his barn. The evening meal was the best they had eaten for some time and the mood of the group lightened. 'That is the end of that sea trip,' said Edmund. 'We have to decide on how we venture further.'

'May I suggest we carry on to the port of Bastia in the north,' said Sir William. 'I am sure we would be able to find a boat to take us across to the mainland from where we could continue our journey.'

'It will be slower by land,' said Edmund.

'Not as expensive though,' countered Sir William. 'We might also find opportunities to add to our purse.'

They all agreed to continue by land after they reached Italy. They retired for the night in a happy mood having decided what to do for the next part of their lives.

Maria and Edmund undressed and Edmund reached for his wife. They were soon in each others arms and moving to the bed. Edmund felt a new vigour and sensation in their love making. They lay wrapped in that personal cocoon that comes after two people in love have reached the ultimate height of passion.

The morning found all the party in good spirits and ready to set out on the next part of their journey. Edmund and Maria kept smiling at each other which brought some comments from Sir William. They kept to the coastal road and trails making good progress north. One afternoon as they were descending to a small village Edmund turned seaward and called to Sir William. 'That ship I can see looks very much like the ship we sailed on.' 'I have been watching it,' said Sir William. 'It's too far away to be sure, what would they be doing this far out of their way for?' 'Perhaps they seek revenge or my money,' replied Edmund. When they left the village in the morning they searched the sea for the ship, but it was not visible.

They reached the outskirts of Aleria, a much larger village with a small harbour. Looking down from a hill outside the village they could see a large black ship anchored just outside the harbour.

'That is Constanta's ship,' said Edmund. 'We must prepare for trouble. I would like to meet him outside the village so we don't involve innocent villagers. Stephan go and find out if it is the captain but be ready to run if there is trouble. Assad go with him.' Sir William and Edmund donned their armour and changed to their destriers.

Stephan returned with the answer that Constanta was there and causing trouble in the village. 'Go back and tell him to meet us and he can fight us for the money.' When Stephan retuned he had Constanta's reply, which was when he wins Sir William is to pay the remainder of the money and more to repay the cost of chasing us.

'Return and tell I accept, and when I win he is to leave here and never return.'

Stephan rode off and the rest of them found a large area where they cleared the ground. Stephan appeared closely followed by Constanta and some of his crew. With them was a tall Moor who stepped forward and drew a long scimitar.

'This man will fight as I am too old, it would not be a fare fight,' said Constanta. 'I agree,' said Edmund. 'I will remove my armour as your man has none.'

Striped down to just a light breast plate Edmund swung Talio in a few practice moves. The Moor approached and Sir William stood between them. 'You will fight with just your swords. If one of you is mortally wounded the other will stand back.' He turned to the Moor. 'What is your name sir?' 'Ahmed,' replied the man.' They both raised their swords and Sir William raised his between them. He raised it further and sweeping it skyward shouted to them to fight!

The Moor attacked immediately with swinging side sweeps and Edmund had to move quickly to avoid the blade and then parry one of the strokes. This allowed him to lunge Talio for the Moor's throat which was neatly parried. The two men circled each other, Edmund thought I have my hands full with this man he is an experienced warrior. They cut, thrust, parried and raised the dust as each one of them tried to find an opening. The ring on Edmund's finger was very hot and Talio was beginning to sing as it struck the scimitar. The Moor began to slow and Edmund pressed him hard, it was only a trick and Edmund found himself backing up. Then Edmund felt a surge in his strength and Talio flew. Cut, thrust, parry and lunge with amazing speed. The Moor staggered back and Edmund pressed forward Talio leapt for his throat and the Moor went down, blood spurted from the wound and with a loud gurgle the man breathed his last.

There was a silence for a few minutes then Constanta shouted, drew his sword and calling to his men, charged towards Edmund. No one moved. Constanta realising he was on his own skidded to a stop and turned to his men. 'Cowards, all of you. There are only five of them, cut them down.' Somebody from his crew said.

'If they all fight like that I am away from here.' They all turned and went back to their ship. Constanta followed still shouting at them. Sir William went to Edmund, who stood shaking with sweat dripping down his face. 'I have never seen such swordsmanship. No one will ever beat that sword.' Maria rushed up and hugged him.

They gathered their belongings together and Henry went ahead with Stephan to find lodgings for the night. They gathered in an old Inn and celebrated over a good meal and wine. News had come to the village about the fight and the people were glad to see the back of the captain and his crew. That night Edmund lay in his bed while Maria fussed over him. He had not come from the fight completely unscathed as he had a small cut on his shoulder. The way Maria fussed Edmund thought he had lost an arm! Her ministrations later that night were far more helpful!

Edmund led the group away from Aleria journeying on northwards. In places the road was just a path on a cliff edge. They could see fishing boats below them and sometimes, in the distance, a large sailing ship. They found the villagers friendly especially when they knew that they would be paid for accommodating the travellers. Edmund kept a check on his purse as the gold was dwindling.

'Our money is depleting,' he said one night as they sat round a camp fire. 'We must camp more often and find our own food for the table. Maria and Chiquita are good cooks and I am sure they will help.'

'If you will catch some game we will prepare a better meal than the Inns we have stayed in.' 'That is settled then,' said Sir William. 'We will camp and forage for ourselves.'

There were a few jokes about being gypsies, Edmund thought about the last time he had been with gypsies, they all agreed to camp and hunt. Initially it was a light relief to hunt and look after themselves.

Chapter 19

The weather was kind to them with bright sunny days and balmy nights. Game was plentiful and they were making good progress towards Bastia. The road, or track, became more busy as the approached the city. The last night before entering the city was spent on a hill overlooking the harbour. They could see that the harbour was busy, a large boat was rowed out at midday and returned late evening. Edmund wondered if it was a ferry to the mainland.

Early the next morning Edmund and Sir William went into the city and made their way to the harbour. Dressed as ordinary travellers they made enquiries as to ways of crossing to the mainland. The boat they had seen, turned out to one of three ferries that travel between the City and Pisa on the mainland. Moving between the people they found the ferry point as one of the boats docked. Edmund asked the skipper when he was making the journey again. 'Should be later today but two of my men are sick and not able to row. We cannot rely just on the sail.'

'We are eight people and eleven horses,' said Edmund. 'We could row if you will take us.'

The skipper thought for a moment. 'I will have to use the larger boat and I will need help on the return journey, if I can find two more men then I will do it.' They agreed a price and would meet at the dock just after noon. Edmund looked at the craft moored at the dock and hoped the weather would remain calm, the craft had seen better days and he did not fancy swimming.

They aroused some interest as they assembled at the dock and boarded the ferry. The horses were a little skittish Assad had to use all his soothing words to calm them. The ferryman looked worried when Edmund's destrier came aboard. 'Is he tame?' he asked. 'Does he bite. He is as big as two horses, I should have charged you more.' 'We are rowing for you so that equals it out,' replied Edmund as he pick up one of the oars. Edmund and Sir William soon found that rowing the ferry was not as easy as they had thought. Stephan and Henry relieved them and they were glad of the rest. There was a small sail that was hoisted which did not help much. Amazingly the horses liked the rolling motion of the craft whereas Maria did not. The town of Pisa came into sight and Edmund and Sir William, who were rowing at the time, put more effort in and the boat increased speed. They reached the harbour where the ferry usually docked, willing hands helped them to tie up. Getting the horses off proved the most difficult as they wanted to stay on the ferry!

Stephan went off to find accommodation for the night away from the dock area. He returned to inform them that there were many military men about and he had been stopped twice and asked what he was doing in the city. The Inn Stephan had found was comfortable enough and had good stables. There were many men at arms drinking and the travellers went straight to their rooms. Maria said she still did not feel very well, she thought it was the fFerry crossing and the smell of the horses so Edmund just kissed her goodnight.

They rose early and set off, Edmund had wanted to see the Baptistry and tower but there was an atmosphere in the City that indicated there could be trouble soon. Soldiers stopped them on the road repeatedly so they took to the lanes and side tracks. Amazingly Henry said he had been this way before when he was part of a crusade, many years ago. The scenery was beautiful, steep hills, long valleys with rivers running through. Forests with plentiful game making ideal camping. They came across empty villages where the population had been decimated by the plague. They kept well away from these and hurriedly moved on. For the same reason they kept to the north to avoid Bologna, Stephan remarked that they were living like gypsies but he could understand them liking the freedom.

They were interrupted in their travels when they came to a great river which they learnt was the river Po. Edmund and Sir William travelled up and down the bank until the found a small village that had fishing boats and a ferry. They arranged a crossing for all of them. Landing on the other bank they moved off towards the next city.

Edmund sat relaxed as they rode, he felt at peace and was remarking to Maria what beautiful countryside they were passing through when they heard screams coming from ahead of them. Sir William looked at Edmund and everyone spurred their horses on. Rounding a bend in the road Edmund signalled the women to stay back. They could see a group of men surrounding a carriage, there were bodies on the ground and the screaming was coming from the carriage. One of the group realised that Edmund was galloping toward them and shouting to his fellow bandits they grabbed one of the women from the carriage. Four of the bandits galloped away with the woman while the rest tried to grab the second woman. Edmund and Sir William were soon among them and Talio went to work with no mercy. When the fighting stopped most of the bandits that had remained, lay dead or dying. Edmund passed the hysterical woman to Maria and followed Sir William who was chasing the fugitives. They led them into the hills round twisting tracks with drops into ravines on one side then another. Finally they found the entrance to a large a cave. Edmund and Sir William dismounted and drawing their swords approached the cave entrance warily. To one side stood group of trees and the bandits horses were tied there All was quiet so they entered and found a huge space with a tunnel entrance leading off. They picked up two branches and lit the ends to form a torch. With the flickering light they entered the tunnel which opened out to quite a large passage.

Edmund held up his hand and they stopped to listen. Faint noises came from ahead so they continued further into the passage. The passage twisted and turned as the rock that it was formed from changed in density. Ahead of them, around a corner they could see light. Dousing their torches they crept forward and came across the brigands sitting on boxes in a larger cave. The could see the woman cowering in a corner while the brigands were arguing amongst themselves as to what to do next. Edmund rattled Talio against his scabbard. The brigands stopped talking, one of them rose and with a sword in his hand came towards them. Sir William pressed himself into a small niche in the wall while Edmund crouched down. As the light from the man's torch illuminated them Edmund sprang up and Talio was through the man's throat before he could utter a sound. Sir William caught him as he fell. One of the remaining three called out. 'Have you found anything, Enrico?' Edmund held his hand over his mouth and muttering through his fingers said that it was nothing and all was well. He picked up the dead mans torch and holding it well ahead of him they walked into the cave. Before the bandits had time to realise it was not Enrico Edmund and Sir William struck. Talio downed the first man and Edmund leapt to the side of the woman to protect her while Sir William threatened the remaining two with his sword.

Edmund signalled them to throw down their weapons to which they obeyed and stood looking at the two knights. Suddenly one of the men cried out and sprang at the woman with a knife. Talio flashed in the dim light and the man's head parted from his body rolling to stop at the other man's feet. The woman screamed and the remaining brigand fell to his knees begging not to be killed. Sir William looked around the cave and found rope with which he tied up the prisoner. Edmund soothed the woman who in fact was only a young girl. She was shivering with shock and Edmund moved her away from the bodies.

The cave was obviously a hideout for the brigands. There were boxes of food, skins of wine and some water. Sir William took one of the torches from the wall bracket and investigated the other exit.

The tunnel was much smaller and ended after a few feet. 'Not very clever to use this, they were trapped in here. I suppose they thought that nobody would come this far.'

'We must find out who this girl is,' said Edmund. 'Let's get out of here into fresh air.'

With Edmund half carrying the girl and Sir William, prodding his prisoner along, they made their way back to the entrance. They all breathed in the air as their eyes became accustomed to the light. They could hear shouts from below and Edmund raised his voice to call out, it was not long before the rest of their party found them. Maria rushed to Edmund's arms saying. 'Are you wounded? Where is this blood coming from?'

'It is not mine, my dear. We are both unscathed as Talio has done his work again. This is Helena Cancharello whom they were hoping to ransom.' The young girl ran to Maria who took her in her arms.

'We must deliver these ladies to their family in Venice and then be on our way.' They made their way back to where the coach was and found, Assad had been busy, all the bodies had been dragged to the bushes on the side of the road and he was digging graves for the guards that had been killed, the wounded ones he had put in the coach. Edmund dismounted and thanked Assad for what he had done.

'We have collected more horses from the brigands,' he said. 'Perhaps the young ladies would prefer to ride until we reach better roads.' Helena and Lucia agreed as there were no springs on the coach, however Maria said she would ride in the coach for a while and look after the wounded, it would be a change from the saddle and Chiquita would accompany her.

They journeyed on towards Venice, camping at night and eating well from their hunting. One night as Maria lay in his arms Edmund turned to her and said, 'I think this country living is getting too rich for you, my love. I can feel you putting more flesh on.' Maria looked at him and said, 'It is not fat, husband, it is a new addition to our family!'

Edmund sat up with a start. 'You mean after all this time it has finally happened? I can not believe it. My dearest, this is the best of news' He reached for her and they embraced. 'When did you know?' he asked. Maria said she had not told him before as she wanted to be sure, she thought she was about two months into a pregnancy. Edmund was trying to get over the shock and the feeling of happiness was overcoming him. He pulled Maria tightly to him and said she must be very careful and look after herself. 'Do not say anything until the morning,' said Maria. Edmund gathered her in his arms and they sank back into the bed.

For the rest of the journey Edmund insisted that Maria keep to the carriage.

Chapter 20

Harold stretched and turned to reach for Elizabeth but the other side of the bed was empty. Sitting up he could not see her in the room. He sat on the edge of the bed for a few moments before putting his feet on the floor and standing up. He still felt pain when he first stood on his injured leg. The leg had been badly broken when he fell from his horse after it reared up when frightened by a loud bang. Harold had been to a gathering summoned by the king to witness his new siege cannon. He had been carried home and took no further part in the preparations for the next stage of the kings war with France. He called for his page to assist him.

Harold found Elizabeth already busy organising the household. She turned and smiled at him with their son beside her.

'I must get to Norwich and see how the shire is faring, now the plague seems to have abated.'

'Don't go near the fens though. That was the worst place, I don't think many survived there,' said Elizabeth.

'I will send a courier to the barons, or whoever is in charge while some of them are away in France. This war is costing us dearly.'

A week later Harold set off for Norwich, he had asked Stephen to accompany him and with a large escort they posed an impressive sight. Elizabeth stayed behind with their son who had been christened John. Harold realised that many of the barons had sent men to the army on demand from the king, some barons had gone with their men. With men at war and the loss of labour due to the plague, land and farms were being neglected as a result wool production was down which is what worried Harold. Arriving in Norwich he settled himself in the castle and called for the sheriff for an update on what was happening in the city.

'Tell the Abbot I will see him in the morning, and do not take any excuses from him,' said Harold. 'I sense he is beginning to throw his weight about again now that he knows Earl John is dead.' The Sheriff smiled and said the Abbot would be there, willingly or not. Harold discussed with Stephen what might occur at the meeting with the cleric and also the meeting with the barons. Harold missed Edmund and wished he was there to lend his military strength to the meetings.

The Abbot duly arrived and they had a fruitful discussion. Harold was pleased to hear there had been no trouble between the monastery and the city. They were more concerned about the loss of population due to the plague.

The meeting with the barons was less convivial. The older lords who had remained in their castles were not enthusiastic to have such a young Earl in charge of the shire. The barons who had left with their men to fight in France had left behind an odd assortment of brothers, cousins, reeves and senior members of their staff to run their estates. Some were competent enough whereas others did not have a clue as to what was needed.

Harold started the meeting by demanding to know why some of the taxes had not been payed. The main problem was that there were not enough workers to produce the crops needed and gather the wool for shipment.

'I know we have lost many good souls as a result of the plague.' said Harold. 'You must now do as I have done and recruit from any source you can. Surrounding shires that do not operate the cooperative farming as we do, or did!' He looked as the assembly pointedly as he said this. 'Many workers in those shires could be attracted to us. We must get back to meeting the demands of the cloth makers or they will look elsewhere. This is not a time to hoard money or to refurbish castles that do not need it.' Several looked at their feet at this. 'I shall look at each estate and visit those that I feel will benefit from my plans. We need to pull together at this critical time.'

As Harold sat down there was considerable muttering in the meeting and the brother of the lord of Holt stood and said, 'We cannot steal workers from other shires, if we do we will have war here as well as France.' Several nodded their heads.

'We do not need to actually steal workers, the news has spread from our estates to others on how our men are treated and that has caused a steady trickle of men and families to seek employment with us, some as far away as Liverpool in the north. It does work if you have the determination. I leave you to think about what I have said and we will meet again tomorrow.' Harold rose and left the room where a general hubbub could be heard gradually getting louder. Harold turned to Stephen and said, 'I will let them think about that for a while and then listen to those who wish to speak to me. Go out and see who is first.'

Soon Harold had a stream of barons or the men who had been left behind. The main complaint was the increase in taxes and the low yield from their farms. Some had listened to him with a positive mind and these he encouraged and said he would help where he could. The free banquet in the evening helped to lighten the day, when Harold entered the hall in the morning most had left. After he had joined Stephen at the table he said he would visit the Abbey to find out what was happening to their wool.

The Abbot was very evasive when asked about the amount of wool he had stored. Harold reminded him that under the agreement that existed half of the wool belonged to Wymondham. The Abbot said that now Earl John was dead a new agreement should be made, Harold replied he did not mind as the new agreement would state he would take three quarters now. A fierce argument ensued at the end of which, the Abbot agreed the existing agreement would stand but there was very little wool in the warehouse at the moment.

Leaving the Abbot, Harold and Stephen walked round the outside of the Abbey and came upon a path leading to some old sheds. They found the door locked but a small window was open. 'I suppose it will be me who has to squeeze through there,' said Stephen. 'I will keep watch,' said Harold. Stephen was about to wriggle through the window when he stopped and said. 'The place is full of bales of wool. There is no more room in there.' 'Come down,' said Harold. 'It is time for another talk with the Abbot.'

They found the Abbot in his rooms and confronted him with what they had found. He twisted and turned with reasons and excuses. Harold looked at him sternly and said, 'The truth is you wanted to defraud the townspeople of their rightful share. I will confiscate all the wool we have found and search for who is in league with you. I shall leave a contingent of guards here to keep an eye on what goes on in this city.' With that he stormed out of the Abbey and returned to the castle.

Harold was in angry mood as he entered the castle, he found some of the barons still there. Flinging off his cloak he went into the hall and sat at one of the tables. 'What do they want now?' he asked the sheriff. 'They wish to talk to you sir. They wish to discuss what to do about their problems.'

Harold listened to them individually and then asked them to meet him in the hall. When they were all assembled he spoke to them.

'You all have various questions, and what you perceive as problems. I invite you to come to Wymondham and you can see for yourselves what I have been talking about in practice. I will expect you all in two weeks time.' With that Harold left and returned to his chambers telling Stephen that he would leave in the morning.

Elizabeth was pleased to see her husband return in one piece. John toddled to his father to be picked up. Harold reflected on how lucky he was with his family and wondered if Edmund had any children yet. Thinking of Edmund brought to mind the barons who would be descending on them soon. He wished Edmund and his mighty sword were here to defend their home.

Harold prepared for the barons by sending his reeve out to the tenants to make sure they were ready. The reeve reported all was well but Harold still felt a foreboding that something would go wrong, perhaps they would only visit Dunston he knew Stephen had full control and was in charge. That would be his plan, keep them close to Wymondham.

The day of the visit from the barons was a very wet day, continuous rain from dawn to dusk. The barons arrived in not very good humour, shedding their wet clothes as soon as they were inside. The son of the baron from Holt, Geoffrey, was particularly vociferous. 'We are looking after our lands quite well without this interference,' he grumbled. 'Coming all this way in weather like this is ridiculous.'

The large meal that evening improved the atmosphere and it ended with much laughter and song, it may have been the imbibing of the wine and mead. Two barons were accompanied by their ladies and before the men got down to serious drinking Elizabeth suggested they retire to another room. Most of the barons had brought men at arms with them to protect them on the route, or that was their reasoning. Harold made sure that his guards were watchful and the visiting men at arms were accommodated in the tower. The evening drew to a close with some of the barons slumped over the table the rest staggered back to their rooms. Harold had intentionally not drunk very much so was fully in charge of himself. He entered their room and found Elizabeth already in bed, turning he bolted the door and went over to her. 'I am not coming to bed yet, my love, as I am expecting someone.'

'Who are you expecting at this time, most of them will be unconscious by now,' queried his wife. They did not have to wait long before there was a hammering on the door. 'Come out here, boy!' shouted a voice that Harold recognised as the Holt baron's son. Harold made no reply while Elizabeth pulled the bedclothes around her. There was more shouting and someone tried to open the door. Suddenly Harold could hear the clash of steel and more shouting punctuated with cries of pain. A more gentle knock sounded on the door and a voice said. 'All clear my lord.' Harold unbolted the door and stepped out to find four men surrounded by guards, one of whom was the young man from Holt. Two more men lay dead upon the floor with another moaning from his wounds.

'These men were trying to gain access to your room, my lord. We have arrested them and will lock them in the dungeon.'

'You can't do that,' said Geoffrey. 'I am the son of a baron. When my father returns he will make you pay for this.'

'I know your father and he was a good friend of my father so I do not think it will be me he turns his wrath on,' said Harold. 'Take them away.'

Harold descended to the Keep and found guards positioned at all doors and gates, as he had instructed. Expecting trouble from the meeting in Norwich he had taken prudent precautions to safeguard his family.

It was a late start to the morning and there were many sore heads. Harold overheard bit's of conversations that were discussing the nights events. Most of his guests complemented him on being prepared and were surprised at the 'old head on young shoulders'.

They all set off for Dunston in sunshine, a definite improvement on the previous day. The mood of the party was quite jovial and Harold began to relax. He pointed out the well tilled fields as they rode past and the quality of the sheep. When they reached Dunston, Stephen showed them his warehouse and the quality of his wool. He explained how the system of involving the workers in the running of the farms produced the results they could see. Returning to the castle they prepared for the evening meal, which was another feast. They stayed overnight in Dunston and when they eventually congregated in the hall the consensus of opinion was that Harold had proved his point and the majority were keen to get back to their own estates to start improving their own lands.

Harold now had to return to Wymondham and decide what to do about Geoffrey. The king did not take kindly to one baron trying to murder another when they were invited guests. On the ride home he thought the best idea was to send them to London and let the Lord Chancellor deal with it. His thoughts then turned again to Edmund, when would he come home?

Chapter 21

Edmund could not keep the smile from his face as he prepared to move on in the morning. They decended from the hills to the plains around Venice, from the occasional high ground the glimpsed the Great Lagoon that surrounded the city. Helena said her home was on the edge of the Lagoon and was reached by land.

Her home turned out to be a palatial building standing within large grounds. The carriage trundle up the drive and stopped in front of the large doors which were opened by a footman. A large portly gentleman and an overdressed lady, equally as large came down the steps and went to the carriage. After the wounded had been unloaded they were surprised when Maria stepped out but Helena called out from her horse, 'I'm here Mama.' There was much rejoicing at Helena's rescue with her parents thanking Edmund and William profusely. They were all invited to eat with the family tonight and rooms were made available for everyone to rest and clean themselves up. Maria said, 'it is so nice to have a proper bed to sleep in and I can have a bath.' Edmund agreed and hoped she did not feel too discomforted from her journey. 'I will be fine, this short rest is just what I need now, do not worry my love I am made of tougher stuff than you imagine.' Edmund laughed and suggested he come with her to bathe and he could scrub her back. 'It will be safer if Chiquita does that,' giggled his wife.

Senior Cancharello provided a superb meal but they were all soon ready to retire. They rested the next day and Edmund recounted to Senior Cancharello all that had happened with the bandits.

'It is very unsettling here at the moment with district fighting district and the bandits picking up what they can steal. The military are too busy fighting to take any interest. Luckily the city is not suffering as our fleet is too strong for anyone to try and attack it.' The count said he would like to show them the city and as he had is own boats they could go whenever they liked. They decide tomorrow would be a good time.

Edmund looked at the boat they were to sail to the city in. He thought it was a strange craft, a high prow and stern with a rear deck. The deck had a cover and he found out, as they boarded, that this is where the passengers sat. There were eight rowers and they bent to their task with a will. The lagoon was much calmer than at sea and the boat sliced through the water at a good speed. They slowed as they approached the main canal that ran through the centre of the city. Helena was busy explaining the buildings to Maria and who lived where. The large houses seemed to rise out of the water like monsters from the deep. Their boat reached a bridge of boats and they turned to return the way they had come.

Entering the lagoon they turned towards the shore and Edmund could see a bridge over what looked like an entrance. 'This is the Ponte della Paglia,' explained Bernardo. 'It is the entrance to the city and to our wonderful basilica of Saint Mark.' They disembarked in a side canal and walked to a large square where the basilica stood in all its splendour. Edmund was impressed and Maria gasped at the ornate exterior of the building. Their wonderment continued as they entered the basilica and could see beautiful paintings and sculptures were everywhere. The high alter was a blaze of colour and gold. Edmund and Maria sat together and marvelled at what they could see.

Returning to Bernardo's villa the conversation was all about what they had seen in this city on the water. Alone in their room that night Maria asked what were they to do now that Helena had been returned to her family?

'Going on to Jerusalem has not the same point as it had,' said Edmund. 'We must take care of you and the unborn child and travelling that far in infidel countries is not a good idea. I will investigate what is the best way to return to our home.' Maria was pleased at these words and hugged him.

Bernardo invited a friend to his house to meet Edmund. This man was a traveller and had a fund of information. His advice was to keep to the coast and make for Genoa then take a ship to a port in Spain that was the nearest to Toledo. Edmund discussed this with Stephan and Assad and they agreed it was the best solution. Eduardo, the friend of Bernardo, suggested that he travel with them as he was heading for Pisa and could speak the different dialects of the regions they would pass through.

The party departed the following morning, Maria had opted to ride as the coach was too uncomfortable and she tried to explain to Edmund that she was fit at the moment. She did agree that once they were over the mountains she would think about it again. They said their goodbyes to Sir William and Henry who were going on to the Holy Land.

Bernardo had been very generous with a reward for rescuing his daughter, after splitting this with Sir William there was still a large amount to fill Edmund's purse. There would be no camping this time and Eduardo knew of several Inns along the way that were good to stay in. The weather was good, the pace was easy and they enjoyed each others company. Eduardo had a fund of jokes and stories of the people in Venice. They met no brigands this time while they were in the mountains and crossing the rivers was easy. When they came nearer to Pisa however there was certainly more militia roaming around. Eduardo said he was worried about the soldiers who were going around in groups. They had no leaders and no military objectives, they were just turning into robbers. 'We are but small in number and with woman we are easy targets. We should move at night when they are in their cups and will not notice us,' he said. Edmund looked at him and said, 'I would prefer to meet them in daylight so that I can see them clearly.' Stephan smiled and Assad looked on the ground. They moved off in the direction of the city which was still a day or maybe two days away. Rounding a large rock outcrop they were confronted by a group of militia who blocked the road.

'Stop and declare who you are,' said the leader. Edmund whispered to Eduardo to keep going. 'Stop, I say. Who are you, do you not understand us?'

Edmund counted five men and their leader. He looked straight at the leader. 'By what authority do you stop peaceful travellers going about their business.' He kept moving forward and the leader, followed by his men, all drew their swords. Suddenly Talio was in Edmunds hand and the leaders head lay on the ground. Stephan and Assad were ready with their weapons and attacked the men on the flank while Edmund dealt with the three in the centre. Talio sang her death song and men fell dying or dead. A few minutes was all it took and the fight was over. Edmund dismounted and wiped Talio clean while Stephan despatched the one injured man who was near death. Eduardo sat on his horse with his mouth open and sweat running down his face. Edmund went to him. 'You can see why I prefer daylight.'

'I have never seen anything like that before, in all my travels. Three men dead in minutes. No one could stand against you. The sword has magical power in your hand.'

'So say some people, all I can say that it cuts and thrusts as I think. The beautiful balance of the blade also helps.' Edmund told him how it had been forged by his grandfather.

They moved the bodies to a gully at the side of the track. Maria watched silently, she did not like fighting or killing but knew that sometimes it was unavoidable. She thought that the sooner they were home the better.

There were more militia in evidence as they decended into Pisa none of whom challenged them. This time Edmund was determined to visit the baptistry and was suitably impressed. Maria was a little frightened that the tower would fall over.

Eduardo said his goodbyes while the Edmund found a suitable Inn. When they had fed and rested Edmund and Stephan walked down to the docks. There were many ships there but none going to Spain. Sitting outside a chandlers and wondering what to do next a man approached and said, 'I understand you are looking for passage to Spain. I am sailing to Barcelona, what is the size of your party?'

'Three men and two woman,' said Edmund. 'We also have five horses.' 'No horses,' said the man.

Edmund looked at Stephan and they asked the man if they could think about that and where could they find him with their answer? The man replied that his name was Garcia and his ship was the Barracuda. Edmund and Stephan returned to the Inn and they all met to discuss Garcia's proposal.

Assad did not want to give up the horses he had grown very fond of them and they certainly liked him. Edmund pointed out that they may never get a better chance of getting home, he also had in his mind that time was passing and the approaching birth was causing him concern. They eventually decided to go and find Garcia and look at his ship to see if they would be comfortable for the journey. Reaching the docks they found Garcia who led them to his ship. The craft was much smaller and sleeker than the ships around it and Edmund could see that there was no room for the horses.

'Come aboard,' said Garcia. 'She is a new design of ship and I hope to gain many orders to build them on my return home. In my native Portugal we have been trying to find a faster design.'

There was an enclosed area at the rear where there were four small cabins. Garcia suggested that Edmund and Maria take one and Stephan with Assad could take one of the others, with a curtain to separate them from Chiquita. Assad said she would share his bed anyway, this raised a few eyebrows and smiles. Edmund could see the craft was very neat and tidy a sign that the sailors took care of their ship. He discussed with Garcia a price and found the man was reasonable, he said if the men were willing to help in the duties on board he would reduce the cost.

When they returned to the Inn, Edmund explained what had been arranged to Maria. His wife was apprehensive as she was not a good sailor and had suffered on their voyages. Now came the part where they must sell their horses, it was a sad occasion and Assad did not say a word to anyone. Once the deals had been done they went back to the Inn to pack their belongings and prepare to board the ship that evening.

Chapter 22

The ship slipped her moorings and sailed out on the start of their journey home. Edmund was interested in the ship and the differences to other vessels. She was narrower in the beam and felt lighter. The sails were different and could be rigged so that she could beat to the wind or using a huge sail forward could run with the wind at high speeds. Captain Garcia was a very competent skipper and they were soon slicing through the water at a great speed. Garcia steered them round the north of Corsica making for Marseilles where they stopped to pick up food and water. Edmund took the opportunity to go ashore and find the Inn where they stayed when they were in Marseilles. The Landlord was pleased to see him and asked if they were staying the night?

'No, we are homeward bound and I wanted to know if you had seen or knew anything of captain Constanta and his ship?'

'I have heard that his ship docked here two days ago but left on this mornings tide.'

Edmund looked at Stephan and shrugged his shoulders. 'Perhaps he will be long gone when we leave, but we had better keep a sharp look out. He is a pirate and if he thinks our ship will be easy pickings we could be in trouble.'

He won't know we are on board though,' said Stephan. 'I would not say anything to Garcia, it will only make him nervous.' They thanked the Landlord and retuned to the ship.

The stores were soon loaded and they set sail on the evening tide. Looking back to shore Edmund stood with his arm around Maria. 'We are on our way home. I shall be please to see it after all the adventures we have had.' Maria nodded and snuggled up to him. 'Come wife, it is time for bed.'

Edmund woke to the noise of running feet on the deck above. He could hear Garcia shouting and his voice sounded urgent. Rising he put on his jerkin and shoes prior to going on deck.

'Stay out of sight.' Garcia was waving at him, he bent low and waited for the captain to reach him. 'We have a ship on our starboard bow that I don't like the look of. They are obviously looking us over and I am wondering if it your old friend?'

Edmund raised his head slowly and looked out across the sea. There was a black ship in the distance and immediately he recognised Constanta's vessel. Bending down again he asked Garcia what was the next move.

'I think he is just weighing us up as a prize, he cannot know you are aboard. The wind is blowing well from astern so we might have a surprise for him.' He quietly gave orders to the crew who prepared to hoist a large sail to the foremast. At Garcia's signal the sail was unfurled and immediately filled by the wind. The ship leapt forward and raced away. A cannon roared from Constanta, but they were well out of range and increasing speed.

'I don't think he will give chase, there are other ships that he can attack who are leaving Pisa.' Garcia said this as he gave orders to the helmsman to alter course slightly and the ship went even faster. Soon the black ship was just a dot on the horizon.

Two hours later the great sale was furled and their speed reduced and the sailing became more comfortable. 'I have to put in to Barcelona for some business. You may go ashore if you wish.' Edmund thanked him and said Maria would like to stretch her legs.

Tying up at the port Garcia told them not to be long as the dock was exposed to the weather and the glass was falling. Edmund and Maria with Stephan quickly went ashore.

They found a small market but Maria's legs began to ache so it was an about turn back to the ship. The clouds were darkening as the boarded and Garcia was ready to cast off immediately. They cleared the harbour just as the storm broke. Maria clutched Edmund and cried that they would all be drowned. Garcia proved how good a skipper he was by guiding his ship through the storm and riding the waves until the wind began to abate. The ship gradually pitched and rolled less and less. Maria and Edmund ventured on deck where Garcia was manning the wheel himself. The crew were busy clearing decks and sorting out the sails.

Garcia called them up to where he was standing.' It will be smooth sailing soon. She is a good craft in a storm and will ride out most waves, I hope it was not too exciting for you.'

Edmund and Maria looked at him and laughed. 'We were nearly parents before the due time,' said Edmund. Holding on to a rail the couple felt the speed of the craft and the thrill of riding the waves. The glorious evening sunset bathed the ship in a golden glow and Edmund drew Maria closer to him. They stayed looking at the sinking sun until Garcia handed back the tiller to his coxswain. Through the night the little ship carried on its southward course.

The next day Garcia reduced speed and the crew set about getting the ship ready to enter port. Decks were scrubbed, sails were stowed, rope was coiled and the cabins cleaned. They reached Valencia the next morning and as soon as they had docked Edmund realised why the ship had been cleaned. They were boarded by some official looking gentlemen in uniform who wanted to know what they were carrying. One of the officers approached Edmund.

'Who are you sir? Where have you come from and where are you going?'

'I am Sir Edmund Ivanson this is my wife Maria Berchello with her maid. The other gentlemen are señor Stephan and Assad who are my friends and business colleagues.'

'Many pardons sir, I know señor Berchello and have heard of you too sir and your fighting skills that are the talk of Castile.'

'We are to disembark here and after resting in your city, we journey home.'

The official bowed and joined his colleague who was already leaving the ship. Garcia was pleased to see them go and said it had only been introduced recently, they were looking for Castilians who would cause trouble in the city as they were laying claim to the area and he thought that eventually it would come to a war.

Edmund checked that everyone was ashore and after settling with Garcia as well as thanking him, moved off to an Inn that Stephan had found for them. The Inn was comfortable enough but Edmund was concerned that there was still pestilence in the city after the plague. Assad went looking for horses

'I think we should start our journey home as soon as possible. I do not want to rush but we need to be home in time for the birth.' Maria smiled up at him and nodded her head in agreement. They were discussing what they would need for the journey when Assad brought two gentlemen to see Edmund. One of the men stepped forward and holding out his hand announced himself as señor Ferranti, an equerry of the king of Aragon.

'Sir Edmund we are pleased to welcome you to Valencia. I have a message from our king. He wishes you to join forces with us to defend our city from the attacks of the Castilians. We would offer gold and a title should you agree. Will you join us?'

'I am taken aback by your offer. We are only three fighting men, we would not enhance your army very much. My home is in Castile and I do not wish to fight against my king.' Edmund said this as he turned towards Maria. 'My wife is carrying our first child so we shall leave for home as quickly as possible.'

'That will not be possible, I am afraid,' said the other man. 'We can not let you fight against us. Your prowess with a blade is known and you must stay here until the Castilians are beaten back.'

Edmund's anger was rising and suddenly he grabbed the equerry and held a knife to his throat. Stephan drew his sword to threaten the other man.

'Tie him up and gag him. Lock him in that little room over there.' The man struggled and Stephan struck him. 'That should keep him quiet for a while.'

Edmund looked at the equerry and said. 'There will be a knife at your back and my magic sword ready to cut your head off if you try to endanger us. Do you understand?'

The frightened man nodded his head, Edmund could feel him trembling. Leaving the Inn they met a contingent of guards waiting for them. Edmund whispered to the equerry who spoke to the guards telling them to march back to their barracks while he accompanied Sir Edmund on horseback. Going to the Inn yard they found Assad and Chiquita with horses., all their baggage had been loaded onto two and the rest were saddled ready. The equerry's horse was also tethered there and once he was in the saddle Stephan closed up to him.

'Should you be foolish and cry out, remember you will be the first to die.' Edmund said this as he moved out with Assad bringing up the rear. No-one stopped them as the rode north until they came nearer to the border with Castile. Here patrols were more frequent and eventually one stopped them, a nervous Ferranti told them who he was and that they were on a mission for the king. Two of the soldiers accompanied them to a small village that was situated not far from the border. Resting at an Inn and out of hearing of Ferranti, Edmund discussed how he planned to get them across the border.

They rose and left the Inn at first light. Assed led the pack horses with the ladies in close attendance. Edmund had bound and gagged Ferranti and locked the room. Stephan kept close to Edmund and the two of them were a few paces in front. They managed to bypass a group of guards and kept going towards the frontier. Edmund called a halt and putting fingers to his lips signalled silence. A small group of men were creeping up on the guards they had just passed. They pounced on the men from Aragon and a fight ensued. Edmund drew Talio and shouting "We are for Peter and Castile,' he joined the fray. There were soon no survivors from the Aragon camp. Edmund was cleaning Talio when the captain of the Castilians came to him and said, 'You are the English knight with the magical sword. I was one of the guards when you rescued us from that village. What are you doing here?' Edmund explained that they were trying to make their way home to Castello Dunston. 'We thank you for your assistance tonight but we must leave here now before more of our enemies come. I will send two men with you who will vouch for you as you go through our lines.' Edmund thanked him and they moved off deeper into Castilian territory.

They made for the river Jucar as this afforded the best pass through the foothills and fresh water. Their mood lightened as they rode knowing they were on the last leg of their journey home. The road by the river was easy and they made good progress. The approach to Cueca was not so easy as there had been small landslides and they had to be careful not to slip over the edge of the gorge. Suddenly Edmund's horse slipped and the knight had to grab the pommel tightly, as he did so the ring dug into his finger. Cursing he calmed the horse and looked down at his finger. The ring had cut it slightly so taking it off he put it into his satchel.

Chapter 23

Harold was breaking his fast one morning when a messenger arrived with a missive from the Lord Chancellor. As Harold read it he became a little concerned as he was summoned to a meeting in London. I wonder if this is to do with Geoffrey he thought. He knew from his contacts at court that Geoffrey had been convicted and had now been languishing in the Tower for several years. Attacking a peer of the realm in his castle did not sit well with parliament or the king. The door flew open and a young man burst into the room. 'Who was that father, did he come from London, are we going to London, shall I tell mother?'

'Calm down John, yes the message is from London and I will discuss it when I have spoken to your mother. Now leave me in peace until I have finished eating.' The young man left and a smiling Harold finished his food.

Harold read the letter that informed him that his presence was required in London. The missive did not go into detail as to why he was wanted, all that it said was that he was to report to the Lord Chancellor on his arrival.

That night as he lay next to Elizabeth he pondered on what he would find when he reached London. His wife snuggled up to him and whispered. "What ails you my love, was it the letter?' 'Yes, it is. I wonder what he wants? I must take a copy of our accounts with me I hope our clerk has them up to date.' They lay close together until sleep took over.

Two days later Harold was ready to make the journey. John begged his father to take him with him but Harold said he would be needed at Wymondham to look after his mother, which seemed to appease the boy a little. They were quite a caravan as they moved off, Harold and his squire Alfred, his clerk Joseph, and twenty men at arms. Harold wondered if the Black Prince would be at court or was he still in France. He did not like the man and he knew the feeling was mutual.

Harold's new squire was a sturdy young man, son of a tenant close to Wymondham. Harold had seen that the lad did not want to be a farmer like his father and asked him to come into the castle. He had watched him develop his fighting skills working with the guards.

Arriving in the city Harold was reminded of the smell that hung over the place, he would be glad to get back to the clean air of the countryside.

Harold planned to stay at the London house, if it was still there. They entered the gateway and could see that the gardens were overgrown but the house still stood. A man appeared at the door to their loud knocking, he said he was the son of the previous seneschal, Harold said who he was and the man bowed and bid him enter.

'I am sorry my lord that the house is not in a very good state. We lost many staff to the plague and as we had not heard from Sir John we did not know what to do. We will do our best to accommodate you but there is only the housekeeper and one girl left.'

Harold could see that the house was indeed neglected and he said that there were no women with them so they would take whatever could be arranged and he would discuss the future with him after his visit to the Lord Chancellor. He thought to himself that his original idea was probably the best, sell the house, why would he want an expensive liability in this stink-hole, he could always stay in good Inns outside the city.

The meeting with the Lord Chancellor was to be at the Tower and they made their way through the throngs of tradesman and beggars in the morning. The city was in a woeful state after the pestilence had passed and Harold hoped he would not have to stay here for long. The anteroom was crowded with people wanting to see the Lord Chancellor but to Harold's surprise he was conducted to a small side room by a fussy little clerk. A connecting door opened and the Lord Chancellor strode in.

'Good to see you Norfolk, sorry to hear of your father's demise, bad business the dammed plague, emptied half the city. How fare you in your shire, do you still follow your fathers farming principles? Lot of talk about it here but nobody else has had the courage to try it.'

'Our shire is surviving after the terrible times we have had.' Harold thought it wise not to tell that they were coping very well. 'We are still following my fathers plan for co-operative farming and so far the tenants are agreeable to stay with the plan Sir John devised.'

'Called you in to tell you of a decision his majesty has made. This is to honour what your family has achieved and the support you have given him, especially young Edmunds prowess in helping to defeat the Scots. Where is the young man now? We have not heard of him for a long time. I digress, his majesty has been pleased to found a new order of knights they will be called Knights Companion and become members of the Order of the Garter. Dam silly name if you ask me but his majesty has his reasons. He is the only one who can bestow this title on a knight and he has chosen you.'

Harold stood dumbfounded for a few minutes. 'I cannot understand why he has chosen me.'

'His majesty remembers the time you first met and has followed your progress ever since. The investiture will take place on St Georges day at Windsor, you will be there at noon on the day before and call next door before you leave. I will see you on the day.' With that parting shot the Lord Chancellor left the room.

Harold turned to Alfred, his new squire who had accompanied him. 'What do you think of that?' 'A great honour lord, not only for you but the family and all your shire.' Joseph agreed.

The went to the room next door where a fussy little man measured Harold for his dress that he was to wear. 'They will be ready for you sire, when you call the day before your investiture.'

As they were leaving the Tower a tall thin man with sallow complexion stopped them and asked if they would be kind enough to come to his masters office. Harold asked who his master was and found out it was the Book Keeper.

'This is what I had expected, come Joseph let us see what the man wants.'

They followed the man to a room adjoining the Lord Chancellors office and introduced to another thin man who looked as though he had never seen the light of day. Harold introduced Joseph and said that he would provide any details that were required. The meeting turned out to be just a verification of their taxes and what had been payed. There was an attempt to exhort more from Harold's estates but Joseph proved that there was no reason to do this and with Harolds new appointment it would be unwise to peruse this further. With a sickly smile on his face the Book Keeper bid them farewell.

Returning to the house Harold called Feathers to him and said he was to get the house in good order, to employ the staff that were necessary and he would stay for two or three days to see how he progressed. Harold realised that St Georges day was only four weeks away so he must return home, collect Elizabeth and John and return. He called Alfred and bid him to prepare for the journey that they must start the next day. Joseph was to stay at the house and supervise the work and keep an eye on what was being spent. Four of the guards would also stay to show that the house was now occupied.

The ride home was uneventful, Harold pushed them hard and they made good time with only two stops. Elizabeth was pleased to see Harold and became very excited when he told of all the news, she immediately began organising packing for the return to London. John went around getting into everyones way.

When they arrived back at the London house they could see immediately that Feathers had been busy. The gardens were tidy and in the house everywhere was clean and almost back to how it was when Harold had visited it with his father. Elizabeth went from room to room saying what a grand house it was, certainly more comfortable than the draughty castle at Wymondham.

Harold presented himself at Windsor on time and was fitted out with his robes and hat. He did not like the hat but was told it was necessary and must be worn. On the day of the investiture the sun was shinning and there was quite a crowd of people lining the short walk from the castle to the new chapel. Most people cheered and applauded the king and his knights as they walked however Harold did hear some disgruntled murmurs from parts of the crowd. They were unhappy at Edwards persistence on waring with France.

Queen Philippa kept them entertained at the dinner with stories, it was obvious to everyone that she was pregnant again.

Harold and Elizabeth were pleased to get back to the house and spent the next day relaxing in the garden. Harold knew he would have to get back to Wymondham as London was too far away to organise his estates. He also knew that you could get sucked into the various groups who wanted to further their own agenda in the court and Harold loathed them.

They hired a boat to sail up and down the river which enthralled John. He had befriended one of the gardeners who had built him a small cabin overlooking the river. He was disappointed when Harold declared it was time to return to Wymondham.

When they reached home the villagers turned out to applaud Harold. He hoped that his new appointment would help in his control of the fiefdom as he was now a friend of the king.

Chapter 24

Edmund left Cueca the next morning wanting to reach home as soon as possible. The road wound through the valley and they all began to relax knowing they would soon be at the vineyard. Coming towards them they saw a group of horsemen, at a distance they could not determine who they were but their flowing clothes made Edmund think of Moors. When they were close enough he could see that they were a mixed bunch of Spaniards and Moors with three women as well.

'Good day to you.' Edmund extended his greeting to the leader. 'Do you travel far?'

'Far enough, we are looking for work but not many are hiring at the moment. We called at a large vineyard but they would not accept us because some of us are Moors. I thought we were at peace now. They told us the owner was away but that was just an excuse.'

Edmund said he did not know the place, they were journeying home and were not looking for work. The two groups went their different ways and Edmund's party moved quickly on through the valley. They stopped in a small village Inn for the night. There were only two other guests who were sullen and hardly spoke when Edmund greeted them. The landlord brought them a substantial supper which they all devoured as they had not stopped for food all day. Edmund and Maria decided to go up to bed, His wife was feeling exhausted as the impending birth was beginning to tire her. Edmund looked up as the door of the Inn opened and the leader of the group they had met on the road strode in. He had two of his companions with him.

'Ah, there you are. We have been thinking you were not honest with us, you knew too much about the vineyard and your accent could be English. You are the owner returning home aren't you?'

'If you have lived in some of the northern areas of Portugal your Spanish can sound strange.' Edmund stood up as he said this. 'We are returning home that is true but not as owners of a vineyard, just to our house in Toledo.'

The man replied that he did not believe him and he would teach him some manners regarding being rude to Moors and his friends. The landlord quickly stepped between them and said he would not tolerate fighting in his Inn. He called out and two large men appeared.

'Come outside, if you dare, and we will soon settle this.' The leader turned and with his two companions made for the door.

'Don't go,' pleaded Maria. Edmund looked at her and said that if he did not settle this now they would only wait for them on the road. Outside the light was beginning to fade, Edmund positioned himself in the best patch of the sinking sun and drew Talio. Everyone else unsheathed their swords and they faced each other.

'This is your lesson to tell us the truth,' shouted the leader and sprang forward. Edmund parried his attack and suddenly realised he was not wearing the ring. Talio was beautifully balanced and made of strong steel, in Edmund's hand it allowed him to use his expertise as a superb swordsman but he did not have that extra speed that he had come to rely on. This confrontation he had to win on his on merits. The fight swung to and fro Edmund started to feel perspiration running down his face. His opponent was also slowing but some of that was deception and he made a vicious attack which drove Edmund back. He felt a blow on his left shoulder but ignored it and stood his ground. The leader started to flag again and Edmund thought another attack would come, he drove Talio hard to the man's throat and was rewarded by spurt of blood in his face as the leader went down.

Stephan and Assad had beaten their opponents. No one had died, the leader was severely hurt and his friends tried to stop the bleeding. Edmund turned to back into the Inn when he found himself in Maria's arms.

'Oh, you have been hurt my love. We must take you to our room so that I can look at your wound.' When Edmund removed his clothes the wound could be seen. The sword had pierced his shoulder, not a large cut but a deep one. Blood was oozing from it and as Maria bathed it the flow quickened. Stephan came to see if there was anything Edmund wanted, Maria said a doctor was needed.

'I do not think we will find one of those in this village. If there is anyone he would only be an apothecary and not very skilled.' Stephan turned to go as a loud knock came on the door and it opened to reveal Gareth.

'We were on patrol it is a pity we did not come earlier. How are you Edmund?' Edmund smiled and said he was all right and there was too much fuss being made. Maria bound the shoulder and they went down to the Inn's only room. There were four other men from the vineyard there.

'How are the grapes this year? We need a good harvest to pay for all the improvements that are needed.' Edmund looked at Gareth as he said this.

'It has been a very good harvest for the past two years and our wine is selling well. I have already made some improvements and there are more to come. The vineyard has settled down and we have a good team around us so you have no need to worry.'

Edmund realised he was out of order in making it look as though he was the only one who made decisions. He had been away so long and so much had happened that he would be out of touch with what was taking place at home.

In the morning after Maria had dressed Edmund's wound they set off for Castello Dunston. Edmund slouched in his saddle due to the after effects of the fight and his wound. There was also his pride that had taken a knock when he realised without the ring he was just a good swordsman, and Gareth had taken over at the vineyard. He still had Maria and the forthcoming baby which cheered him a little. Maria kept up a stream of questions to Gareth wanting all the news.

They sighted Castello Dunston as the sun was setting and all their spirits rose. There was quite a welcoming committee and concern that Edmund had been wounded. Edmund took his place at the head of the table that night and saw the looks exchanged between Gareth and Stephan. While he was at home he was lord and that was that.

It was late in the morning when Edmund rose. Maria wanted him to stay in bed and rest. He wandered around the barns and sheds not knowing what to do. Everything seemed to be in order and it was obvious that Gareth was doing a good job. Maria was resting as she had not felt well these last couple of days but the woman who was looking after her said this was quite usual. His first call was to the forge where the new blacksmith was working. Edmund explained he had a valuable ring that he would like him to look at. When the man looked at the ring he was impressed with the strength of the metal. "It looks like gold but it is harder, I will smooth the edge where it has been uncomfortable for you.' When the Smith had finished Edmund tried on the ring and found it fitted much better. He thanked the Smith and continued his walk. He reached the stables where Assad was saddling a horse.

'Saddle one for me please. I feel like a getting out into the country for a while.'

'I will come with you sir, it is not wise to ride alone with these bandits and Moors around.'

Edmund agreed and when the horses were ready the two of them rode out. His shoulder was still painful where the sword had penetrated. This was the first serious wound he had received since he had become a fighting man, thanks to the ring and the sword. Now he had the ring back and he assumed that the magic in the sword would return. Reaching the village of Largasera they stopped at an Inn to refresh themselves. Sitting outside they could see a rider approaching at great speed. He saw Edmund and pulled to a stop, jumped down and rushed over to them.

'Sir Edmund you must come home quickly. Your wife is unwell with the baby and she needs you.'

Edmund and Assed set off at a full gallop, urging their horses to maximum speed. Arriving at the house Edmund dismounted and rushed inside. He brushed aside a man who tried to stop him and bounded up the stairs to their bedroom. Several women were around the bed, one turned and spread out her arms to stop him. 'There is nothing you can do sir, just wait outside while we clean up in here.' Edmund did not understand and tried to push past when another of the maids helped to restrain him. He could see blood everywhere and just the form of Maria, not her face.

'What has happened, let me see my wife.'

'There was nothing we could do sir, they have both succumbed and are with God.'

Edmund collapsed with shock, the woman who had been looking after Maria came to him and told him what had happened.

'Your wife started to give birth and there was a sudden great burst of blood. The baby came out but was stillborn. We could not stop the bleeding from your wife and she died a few minutes ago. Let us clean up before you go to her, please?'

Edmund sat in a chair and buried his head in his hands. Why had he gone riding, why had he not stayed here with Maria. One of the women touched him on his arm. 'You can go in now.' He rose and went back into the room. They had cleaned it up well and Maria lay in the bed white faced, very still with her eyes closed. Edmund knelt beside the bed and clasped one of her cold hands.

'I am so sorry, my love.' with that he rose and went down to the yard and then walked out to the vines. Once well away from the house he dropped to his knees and burst into tears.

Chapter 25

The sun was setting as Edmund made his way back to the house. There were people milling about in the yard and he recognised some of Berchello's men. Hurrying inside he mounted the stairs and found Maria's father kneeling by her bed. The man rose and embraced Edmund.

'I am so sorry, my boy, you had so much to look forward to. We would like to take her to Toledo to be interred in the family vault. Do you have any objections? We must act quickly due to the heat in this part of Spain.'

'I have no objections, she should be with her family.'

'Good, then I will have caskets made for her and the little one. I am sure your carpenter is quite capable and we will leave tomorrow. I will go now to make the arrangements and will see you in the morning.'

Edmund sat next to his wife's body and looked at her face. There was a knock on the door and Gareth came in.

'Is there anything I can do. señor Berchello has told us of the arrangements and Andrea, the carpenter, has made caskets before. We would all like to come to Toledo for the funeral. Emile will stay and look after things here.' 'I would like that, to have all our friends there to see Maria put to rest,' said Edmund.

They all set off early the next morning as the mist was rising. A quiet and sad convoy heading out towards Toledo. The coffins, one large and one very tiny, were secured on a cart that was dressed in black. They stopped at noon and their priest who was travelling with them, led them in prayer. As night crept over the land they entered into Toledo and the cortege arrived at the cathedral where the bodies would lay overnight. Edmund was exhausted and longed to be alone, Berchello insisted he accompanied him to his house. All the family were there, this is what Edmund wanted to avoid, he was full enough with his own grief, as soon as was polite he escaped and went to the old house where he lived when first coming to Toledo. Gareth and the rest of the men were just sitting down to a meal and invited him to join them.

The next few days Edmund was in a trance, the funeral in the cathedral, the internment in the family vault all passed as if in another world. Sitting with Gareth he finally started to get himself together and think about his next steps.

'I do not want to go back to Castello Dunston now, will you carry on managing the place for a while, I need time to decide what to do?'

'Of course, Edmund, how long do think that will take?'

'I don't know, I thought I would contact Isaac and go with him for a while.'

Assad immediately said he would stay with him. Edmund agreed and replied that it would be good to have a friend with him. Stephan said his father had asked him to return home and he felt duty bound to do so now that his sister had gone.

Several days later, after the Castello Dunston party had gone Edmund contacted Isaac who agreed that he had a couple of trips to make that Edmund would be a most agreeable companion for him. Having something to do eased the pain of the loss of Maria. The first trip went without incident and Edmund began to relax more. The next journey was not so easy, anti-Jewish feeling was still rife in the area. There were many killings and so called executions.

'I have to go to Cordoba with some money (Edmund knew that this usually meant a lot of money!). I will need you to accompany me. I will be meeting my friend David, we will be as discrete as we can but you never know who is watching.'

'We will be ready. Where is this meeting to take place?' asked Edmund. 'At his house on the edge of the city.'

They reached the house in the early evening as the sun was setting. The first thing Edmund noticed was that in the shadows he could see men congregating.

'Stay back Isaac until we see what is going on. Assad come with me and keep your sword arm free.'

They approached the men and greeted them. This was met by a gruff response. Edmund enquired whether this house belonged to señor Enrico, he had no idea who that was as he had just made the name up. A big burley man stepped forward and said he had never heard of him and this house belonged to a 'dirty Jew' but not for long as they were about to force him out.

'What has he done that is so wrong that you want to force him to leave his home?'

The man looked puzzled at this and said. 'It is none of your business so be on your way and don't get involved.' There was a murmuring from the rest of the men as Edmund stepped in front of the door.

'I am a defender of persecuted people and this is called Retribution,' he said as he unsheathed Talio.

The big man drew his sword and leapt at Edmund with a loud cry. Talio described an arc in the air finishing at the man's neck and his head fell to the floor. No one moved and Edmund stood twirling Talio around his wrist.

'Does anyone wish to be next?

There was a moment of stunned silence and then they picked up the body and moved off with a parting shot that the authorities would hear of this.

When they were well out of sight Isaac came and they approached the front door. An upstairs window opened and a voice called, demanding them to state who they were. Isaac called out to his friend and soon the door opened and they were welcomed inside. David was full of thanks but he said they would be back with more men and the militia.

'I must pack and take my family south, we have friends near the Portuguese border. This persecution is going to get worse.'

'We must be on our way too, we need to get Isaac home in one piece and I must get back to Castello Dunston.' With that they mounted their horses and started the journey home.

Edmund and Assad neared the vineyard and Edmund called a halt.

'I have made up my mind to return to England. Gareth is now a family man and has proved he can manage the business here. Will you come with me? We have been together so long I would miss you.'

Assad smiled. 'How would you manage without me? You could never look after your horses. I would like to see your home in England, you have talked about it so much.'

Edmund laughed and they entered the vineyard in a happier mood than when they left it. Edmund went to find Gareth and tell him of his decision, he found him by the wine presses. Gareth looked up as Edmund entered.

'How was your visit to Isaac? Did he want you to be bodyguard again?'

'Yes, he did, it will be the last time though. I have a proposition to put to you. I am not a person who can be tied down, as you must know. I have always been on the move finding adventures.'

'Or trouble,' said Gareth.

'I must admit trouble does seem to follow me. I want to hand over the vineyard to you, that is you would have full control and I will be gone, probably making my way back to England. The property would remain in my name and I would expect a small percentage if you make profit. In three years you can make me an offer to buy it if you wish. What do you think of the idea?'

'I will talk it over with Chiquita and Cuthbert.' Gareth walked off in the direction of the house and Edmund stood looking after him. He had left England a long time ago and much had happened in his life. He still had the wander lust and the habit of getting into trouble. At the end of the day he was an Englishman and the pull of home was stronger than it had ever been, probably due to the loss of Maria.

Chapter 26

The evening before Edmund and Assad's departure they sat down to a quiet meal. Gareth had agreed terms with Edmund and a paper had been drawn up at the insistence of Gareth. He was pleased in some ways that he could now run the vineyard as he wanted and Edmund was also relieved that he no longer had the responsibility.

They set off early on the morrow with four pack horses laden with their belongings. They had decided to head east to find the nearest port and then set sail for England.

They made an easy journey towards Avila, topping a small hill they looked down at the city in the distance. The walls and towers showed why it had not been defeated. Edmund remembered the last time he was there and they had been captured by bandits. Señor De La Cruz had been most generous after his rescue, he also wondered if his daughter, Rhyannon, was still as beautiful.

They entered the city by the south gate and wound their way to a large Inn where they could stable their horses. They sat eating a meal and looking at their fellow guests. A man broke away from one table and came over to them.

'Sir Ivanson, you may not remember me, I was one of the guards when we were attacked and captured. I will never forget that event and the way we escaped and beat the bandits. A pleasure to see you again sir.'

Edmund rose and shook the man's hand, several other diners were now beginning to stare at him, one shouted that he was there too and banged his drinking pot on the table. There was soon a chorus of pots being banged on the tables. A man rose and shouted above the din. 'Show us your magic sword, get it to do a trick or a dance for us.' Silence decended on the room and a friend of the drunk tried to calm him. Edmund sat down and smiled at the man.

'There's more magic in my fists than in that sword,' continued the drunk and he staggered towards Edmund. The landlord came behind him and pushed him towards the door telling him to go outside and sober up. When the man had gone the barroom settled down and the drinking resumed. Edmund and Assad made their excuses and retired to bed.

Leaving the Inn the next morning they were confronted by the drunk of the night before with two other men. 'Now we will see how magical that weapon of yours is. There are only three of us so it should not take long to show us what it can do.' The three drew their swords and advanced on Edmund and Assad. Assad move to one side and drew his weapon. Edmund moved to the other flank and drew Talio. Edmund quickly sent one of the men's sword flying into some bushes and turned just in time to parry the drunks attempt to run him through. He fenced for a moment and the then with a quick twist of his wrist disarmed the man cutting his wrist in the process. Assed had also disarmed his opponent and the three of them, cursing loudly beat a hasty retreat. Edmund collected the weapons of the three and gave them to the landlord, who had come out to see what all the noise was about.

'About time that braggart was taught a lesson, you will have to keep a sharp lookout as he is likely to strike one dark night when you are off guard. Come in and eat before you go.' The landlord turned and went back into the Inn. Edmund and Assad followed him and sat down at a table. The other residents had not yet risen so when they had finished eating they saddled up and left.

Arriving at De La Cruz' house they enquired if the count was at home? When the servant returned De La Cruz was with him and rushed over to embrace Edmund

'Come in, come in dear friend. I had heard you were in the town and expected you.' 'We had a small delay, sir. How is your family?'

'They are well, thank you Edmund. I heard of your loss and we all pray for you. Jolentia and Rhyannon are both married, in fact they are on an extended honeymoon, travelling around Spain.'

They had now reached the large family room that Edmund remembered. De La Cruz invited them to sit and sent a man away to fetch refreshing drinks.

'What are your plans now, Edmund? Where are you heading?'

'We are hoping to make it to the north and find a ship sailing for England. I have been away too long from my brothers side.'

They finished their drinks and De La Cruz suggested they stay the night here and he knew a man who could guide them north. Edmund thanked him and said it would be most useful.

'It is the least I can do in repayment for my rescue from those bandits.' De La Cruz said this as he called his manservant to him and told him to arrange rooms. Assad excused himself and said he would go and check on the horses.

'There is no need to go, my stable lads are very good and will care for your animals.' Edmund laughed. 'They are like his children and like a father he must see for himself.'

A manservant entered accompanied by a man dressed for the country. He was introduced to Edmund as Domingo, his guide to take him north. Edmund thought he looked like Garaile, the Basque man they met in the mountains. Domingo told them he was from Santander and knew all the Northern regions.

'My friends wish to start their journey in two days time.' De La Cruz informed him, Domingo said he would be ready. Edmund thanked him and they fell to discussing plans for their trip.

The morning of departure arrived and the little party set off towards Salamanca which would be their first objective. Domingo was a talkative man and kept them entertained with stories of life in the Basque country. Edmund doubted that they were true but it lightened their mood as they rode. The first night they stopped at a small village Inn and as Edmund sat outside watching the sun disappear he thought of England and his brother, Harold. He had not written to say that he was returning, would Harold want him after all the time he had been away. Would there be a place for him? These thoughts were still with him as he went to his bed.

They pressed on the next day towards Salamanca. Domingo still chattered away to them, it did not slow their progress however, they soon saw the great city of Salamanca before them. Edmund thought on the fact that so much had happened to him since his last visit here. Entering the city they made their way to an Inn that Domingo recommended. The rooms were very comfortable and Edmund felt relaxed and at ease for the first time in a long while.

After a good nights rest Edmund proposed a walk through the city. Domingo said he would find it very busy as it was the time of the Annual Fair, Edmund remembered the last time he was here He joined the crowds milling around the market. He spotted a stall selling bright scarves and cheap jewellery

'I bid you good day, señor Milosh. I trust you and your band are in good health.' The man spun round and let out a shout. 'Edmund, my friend, where have you come from?' He came round from the table and grasped Edmund in a bear hug.' Come let us sit and you can tell me all that has happened to you.' Milosh took his arm and they went to a nearby taverna and ordered wine. Edmund told him a shortened version of what had happened to him since they last saw each other.

'I am very sorry to hear of your wife and child. Is this what made you journey back to England?'

'Yes, it is time I went back to my brother too. I have land there as well as here so I will return to Spain at some point in the future.'

They sat chatting, drinking and watching the people enjoying the fair. A tall knight approached them and Edmund leapt to his feet. 'Alberto, how good to see you. How are your friends? Are you here for the tournament?'

'This is a surprise,' answered the knight. 'Last I heard of you was that you were running a vineyard in the south. What happened, did you drink all the profits?'

Edmund quickly explained what had happened and the knight apologised and sat down to listen to Edmund's story. Alberto asked him if he was competing in the tournament. Edmund explained he had no destrier so an armoured fight was out of the question.

'There are competitions you could enter, archery and the sword fight for knights in armour on foot. Come with me and I will take you to the marshal.'

They took their leave of Milosh and went to the tournament ground. There Edmund entered for both events. Alberto said he would meet him at the grounds in the morning.

Edmund went back to the Inn and found Assad had already returned. Edmund told him that he had entered the tournament and asked if he would squire for him, to which Assad readily agreed. They unpacked Edmund's armour and Assad said he would clean it while Edmund prepared his weapons.

The morning was clear and bright, and warm as they made their way to the tournament. Archery was first up and Edmund joined the other contestants at the first target. They were arranged in groups of four and told to fire in sequence. Edmund found himself in third place after the first target. They moved to the next target and split into fours again. Edmund realised this target was further away, he adjusted for the wind and loosed his arrows, second this time. They went through two more targets with the spacing increasing each time. Edmund held on to second place much to the annoyance of some of the locals. He went back to the tents that had been allocated, with Assad's help he put on his armour and belted Talio around his waist. The first part of this event was a general melee. They were split into three groups to start with and positioned around the arena. The start signal was given and everyone charged to the centre where the fighting began. The rules were that no-one was to receive killing wounds, that had been the instructions from the marshal. Edmund hung back as he was aware that old scores were often settled at this type of event. Edmund picked his target and was soon fencing with a young man, he disarmed him easily and moved on to a large knight in black armour. This man was experienced, he turned and faced Edmund and attacked him viciously. Edmund parried and then attacked himself. The knight muttered something through his helmet and started to go for the killing strokes. Talio came alive in Edmund's hand and the knight was soon backing up trying to parry Edmund's attack. His sword suddenly spun out of his hand and the point of Talio was at his throat.

'I yield,' he cried and dropped to his knee. 'Who are you sir, I have not been beaten in single combat before.' Edmund did not answer as the marshal came to take him to the Count. Edmund removed his helm as he stood before count Alfonso Deride, the lord of the area.

'Well done sir knight, I do not think we have met before. What city are you from?' 'From England originally, my lord, I have lands in Toledo.'

'You are welcome here, will you be in the joust?'

'Unfortunately not, sir. I have no destrier and my own horse would not be suitable.'

'Then you shall ride one of mine. Bring Medianoche here to me.' One of the Count's men went off and returned with magnificent black destrier, ready saddled, armoured and with bright red trappings. Edmund expressed his thanks, took the horse from the servant and lead the beautiful animal over to Assad. The great horse lowered its head to Assad and Edmund could see a white stripe down its nose and one hoof had a covering of white hair. Edmund went to his tent to prepare for the joust.

Edmund had not competed with a lance for some time, he started nervously until he remembered the technique he had used successfully before. He eventually found himself in the last run and facing the Black Knight again. They had one fall each when Edmund faced him for the last time. Medianoche pawed the ground and when Edmund dug his heals in he bounded down the track. Edmund lowered his lance, instead of jinking it down and to the left he brought it up and lifted his opponent completely out of his saddle.

The Count was pleased Medianoche had done well, he awarded Edmund the prize of a large purse. 'You ride very well sir, you now have a destrier as I gift him to you.'

Edmund was taken by surprise and wondered what he would do with such a powerful animal. Assad was pleased, horse and man had taken to each other almost immediately. They walked back to Edmund's tent where Assad helped him remove his armour. He sat for a moment to get his breath back and see what was in the purses, there was a lot of money which was very welcome, it meant he would not need to use the facility that Isaac had set up for him.

'May I enter?' Milosh stood at the entrance with a big grin on his face. 'Congratulations, you have not lost your skill at arms I see.'

'It's more exhausting as you get older though, are you staying long in Salamanca?' 'A few more days and then we return to Segovia. Our camp is just outside the city to the north, come and visit us.' Edmund thanked him and said he would try.

Edmund and Assad were packing up their equipment when a messenger came up to them with and invitation from the Count to join him for dinner at the castle. Dressed in his best clothes Edmund set off for the castle. He guessed that the Count wanted him for something and it was not just to share his meal with him.

He was announced by the servant. 'Sir Edmund Ivanson of Castello Dunston and England,' said the pompous little man. Edmund felt a sense of sadness as he heard his full title. 'Welcome,' said the Count as he grasped Edmund's hand and led him into the room where the large tables were full of knights and finely dressed men. There was a burst of applause and Edmund felt his face reddening. The Count led him to a seat by his side and the dinner began. The food and the wine kept coming and Edmund was beginning to feel satiated. The Count held up his hand and stood. 'We have seen today a feast of talent and no more so that the performance of our guest (there was more applause). I crave your pardon for I must speak to this young man privately.' The Count signalled to Edmund to follow him.

Chapter 27

The Count led him to a side room and they sat down. Looking around Edmund noticed the room was richly furnished, obviously the count was not a poor man. Edmund sat in anticipation of what the Count wanted.

'I have a problem that I hope you can help me solve,' began the Count. 'A Romany group of entertainers came to the castle and when they left we realised our son was missing. I sent guards after them but when they were stopped there was no sign of our son. This morning I received a message telling me my son had beed abducted and if I wanted to see him alive again it would cost me 1000 gold reals. I want you to find him for me. All my staff are known to him and he would cry out and warn the bandits, but you could find him secretly, I know your prowess with a sword and you would soon release him. Will you do it for me?' Edmund sat silently, a little stunned at the request.

'You are not sure who has him captive. Was there no indication in the message? What is your sons name?'

'No, They will contact me again to give instructions where the money is to be taken. His name is Alfonso. I have the money and my son is worth several times that amount to me. You would be rewarded if you can recover him.' Edmund had a strange feeling that this was no ordinary hostage taking. He couldn't say why it was just a feeling.

'Have you one man they have not seen? That would help and I will take my squire too.'

When the discussion was over Edmund said he would do his best but with no promises. They found the Counts man who had been working in the kitchens so the son would not know him. Edmund explained to Antonio, the Count's man, and Assad what he planned to do. Leaving them he went to find Milosh to ask if he knew this band of gipsies.

They caught up with the other gypsy band as they had stopped for a break. Milosh and his group were invited to join them and soon there were several cooking fires and the groups began to intermingle. Edmund spotted a young boy who was dressed as a gypsy but seemed out of place. He stood quietly at the edge of the group at first and then spoke to the leader of the other gypsy band. Edmund moved gradually through the crowd chewing on a chicken leg, working his way round until he was standing next to the young man.

'Were there good pickings for you in the city?' asked Edmund. They young man looked at him quizzically. Edmund was dressed as a gypsy and spoke in a rough way so raised no suspicion. Edmund looked around and found the man from the kitchens who nodded his head.

'Why do you need 1000 gold reals, Alfonso? You would not have them for long if this band of Jolly Robbers got to hear of it.'

The lad stood shocked for a moment and then turned to run but found Assad in front of him smiling.

'Just come with me quietly and we will sought this out between us.'Alfonso followed Edmund to a small stand of trees.

'Now my lad, what was your reason for deceiving your father?'

'I wanted to travel and he wont let me out of his sight. I thought I would not be noticed among the gypsies, they have some of my age with them and they travel all over Spain. Their leader said he would write to my father to tell him that I could travel with them. I did not know he was going to ask for money.'

'I am sure your father would listen if you spoke to him about wanting to travel. You must speak to him seriously and beg his forgiveness for running away. We will return you to your father and you must apologise and accept whatever punishment he gives you.'

'But I am never listened to as my elder brother will be the count when father dies, there is nothing for me there.'

Edmund left him with Assad and sought out the leader of the gypsies. He found him talking to Milosh. The man said he knew Alphonso was a nobleman's son as his son had befriended him and brought him along with them. Edmund guessed the man knew all that was going on and told him he would be taking him home. He also told him he knew the full story and said that he should report him to the Count. The man pleaded with him not to do that and said he would be back in the mountains soon and away from the area. He tried to blame Alfonso for the whole escapade.

Edmund with Milosh and his group returned to Salamanca keeping a close watch on Alfonso. The city was in sight when Milosh told Edmund he would be journeying on to Segovia so they said their farewells. Edmund with Assad, Antonio and a very nervous Alfonso went on to the castle.

Edmund was taken to the Count while he told the rest of them to wait. He explained to the Count what had happened and his son was desperate to travel and find his way in life. As the second son he saw no place for him at home. The Count realised that some of it was his fault in not including his son more.

'He is very repentant and is ready to take whatever punishment you deem fit. I have and idea that I would like to discuss with you.' When Edmund had finished he called Alfonso to go to his father. Assad asked if the Count was very angry and what punishment would he impose. Edmund replied that he had put a proposal to the Count that could satisfy both of them

'What is it?'asked Assad.

'I have suggested that we take him with us back to England. That should be travel enough for him. He has been taught Latin and French and we can teach him the rudiments of our language.'

'I don't fancy wet nursing a kid for all that time,' said Assad.

'I will take responsibility for him and I think you will find he will behave.' Assad shrugged his shoulders and said that time would tell.

Edmund went back to see the Count and found Alfonso standing in front of him with a smile on his face. 'Father has told me of your suggestion and I would be honoured to be able to journey with you.'

Edmund looked at him and told him it would not be easy, sleeping rough and maybe fighting bandits. He asked the Count if he could take Antonio with them to help Alphonso. The Count agreed saying that he should stock up with food for them. Edmund said to Assad that he should find Domingo and prepare for an early start in two days time.

The time came for them to depart, Edmund felt excited, Assad was worried over what to do with the destrier and Domingo started telling stories. Arriving at the Castle they found Alphonso ready with Antonio and their pack animals. The Count was there to see his son off and wished him God's speed.

The cavalcade moved off heading North. Edmund felt an anticipation and excitement. He was on his way back to England and Home. They had not gone far when it began to rain, another reminder of home thought Edmund. They sheltered under some trees until the rain ceased. Moving off they noticed how the rain had cleared the air which invigorated them and Domingo burst into song which amused Alphonso, and made the others cringe.

The party moved into the foothills journeying on their way to Zamora. They reached the city one cool but sunny evening. They could see the dome of the cathedral and the imposing castle. Alphonso had a letter of introduction from his father to the ruling Count.

Chapter 28

The Count of Zamora welcomed them and offered food and shelter whilst they were in his city. They visited the cathedral and rested for several days. Edmund had to keep a close watch on Alphonso as there were many pretty young ladies casting glances in his direction. There had been a surfeit of girls born in the city over the past twenty years and not enough males to keep the balance. Edmund too found himself being smiled at by the young ladies when walking in the streets. He decided that they must leave before temptation became too great. They headed off towards Ponferrada. Alphonso, though young, had male urges and Edmund did not want trouble while in the city.

Travelling through the hills and valleys, Edmund could see the beauty of the country. The north was much greener and the air cool and sweet smelling from the trees and shrubs. This time they had no letter of introduction so their first action was to find an Inn that could accommodate them and their horses. The Innkeeper informed them that the alcalde lived in a large house by the castle. When the animals were settled Edmund asked Alphonso to accompany him to visit the alcalde. They were met at the door by a young girl who conducted them to a large well appointed room. A half an hour passed and the door opened to a round portly man with a red face.

'I am sorry to have kept you waiting sirs, I had some problems that had to be dealt with. It is a very busy job keeping this town peaceful and calm. What can I do for you? Are you travelling the Camino de Santiago?'

'I am Sir Edmund Ivanson of Wymondham in England, my party and I are returning home and normally we would call on the count but I understand he resides in Lemos. Hence we called on you.'

The alcalde made a shaky bow and began to apologies but Edmund cut him short and asked if there was anyone living in the castle.

'There is nobody there at the moment, sir. The Count only comes occasionally, it does have staff who look after the castle in his absence. I am sure the Count would offer you hospitality there, I will send word that you are coming. Would you and your friends dine with us while you are waiting?' Edmund accepted and they all relaxed, glad of the rest from all the riding they had done over the last days.

The sun had begun to sink in the west as they approached the castle. Edmund could see that it had been built to withstand attacks and siege. An imposing gateway led through to courtyard where they were met by a young man who declared himself to be the son of the steward. Having seen the horses cared for and their baggage unloaded they followed the young man into the castle. They were greeted by an older man who announced himself as the steward. As they had already eaten he conducted them to the bedrooms. They were spacious but sparsely furnished. Edmund said he would meet them all in the hall in the morning.

When they met, a large table had been laid with platters and knives, a large jolly woman brought in food helped by a girl and the young man they had already met.

'I hope that you were all comfortable last night sirs, we always keep beds ready in case the Count pays us a visit. These are my offspring and will look after your needs while you are here.' Edmund spotted Alphonso smiling at the girl and thought he had better keep an eye on him. The meal finished Edmund suggested to Assad and

Alphonso that they look around the castle. Antonio and Domingo said they would attend the horses.'

This was once a castle of the Knight Templars,' said the steward. I understand it was the centre of their banking venture in this region. Isaac told me the history of the knights in Spain up until they were disbanded by Philip of France.

It was a bloody time, however he needed their money. When Assad returned Edmund met him in his room. 'We must keep our eyes open to see if there are any secret places that they might have hidden any documents.' They set off looking in all the rooms and then climbing the winding stairs in the towers to come out on the battlements and the magnificent views over the town and countryside.

'We have come to the top now I think we should look at the bottom, I expect there are dungeons here.' Edmund started the decent.

On the ground floor they looked for the entrance to the dungeons. The steward met them and wanted to know what they were doing.

'This is such a fascinating castle, full of history, we could not miss the chance to explore a little. Are there dungeons?' The steward eyed Edmund with suspicion before explaining that they were on the lower floor, he would not be able to show them as his back was bad and he could not manage the stairs. Edmund sympathised with him and said he was not to bother as they would find the way and before the man could protest Edmund was down the stairs quickly followed by Assad and Alphonso. At the bottom of the stairs there was a dark room. Edmund lifted a torch from one of the wall brackets and lit it. They could see the barred cells around the sides of the room, a dismal place for prisoners awaiting their fate. Edmund spotted a shadow in one corner and found what looked like a tunnel entrance. They tentatively walked into the entrance, they could see the floor gradually descending so decided not to investigate further. Returning to the room of the cells they were confronted by the steward's son. 'Can I help you, sirs?'

Edmund explained they were interested in the castles of the Knight Templars. The young man said the tunnel probably went as far as the next castle but he had never gone very far along it as there had been a roof fall. They all returned to the hall where food and drink had been prepared for them.

Edmund stood looking out of his bedroom window, it was a fine night which boded well for the morrow. Perhaps they should move on. He turned to look around the room with its panelled walls. He walked around and passing one panel felt a draught. He stopped and felt round the edge of the panel, there was a click and the panel swung back revealing a small space in the wall. There was a tiny gap in between two stones of the wall, hence the draught. There was also a dust covered chest sitting there. Edmund tried to move but it was too heavy he looked at the old and rusty. Using his Toledo dagger he broke it open and stared at the glint of gold. He closed the lid and pushed the chest back into the space. Closing the panel he looked to see if there were any tell tale signs that it was there, satisfied that no one would guess a door was there, he climbed into bed.

Edmund lay in the bed thinking about what he had found. Should he tell the others? Should he take it at all? If it had belonged to the knights, they were now disbanded and classed as heretics, he assumed. With this analysis he convinced himself that the find was his.

He had spent a restless night and was quiet at their morning table. Assad asked him if he was ailing and Edmund was a little sharp with his reply. The find was still praying on his mind when the steward appeared to inform them that there were two knights at the gate who wished to see the Count. He had told them that the Count was not in residence and they had asked to meet the knight who was staying there. Edmund rose and followed the steward to the gate. There were two knights and their squires astride their horses, there was also another man on foot. Edmund looked at them and said, 'What do you require?'

One of the knights replied. 'Quid agis sir.' 'Salve,' replied Edmund.

'Ingressique possumus loqui,' responded the knight 'Quari?' said Edmund.

'loqui ad vos solo.'

Edmund looked hard at the knight and said, 'it would be better to speak in french then all will understand. You and your friend may enter, the rest of your men may wait here. Dismount and follow me.' The steward led them to a room next to the hall. There was a table and chairs and Edmund invited them to be seated and sent the steward to bring wine.

'My name is Philip de Calveree and this my companion Paul Guardery. We are visiting castles in the area as we make our way to Santiago. We would be grateful if your steward could show us over this splendid building.'

'I am afraid that is not possible as the Count is not here and I, Edmund Ivanson of Wymondham, am not inclined to allow strangers to wander around the castle. I see from the insignia on your pommel and the ring that you wear, that you were Knights Templars!'

Both knights rose to their feet and faced Edmund.

'These are just things we have picked up in our travels and we are insulted that you think us members of that foul breed,' shouted Guardery.

'Sit down gentlemen, you protest too much. This was once one of their castles and I expect that is why you are here.'

The knights sat down and did not say if Edmund was right or wrong. They asked questions about the building, had there been any discoveries of note and they were trying to trace one of the brothers. Was there any small place he could have been held prisoner, there might be hidden documents that would lead them to him. Suddenly Guardery leapt to his feet. 'We have talked enough now we will search the castle and you will not stop us.' Edmund and de Calveree stood as Guardery drew his sword, they also drew weapons and Edmund shouted for Assad. The two knights moved to the edge of the room as the door opened and Assad, closely followed by Alphonso entered. They also drew their swords and the three of them stood facing the knights. Guardery called to Edmund. 'Face me Englishman and find out how a true knight fights. If I win then we search the castle.' He immediately lunged at Edmund who parried the blow and the fight was on. The others stood back as the two protagonists traded thrusts and slashes.

Edmund realised this was an accomplished swordsman seasoned from many battles. His ring was now burning on his finger and Talio was starting to speed up.

Edmund felt a sword thrust home in his side and countered by forcing Talio through his opponents shoulder. The knight began to weaken and Edmund forced home his advantage with Talio cutting and thrusting so fast the end was obvious. Talio swept round in and arc and Guardery's head fell to the floor. Assad and Alphonso moved towards de Calveree but he dropped his sword and raised his hands.

Assad went to Edmund and looked at his wound. 'We must clean that as soon as possible and bind it.'

'Don't fuss, it is nothing. We must sort this mess out first.' As he was saying this the steward arrived with his son. He was aghast at the blood and immediately sent his son to fetch cleaners. Assad, with Alphonso, rolled Guardery's body in one of the rugs, with the head.

Edmund spoke to de Calveree. 'You will leave Ponferrada immediately and take this body with you. If I hear you are still in this area by tomorrow nightfall I shall follow you and deal with you in the same way.' The knight nodded and said he would be gone.

'Alphonso go and fetch the squires to carry this out.' He gestured at the rug, where de Calveree was kneeling in prayer. Edmund sat down as the wound he had received was beginning to hurt. The steward's wife came in with a bowl of water and began to dress Edmund's wound, it was not deep and by the time she had bandaged it the blood had stopped. The two squires came in and saying nothing they picked up the rug. De Calveree turned to Edmund. 'You may encounter other knights who will want revenge for killing a brother. I shall leave this area but will not forget what happened here.' He bowed and left the room. Edmund signalled Assad to follow him.

The steward was supervising the cleaning up after the fight and muttering to himself. Edmund's wound had been dressed and he found no restriction, although it hurt a little. He went to the gateway just in time to see de Calveree and his party riding away, the rug had been tied securely on Guardery's horse.

'Gather up our belongings, we will move on ourselves. Assad come with me.' Edmund returned to his room and revealed the hidden space to Assad.

'Help me to bring the chest onto the bed, we will be taking this with us.'

When the chest was on the bed Assad wanted to know what was in it that was so heavy. Edmund opened the chest and there was a gasp from Assad as he gazed at the gold pieces.

'Not a word to the others. We will divide this up when the time is right. Now we must find some way of transporting it. Put it into these saddle bags.'

Chapter 29

Edmund gave the steward a very generous amount of coins which changed his attitude to his visitors and he was all smiles as he saw them move off.

Their next objective was the city of Lugo another stopping place for the pilgrims. They came upon the view of the city from a hill. Edmund thought it resembled Avila, with it being behind walls. The main difference was that this city was almost surrounded by water.

'What a place to defend,'said Assad. 'What a place to try and attack,' countered Edmund. 'We will camp here tonight and go into the city tomorrow.' They unloaded the horses so that they could rest. Assad and Edmund unloaded Medianoche who was carrying four large leather bags. 'Try to keep these out of sight and guard them well,' said Edmund.

It was a pleasant evening and they sat chatting round the camp fire. Domingo was well into his fourth story when Alphonso asked Edmund what was in the leather bags as he had not seen them before Ponferrada. They all looked at Edmund and waited for his answer.

"I found some artefacts that the knights were after and I am taking them to Santiago to discuss with a friend what should be done with them.' Edmund thought it was a weak explanation but it was the best he could come up with. Then he remembered something that Isaac had given him, it was a letter and a list of names. The names were members of the banking group that he had used to transfer money from Harold to himself. Looking down the list he found a name for Lugo, a señor Raphael Tailor. This was the answer, he would take the gold to him as he must have somewhere secure.

Arriving at Rafael's house Edmund explained how he had is address. 'I wish to deposit this gold with you until we leave.' Rafael explained that he might have to move soon as he had heard how other towns were expelling Jews. He looked at the bags and explained to Edmund that he could not be responsible for such a large amount of gold. He also explained that the Jews were likely to come under threat again and he would have to move. 'It is true,' said Edmund, 'but it is mainly further south. Will you look after it until we move off again in two days time?' Rafael agreed. Edmund returned to his party and they found a suitable Inn.

That evening, as they sat round the table digesting their evening meal, Edmund spoke to them regarding the forthcoming sea journey.

'When we reach Santiago we shall rest there for some days and then make our way to the port of Caruna. There I hope to find a ship that can take us to England. It will be a long voyage so I hope you are all good sailors, except for Domingo who will leave us at Santiago.'

'I have never been on a ship,' said Alphonso.

'Well you wanted adventure and travel. You will soon get used to it when you are at sea.'

The next day they visited the cathedral, a magnificent building. There were many pilgrims there on their way to Santiago. Edmund decided to leave at night so that they were ahead of the pilgrims. Collecting the bags of gold and securing them on Medianoche, Assad remarked that this would be too obvious to an onlooker that there was something of value there.

'How else are we to carry them? We cannot put them on the other horses it would be to heavier load.'

Assad looked thoughtful for a moment and then said, 'We should sell some of our horses, they will have to be sold before we board ship. Distribute the gold among our own bags, especially your armour, and buy a cart. Two of us can ride the cart.'

Edmund thought for a moment and said, 'one of us must always be on the cart and it will slow us down. We have plenty of time, however. I agree let's put the plan into action. We will make for Caruna and not Santiago, it will keep us away from some of the pilgrims.'

Edmund managed to find a man willing to do a deal with horses for a well built cart. He explained to Alphonso and Antonio that this was the best way to travel with their luggage. Their little cavalcade now consisted of two of them mounted, two on the cart with Medianoche tied on behind. Domingo said farewell and went off towards the Pyrenees.

They journeyed on in company with pilgrims until it was time to branch off towards Caruna. Edmund was disappointed that he would not get the chance to visit the shrine in Santiago, they had to get the gold to the port as soon as possible. Rafael had written a letter to introduce him to a friend in Caruna who had a hidden room where he could store items of value for his customers. They eventually reached the port, it had taken longer with the cart. They searched for the house of Michael, finding, eventually, an imposing house where they were invited in immediately.

The cart was taken to the rear of the house and when Edmund explained what he wanted. Michael soon had it unloaded and certain bags taken to the hidden room. Edmund noticed the door was made of strong thick wood with metal bars and large locks. Edmund thanked Michael and rejoined the others. They found an Inn that could stable the horses. They settled themselves in and after eating their evening meal Edmund suggested a walk down to the docks. Even at this time of the evening the place was alive with ships being unloaded and loaded. Edmund could recognise some of the flags from France, Spain, Portugal but none from England. They entered an Inn and sat at a table drinking a strong ale.

'We may not get a direct passage to England from here,' said Edmund. 'We may have to get to France and try again from there. I will go to the docks tomorrow and try to talk to some of the captains.'

The visit to the docks proved to be frustrating for Edmund. Nobody was sailing to England, he also attracted many suspicious looks as though he was a spy. He found out that relations with France were deteriorating and the only way to get home was on a Spanish or Portuguese ship.

Several days past with their routine of checking at the docks and exercising the horses beginning to wear on their nerves. Edmund found himself berating Alphonso for no reason. On one of their visits to the docks a man approached them and asked if he could speak to Edmund privately. Edmund invited him to the Inn where they were staying and that same night he turned up.

Edmund escorted him to his room and when they were settled the man spoke. 'My name is Henry Fisher and I am captain of the Hippocampus. I hear you are wanting passage to England.'

'That is true,' said Edmund. 'There are four of us and one horse.'

'The horse would be difficult, we have no accommodation that would be suitable and there is the problem of getting him on board. Let me think about it after I return to my ship. England is only just recovering from the Black Death so most people have been sailing to Spain, you are the first I have known wishing to return, have you family there?'

'I had family when I left several years ago I pray that they have escaped the Plague. I would like to accompany you to your ship to see if it is possible to take my horse.'

They went down to the stables to see Medianoche. Captain Fisher was surprised at the size of the destrier. He said he could see there was a bond between the horse and Edmund and understood why Edmund did not want to leave him behind. He also explained that the crossing was not without risks with pirates and the French patrolling the Channel as there is still a war between the two countries.

At the docks they were able to see for themselves that it would be extremely difficult to get Medianoche onto the vessel, let alone stable him. Edmund also noticed there were strange square flaps along the side of the vessel.

'Thank you for your interest in us, captain. I will wait a little longer and see if a suitable ship docks here.'

'I do not think you will find one that will be able to take your horse. Sell him here and buy another when you reach England, that's my advice. I sail in two days time should you decide to come with us.' Edmund thanked the captain for his offer and said he would let him know.

Walking back to the Inn Edmund discussed their visit to the ship with Assad and they both agreed that they had not been told the whole truth. It was decided that they would not travel on the Hippocampus. Finishing their evening meal Edmund decided to return to the docks and tell captain Fisher they would not be travelling with him. Fishers comment was that he thought Edmund crazy to try and take the huge horse by ship and he should sell him. They left the Hippocampus and returned to their Inn.

Edmund liked to exercise Medianoche early in the morning, he explored the surrounding countryside and coast. During one ride he came across a large inlet which had a small dock, moored at the dockside was an unusual ship. Edmund went down see what it was. He found a hive of activity with men loading white horses onto the ship. He asked one of the men where was the captain and was directed to a large swarthy man shouting at someone in the ship. He finished his tirade and Edmund spoke to him in Spanish.

'I don't understand that lingo, use French if you can. What do you want.'

Edmund smiled as he heard the rough voice of a man from the Eastern Counties of England. 'Is it Norfolk or Suffolk you hail from captain? Norfolk is my home shire.'

The startled captain turned to Edmund with a broad grin on his face. He thrust out his hand which Edmund took and shook heartily.

'Captain Salmon sir, Lowestoft is my home, and I shall be glad to get back to it. These rogues know nothing about animals and are frightened to death of the horses. I don't have enough crew to do everything so I have to employ them. What can I do for you sir?'

Edmund explained that he was looking for a passage home for him, his friends and his horse. The Captain looked at Medianoche and said he had never seen such a large destrier and there was room on his ship if he wanted to go.

'Accommodation for you and your friends will be a bit basic, you will have to bunk in two cabins aft. We have to leave on this evenings tide.'

'That wont be a problem we want to get home,' said Edmund. They hurried back to the Inn. Edmund set everyone to work to get ready for the trip. He retrieved his bags of gold and wondered how he was going to conceal them from the captain. He decided on two wooden trunks, one to house his armour with some gold and the other with gold and their other equipment. They loaded the cart and set off for the dock. Alphonso was excited and Edmund could see that Antonio was very nervous but he still looked after the count's son.

They reached the ship and captain Salmon looked over what they had to take on board. He turned to Edmund and they discussed how much the captain wanted for transporting them all to England. Edmund thought the price was fair and said to Salmon that there would be a bonus if the horse was looked after. A sling was wrapped under Medianoche and with a lot of grunting and heaving the horse was swung into his stall and secured. Edmund watched carefully as the two trunks were placed in the hold and they all boarded.

Edmund turned to Assad. 'We will take it in turns to watch those trunks, they are near Medianoche so we can say we are looking after him.' Assad agreed and they went to look at their quarters for the voyage. The cabins were small and only just big enough for two people in each.

As evening fell the ship rode low against the dock wall. The crew were busy getting the vessel under way and Edmund went to the bow as they left the estuary. The sea looked calm and with the setting sun in their faces Edmund felt a strong emotion, he was on his way to a home that he had not seen for many years. Assad, Alphonso and Antonio came to stand beside him, for them it would be a new country and culture that confronted the trio.

Chapter 30

The start of the voyage was peaceful enough, the sea was calm and the wind fair. The ship made good progress and the crew were merry as they had recovered from the exertions of loading. Edmund decended to the hold where the horses were, looking for Assad. He found him talking to Medianoche, the great horse appeared to be listening to him.

'I don't know how you can stand it down here, the smell knocks you over,' said Edmund holding his nose.

'You get used to it, it keeps your brain clear!' Assad said this as he moved over to the white horses. 'These are beautiful animals, but not very useful. Not strong enough for an armoured knight and not trained to for battle, so I'm told. Antonio was telling me a little about them and how they are trained for show.'

'Well come up on deck now, I want to talk to you.'

They both appeared on deck as captain Salmon came looking for them. He said that they were running into a squall and they would be better in their cabin as the men would be altering the sails and they would be in the way. As the squall reached them the ship began to increase in movement and Antonio was soon running for the side of the ship. Alphonso went quiet as did Assad whereas Edmund, who had sailed before, enjoyed the roll of the vessel. Rain started to lash down and Antonio came back into the cabin looking ashen. He lay on his bunk and grasped the sides. Looking outside Edmund could see that the rain had eased, the ship was bowling along with the increased wind.

The sun was setting as Edmund came out on deck. The wind had lessened a little but the ship was still sailing fast as the crew trimmed the sails.

The captain was by the wheel and spoke to Edmund. 'With this wind we will soon be home. Your horse withstood the squall better that some of your men. Come join with me in a jug of ale.'

They sat on a hatch cover on the deck and the captain asked Edmund about himself. 'You have had quite some adventures whilst you have been away. I have never been inland myself in all the years I have been coming to Spanish land. The sea is my home and when on land I have small cottage in Lowestoft.'

'I know Lowestoft. My father was Sir John Ivanson of Wymondham, that is where I am making for.' Captain Salmon looked at him and Edmund explained what had happened to his father and that Harold was now the Earl.

'I heard of your fathers death, the plague is a terrible malady. England is only just recovering from it. We are bound for Portsmouth with these horses and then on to Lowestoft. You are welcome to stay with us until then.'

'Thank you but we shall disembark at Portsmouth and make our way home from there.' Edmund rose and went to find the others to tell them of his plan. The ship ploughed on and soon it was time to sleep, to be ready for the morning when they should have arrived at Portsmouth. Edmund did not sleep well, he lay worried about what he would find at Wymondham. Had Harold escaped the plague? Where would he live? Should he join the king's army? Eventually sleep overcame him.

Edmund was woken by Assad who said that they were standing off Portsmouth waiting for the tide. They went on deck and Edmund gazed at land, England at last. The captain came up to him and said they would dock within the hour.

The harbour was very busy and going ashore Edmund made his way to where ships of the line were discharging soldiers. Some were wounded and most looked tired.

'Fighting the French again, about time we finished that. What with the war and the plague we soon wont have enough men to plough the fields.' This was said by an old man standing looking at the men as they disembarked. Edmund wondered if this was affecting their farms in Norfolk, he needed to get home. They found an Inn on the outskirts of the town that had stables. Medianoche drew many a glance as he went through the town. Once settled Assad went out to purchase a cart and horses and brought all their baggage to the Inn. They carried the trunks to Edmund's room with Alphonso complaining of the weight.

After a good meal they settled down for the night. Edmund found it difficult to sleep, he missed the movement of the ship. Rising early he went down to the stables, Medianoche greeted him with loud neighs and Edmund could see he wanted to get out to stretch his legs. Edmund saddled him and set off for a ride out. The weather was much colder than they had been used to, Edmund put the great horse to a trot then galloped onto some heathland. The ground shook as Medianoche got into his stride. They circled back to the Inn where Edmund rubbed the horse down then went back inside. Assad met him and said he was concerned when he did not find him in his bed. They ate a hearty breakfast and discussed their forthcoming journey. Edmund decided they would travel to Farnham and then on north of London before heading east. Alphonso wanted to see the capital city, Edmund told him to curb his curiosity until he had talked with his brother to find out what was happening in the land. They stayed another day at the Inn and then set off on their next adventure.

Edmund had mixed feelings as they set off the next morning in drizzling rain. He missed the sun and the free and easy life in Spain. He wondered how his brother would receive him. The previous afternoon he had found a courier and sent a letter to Harold telling him of his arrival in England. He was missing Maria too, he had not had a decent woman in his arms for many a day. Perhaps he would meet someone in Norfolk. They journeyed on, passing deserted villages that had been struck with the plague. Occasionally there were beggars with wounds from the war in France.

'We will stay in the next village and rest.' Edmund informed them. They were all tired after the travelling. The village Inn had seen better days and the stables were poor. Assad did the best he could to make the horses comfortable while the rest of them unloaded the cart. The landlord was overjoyed that he had guests who looked as though they could pay. A girl was rushing about trying to make the rooms presentable, with not much success. Edmund and Assad took it in turns to keep watch through the night. They had noticed some locals eyeing the trunks as they carried them in.

'I can't say I'm sorry to be out of that place.' Assad looked at Edmund as he said it. 'Not all Inns are like that one, our Shire has a very good standard,' replied Edmund. They rode on heading North East, Alphonso talked of how green everywhere was and how wet! Antonio was interested in the crops in the fields and how good the soil was, he explained that his father had been a farmer. When his father died there was no place for him as the third son so he had taken the job at the Castle.

They reached the south west corner of the shire and immediately could see an improvement in the way the fields were kept. They met a band of armed men who stopped them and enquired why they were travelling in this part. Edmund explained they were making for Wymondham to call on Sir Harold with messages from Spain. One older man at the back of the group kept staring at Edmund. They were sent on their way and told to watch out for bands of cutthroats that were around this area.

When they first saw the Castle it was raining and even so Edmund felt a surge in his heart. Home at last. They rode on, with Alphonso complaining that he had never been so wet. Approaching the main gate Edmund hailed the guards saying he had messages from Spain. Moments later the great gate swung open and they rode in and made for the keep. They arrived at the castle main door as it opened and a tall man asked them who they were and what was their business. A second man came out and stared at them. 'Edmund?' he queried. Edmund realised the beard he had grown on the journey disguised him, dismounting he walked towards Harold. 'It is me, brother, behind all this hair.' The two men clasped each other. 'Welcome home Edmund. I recognise Assad, introduce me to your other companions and come in out of the rain.' Men appeared to unload the cart and take care of the horses while Harold ushered them all in to the great hall.

Chapter 31

Harold ordered hot drinks to be brought while the weary travellers took off their wet cloaks. The door opened and a young boy appeared, he stopped and stared at all the men gathered in the room.

'Come here William and meet your uncle who has come from a long way away.' Harold introduced his son to everyone.

'Two sons now,' said Edmund.

'Two sons and a daughter, brother. You have been away for a long time, you will meet them tonight at our meal. When you have finished your drinks you can rest in your rooms.'

Edmund made his way to his old room that had been prepared for him. Many memories came flooding back as he sat looking out of the window. Special memories of his father, mother and sister. His concerns of how he would fit in and find a place for himself raised themselves again. There was a knock on his door and Assad came to enquire how he was. Edmund noticed he looked at the trunks that now lay open in the room.

'I have moved the bags of gold from the trunks to a safe place. Tomorrow I will give you your share and we will discuss what we should do now we are here.'

There was quite a gathering at the table that night. The young boy, John, was now a tall young man, by his side was a dark haired girl whom he introduced as his sister Tania. Elizabeth sat next to the young William. Edmund felt the loss of Maria and their baby. After the meal Elizabeth excused herself and departed with Tania and William. The men sat and talked with Harold who relaxed and lit his pipe.

'What do you plan to do now that you are here? You are welcome to stay as long as you like, I expect your friends would like to see something of England.'

'Thank you, Harold, I think they saw enough on their travels here. We would be grateful of a rest for short while.'

When Edmund reached his room that night he made sure his special hiding place was secure and then made for his bed. He lay thinking, what was he going to do? He would discuss it in the morning.

He found Harold on the battlements in the morning. 'This was fathers favourite place to think too.' Harold looked at his brother and smiled. 'Did you see his grave when you went to France?'

'Yes, it is well tended. How long for I do not know, with the situation in France. We came across many wounded men going home. Has this affected the shire?'

'We have lost men to the war and the plague, we have also gained people who have come to us from other areas,' replied Harold. 'The way we farm has attracted them, on the down side it has alienated some Lords which has resulted in threats to us. There has been one great loss to us, Stephen, his wife and child were taken by the plague. He was not in good health and could not fight the disease. I have placed a reeve there at the moment. If you are going to stay why don't you go back to Dunston and take over the fiefdom?'

Edmund was taken aback both by Stevens death and the offer of Dunston Castle. He said to Harold that he would like a little time to think about it and talk to his friends. Edmund left the battlements and went down to the stables to check on Medianoche. The big horse whinnied when he saw him and Edmund had him saddled to take him out. Edmund put the big horse to the gallop and the wind cleared his head. He found himself on a familiar route that led to Dunston Castle. In the morning sun the castle stood out, proud and commanding over the countryside. Edmund reigned in and sat looking at the scene, men going about their work and he could hear noise from the smithy where his great grandfather plied his trade and made Talio. He still felt an urge to fight, every time he settled down something happened to take him away, perhaps this was his destiny. Edmund turned Medianoche and rode back to Wymondham.

Walking into the castle he met Assad and asked him to come with him. Up in his room Edmund gave Assad two leather bags. He had found the bags in the stables they were the right size for the gold he had measured out for his friend. Assad held a bag in each hand itching to have a look inside.

'Have a look Assad, and you will see that you are a wealthy man.'

Assad opened one and gave a broad smile to Edmund. 'Thank you my friend, this is more gold than I have ever seen.'

Edmund laughed and grasped his arm. 'Don't spend it all at once. They are Spanish Doblas so it would be wise to change some of them. I will see if Harold knows where we can do that.'

Edmund met Harold in the Great Hall looking out of the window. He had prepared two larger leather bags and now carried them over to his brother.

'Have you come to a decision, Edmund? Do you wish to return to Dunston? The family would then be strong and ready for most events. Those bags look heavy, put them down on the table.'

'They are a present for you from Spain. I have made my decision and I will take your suggestion and go to Dunston.'

Harold grasped Edmunds arms and smiled. He looked into one of the bags and stood back with a gasp. 'Where did you get all this gold?I hope it was by honest means.'

'I will tell you the story later but I did not take it by force. They are Spanish Doblas, do you know anywhere they could be exchanged?'

'The man who dealt with our money exchange to you should be able to arrange something. We will see him tomorrow. Thank you, this can make a big difference to our future. I will put it away.'

The door opened and John strode in. He was a fine young man with a commanding air. Harold called him over and explained the increase to their fortune.

'Did you win this in war or conflict uncle?' he asked. Edmund told them that at an uninhabited castle where they were sheltering he found it in a hidden place, it was somewhere near the truth. He said he had kept a little in case he needed money at Dunston. 'You intend to go to Dunston then. I am very pleased Edmund, it is just what we need in these troubled times. Tomorrow we will ride over there and you can meet the reeve, William Thatcher. If you want him to stay that is agreeable to me.'

They passed a couple of farms on their way to Dunston. Edmund remarked that the fields had good grass and the sheep looked healthy. Harold replied that their wool trade still payed for most of what they wanted as long as there was no interruption crossing to the Flemish coast. When Dunston Castle came into sight Alphonso said it looked very old. John, who was riding with his father, said that it was one of the strongest castles in the shire.

William Thatcher met them in the Bailey and after introductions were made he suggested a tour of the castle. Edmund could remember most of it, he noticed that there had been one or two improvements. They returned to the hall and Harold announced that Edmund would be moving into the castle. He thanked Thatcher for looking after it. Thatcher said nothing but Edmund noticed he did not join in the well wishing. I will have to watch him before he causes trouble, I wonder why he does not want to go back as a reeve at Wymondham.

Chapter 32

Edmund and his three companions moved into Dunston Castle and soon settled down. They decided to visit all the tenants to find out how they were governing their land. William Thatcher led the party, Edmund noticed that he was not enthusiastic with this task. The first farm was only a short ride and a jolly farmer greeted them. He was pleased to see Edmund and could remember him as a little boy. On his land he mostly grazed sheep and said his wool was the finest. Sitting down and looking at the records he kept Edmund found it to be profitable farm with happy staff, all working together, just like his father had wanted. They moved on round the shire and Edmund found most of the tenants were tending their lands and flocks successfully. They stayed overnights in village Inns which was another way of finding out what was happening in the local area.

The Fens proved to be a little more difficult. Aelfraed's son, Athelard, welcomed them to his home but Edmund sensed that all was not well.

'We have many strangers roaming the Fens, poaching the game and damaging he reeds. They steel our pigs and our women, we are not strong enough to stop them as the plague took many of us.'

Edmund sympathised with him and said that as he had only just returned home and had not had time to organise his men. He would try to provide a guard for the area if it is possible. Athelard thanked him and said it would be helpful. They decided to take Athelard's offer to stay the night. After a hearty meal consisting of game from the Fens they sat chatting and drinking. Suddenly Athelard raised his hand to silence them.

'I can hear movement out in the Fen. Move quietly to the entrance of our village.' He signalled a man to check on the horses and keep them quiet. They started talking again as they made their way to the entrance as though nothing was the matter. The village was surrounded by a whicker fence with a gate at the north and south ends mainly to keep the children and animals in away from the bogs of the Fens. Before they could get to the entrance the gates were flung open and several men barged in, swords in their hands. Edmund stepped forward and demanded to know what they wanted, he spoke this in gutter French. One man stopped and spread his hands holding the others back.

'We want food and money or you die!' was his response.

'Then death has come to you.' Edmund drew Talio and stepped towards the man. The Frenchman leaped at Edmund swing his sword wildly. Talio sang in Edmund's hand and the ring was hot. Talio sliced across the mans heart and as he went down Edmund carried the stroke on and took the following man's head off. The rest of the village men with Assad, Alfonso and Antonio, with John a little behind, fell on the remaining rabble. In a very short space of time the battle had finished and the brigands lay dead or near death and were being finished off by the village men. John stood by Assad and was visibly shaking. Assad was speaking to him as Edmund strode over to them.

'Are you injured John?'

'I'm all right thank you. Just a bit shaken, it all happened so fast. I din't kill anybody.' The lad was still shaking as Edmund took his sword from his hand and sheathed it.

'You were a brave man, John. You took your sword to defend our friends. Well done.' Edmund grasped his arm and slapped him on his back. He turned to speak to Athelard and found him standing in front of his men looking at Edmund.

'I remember my father telling me of the magical sword from Dunston. I always thought it was a story but now I have seen it with my own eyes. You were so fast, is it magic?'

Edmund told them that story that he had told many times before but left out the ring. When they had cleared out the dead to a place that Edmund did not ask about and the wounded had been tended to, they sat down to a simple but ample feast. Everyone was in good humour however Edmund noticed they kept their distance and had become very polite to him. Edmund spoke to Athelard telling him he would send soldiers as soon as he returned to Dunston.

They left the next morning and travelled on to Yarmouth. They made straight for the mayors house who was surprised and began fussing about calling maids to get ready for their guests. Edmund wanted to see the information he had on the export of goods. The mayor, Walter Shipman, became a little nervous at this point as he searched for the papers. Edmund studied what he had been given and found the information to be up to date, maybe this was Harold's influence. John said they often came to Yarmouth and his father spent many hours with the Mr Shipman. The mayor invited them to stay, he had rooms and the escort could stay in the barracks.

They moved into the dining room where there was a large table ready for them all. Waiting were two ladies who were introduced as Ann his wife and Margaret his niece. Edmund was struck by the looks of the niece and wondered where her husband was. In conversation he found out that her husband had been killed in London by thieves. There was one son who was being trained for the military somewhere in England, probably in London. For the first time since Maria's death Edmund felt at ease and comfortable in the company of a woman. He looked up and found Margaret looking at him, he smiled and it was reciprocated.

They spent a comfortable night at the mayors house and the following day visited the warehouse that dealt with their wool exports to Flanders. They took the opportunity to walk round the docks. There were not as many ships in the docks as Edmund remembered, perhaps the unrest with France had limited the number of cross channel voyages.

On their return to the mayor they found food and drink ready for them. Edmund thought he could get used to this life. Margaret sat with them and he found her a pleasant companion. She suggested a walk in the gardens, Edmund readily accepted. It was a very pleasant evening though a little cold. He placed his cloak around Margaret's shoulders. He learnt a lot about this fascinating woman on their walk, the more he found out the more he found himself being drawn towards her. She missed her son and hoped he would return soon, he found it difficult to accept his fathers death and wanted to search London for his killers. Returning to the house they found that a messenger had just arrived from Wymondham. The message was from Harold telling Edmund to return home with all speed as there was trouble in the north of their lands and his military experience was needed. Edmund sent Assad to gather his men and told the others to get ready to ride at once.

They said their goodbyes to the mayor and Edmund took Margaret aside to say he would very much like to see her again. When this problem was solved would she like to come to Dunston. She smiled at him and said she would think about it and would write to him and to take good care of himself.

They left in the gathering gloom of twilight and struck out for Wymondham at the best speed. Stopping for short breaks they ate up the miles and made good time to arrive at Wymondham in the early morning. Harold was pleased to see his brother to explain why he had sent for him.

'We have reports of a large gathering in the woods at Thetford. I have had to send some of my men to Lynn to assist the mayor there. I am not a military leader and I need help with these troubles.'

Edmund studied the information that had come from Harold's contacts. There was obviously some unrest and this was not helped by men deserting from France.

'I will look at our defences here then I must get to Dunston. There appears to be a lot of unrest among the peasants, have you experienced any among our own?'

Harold said he hadn't had any trouble and most of the farms worked well but it did not take much to cause unrest if someone was determined to make mischief. Edmund went out to look at the defences and the mens readiness to defend the castle. John was very attentive and asked lots of questions, perhaps thinking of his future.

The next morning Edmund left for Dunston, Alphonso and Antonio accepted Harolds invitation to stay at Wymondham as this was the larger castle. Edmund and Assad made good time to Dunston and immediately set about organising training for the guards. They certainly needed it as they had been left to their own devises for too long. Assad and Edmund spared with the men and encouraged them to improve their skills. Edmund selected two to ride out and find any large bands approaching the castle. He sent men to check that the moat was full and the streams feeding it were clear. Edmund went up onto the battlements, he smiled to himself as memories came flooding back when his father always came here to think. He noticed a rider approaching at a gallop, he could see it was one of the patrol he had sent out. Quickly descending to the bailey he met the man as he jumped from his horse.

'There is a large force of rebels not more than ten leagues away, my lord. We have also seen a second group, a lot smaller, several leagues to their east. This group looked like soldiers and are all mounted. I left the others to watch and came back to report.'

Edmund listened carefully, he wondered who this second group were. Turning to the man he commended him for his vigilance. 'Go and refresh yourself then come back to take watch on the tower.' He was puzzled as to the second group, who were they, what did they want?

It was not long before the rest of the patrol were spotted. They were being hotly perused by a large force. Edmund assembled his mounted men and rode out to defend them. He organised his men into a wedge formation and charged at the enemy. Edmund's men were armoured, as was he, and they hit the advancing foe hard. He quickly realised that most of the men he was fighting were poorly armed and only a small number had any sort of armour. This was not a fair fight, he decided to swing his men to the right and ran out into an open area. Maintaining the charge he drew away far enough to pull up, turn and face his enemy again. The rabble, for that is what they were, had also stopped and appeared stunned at the ferocity of Edmunds charge. Talio had been at work and there were many bodies on the ground. Loud shouting could be heard coming from the rabble, Edmund guessed someone was trying to stir them into fighting again. As they sat watching Edmund could see another group of horsemen coming into view the other side of the rabble. Some of the enemy had started to move away from the rear and were obviously attempting to escape.

'Cut them off,' called Edmund as he spurred Medianoche forward. The rabble thought he was charging again as did the other group. They were converging on the rabble when they started to throw weapons on the ground and hold their arms in the air, some fell to their knees. Edmund signalled his force to circle them to prevent any more escaping. One of the other group of armed horsemen rode over to him.

'I bid you greetings sir, I am Sir William deGrass. We have been following this rabble, but we were not enough in numbers to attack them.' Edmund inclined his head and replied.

'Sir Edmund Ivanson, that is my castle that you see. I intend to take the leaders of this rabble to my dungeons and then question them later. We have barns where the others can be kept for a while.'

'We will help you to get them there. My men are young and under training that is why we were following.'

They all moved off to the castle where the prisoners were secured and Edmund invited deGrass into the hall. deGrass explained they had been out looking for a certain criminal. Part of their training included catching villains that were known to the authorities. He said that the young men came from all over the south east and would eventually end up in the king's service.

'There is a young man from your fiefdom, from Yarmouth. Perhaps you know his family, the Shipman's.'

Edmund said he did know the family and would like to meet the man. deGrass sent for him and a tall dark young man stood before them. Edmund exchanged a few words with him saying that he had met his mother. He said he would like to speak with him before they left in the morning. Edmund asked deGrass when would Shipman be ready to leave his training.

'You have an interest in the lad? He is ready to join the kings army now. He has a close friend and both of them will make good cavalry men.'

Edmund was on the battlements, greeting the dawn when he heard movement behind him. Spinning round he encountered the young man from yesterday.

'I did not mean to startle you sir. Sir William said you wished to see me.'

'That is correct young man. I understand you will soon be leaving Sir William and joining the kings army. Is this what you want?' Edmund looked keenly at him as he said this.

'I must serve my king and country sir, it is what I have been trained to do. I would like to that in England but the army is in France at the moment.'

Edmund decided to take the bull by the horns. 'You could serve your country by joining my men here. We fight for the king to keep peace in his land, would you not say this is just as important?'

The young man thought for a moment and looking at Edmund said that if Sir William would release him and his friend they would be honoured to join his guards. That is how Margaret Shipman's son and his friend joined Edmund's household.

Chapter 33

deGrass wanted to take the leaders of the rebellion back to London to make examples of them. Edmund agreed and said he would take care of the rest. After deGrass had departed with his prisoners Edmund set about what he should do with the remainder. Some were not dyed in the wool revolutionists and these he moved to better accommodation, still under guard. He decided he would try them all over the next week. While they were waiting he took six of the better prisoners and went to two of his farms, he made certain Arthur Shipman and his friend Edward Archer were part of the guard. While at the farms he surreptitiously let some farm workers talk to the prisoners. Arthur was very impressed at what he saw at the farms and how happy the workers were. The second farm supplied bread and beer to everyone which was gladly accepted.

Back at Dunston the prisoners were sent back to join the other rebels and Edmund could hear them being questioned about their day. Edmund called for Arthur and Edward to meet him in his room. The two young men stood nervously before him.

'Sit down and relax,' said Edmund. 'What did you think of the two farms we visited?'

'They have a very interesting way of including the serfs in the working of the farm. I am surprised at how happy everyone seemed to be.' Edward nodded his head in agreement at what Arthur had said.

'My father began this system many years ago and it has improved our profits, which has improved the lot of the families who work on the farms. We have many second generations following their father and this again improves their wealth.'

Arthur looked up at the ceiling, down at the floor and then straight at Edmund and asked him. 'Is that your fathers sword? We heard so much about it back in London. From what I saw of the fight against the rebels you were just a blur.'

Edmund told them the story that he had told many times before, of how his grandfather made the sword. He missed out the effect the ring had.

'Talio and I have been together in many fights over the years. The balance of the blade is so good it makes it easy to fight with. Perhaps it is my skill that you saw and not magic.' Edmund could see the two young men were not convinced.

'Tomorrow I will watch you train in the practice yard. The rest of the guards will be there so give a good account of yourselves. I must decide your duties and watching you will help me make up my mind. That is all, goodnight.'

Edmund went down to the practice yard in the morning hoping that he would see skill at arms from his two young men. They were sparing with each other when he arrived. He called to Arthur and asked him to come to him.

'I shall pick a man for you to spar with, one who is not your friend.'

Edmund called to his captain and told him to fight Arthur. The captain was a little nervous at first. He soon realised that Arthur wanted to impress Edmund and came at him with all the vigour he could muster. The captain fought him off and then attacked. Arthur was soon retreating as the captains experience gained him the advantage. The young man started to stand his ground and parried well until he saw an opening and drove forward. Edmund called a halt and beckoned Arthur to him. He complemented him on his sword play and said he wanted Arthur to take a patrol out. 'Take eight men and report to me when you return.'

Returning to his room Edmund put pen to paper and wrote to Margaret Shipman inviting her to visit him and her son. He only told her that Arthur had arrived with deGrass and not that he was now part of the castle.

Arthur proved to be a natural commander, even though he was still young. The men responded to him and he led well. Edward was more for fun and Edmund had not given him responsibility yet.

The prisoners were brought before him the following day. Edmund had split them into two groups, the ones who were calmer and were not as argumentative as the second group. To the first group he said. 'You have seen how my workers are treated and enjoy much of what you have been agitating for. My men at arms are also well treated. I know you have been talking to them so you know what I say is true. I propose to offer you work on the farms or to enlist in my men at arms, You will sign to do this for five years and then you can leave or stay. The alternative is you will be sent back to London to be judged by the magistrates there for rebellion and treason. Now is the time to make up your mind and go to the two tables there and make your mark.' There was a rush to the tables as the rebels realised the opportunity Edmund had given them. Edmund smiled at Assad as they both knew they needed men desperately to secure the prosperity of the shire. Edmund had the second group brought in and he told them the same story. Some of these men he did not want and when they started to criticise his decision he had them removed back to the cells. All in all it had turned out well he had a good influx of men and only a small number to send back to London.

A letter arrived from Margaret that said she would be pleased to accept his invitation and was surprised to know that her son would be there. Edmund gave orders to tidy up the castle and fussed around getting everyones way. He told Arthur that his mother was coming to see him. The young man was pleased but puzzled as to why she would want to come this far. Edmund said that when he had met her in Yarmouth, she missed her son. He did not say he missed her in his message but he sent an escort for her.

A rider brought a message to Edmund asking him to go to Wymondham. When he arrive there Harold was very agitated and they went to his room to talk. Harold paced up and down the room as he told Edmund that a patrol had returned and brought the news that the Earl of Leicester had put together an army consisting of his troops and that of Nottingham, their lord was away fighting for the king.

'He intends to invade us I am sure,' said Harold. 'I have not many men and he could overrun us and take our lands. What are we to do?'

Edmund calmed his brother and said he would send Assad out with a small patrol to asses the situation. Meanwhile he would return to Dunston and assemble a force to bring to Wymondham.

'While I am gone get messages to your farms and tell all the tenants who have promised fighting men to meet here in two days, no later.' Edmund then left for Dunston leaving Harold to carry out his instructions.

Arriving at Dunston Edmund went straight to the blacksmith.

'How much armour have you repaired and made? I told you it was urgent when I went away to the farms. Did you find more weapons where I said for you to look?'

The blacksmith bowed and said that he had all three fires working and the smith from the village had also helped. 'We can fit out 500 men all together my Lord and more is being made as we speak. We have good weapons for 1000 and many arrows for the archers.'

Edmund thanked him and called for his captain to get all the men together. He sent four men out to the farms to bring in the men who would fight.

'I want them all to be ready to move in two days. We move to Wymondham first and join with their men.' He finished speaking as Assad came to him and gave his report. He had found Leicester's army, which numbered about 5000. There were some armoured knights but most were men who had been promised rich pickings if they succeeded in overthrowing Harold. These were poorly armed with scythes, pitchforks and a few swords.

Edmund left Dunston with a force of 1200 men. 500 of these armoured and mounted and were being led by Assad. The rest were well armed and determined to fight for their lord and their land. They met Harold who had gathered together 2000 men, all well armed. John was there, in armour, with Alphonso and Antonio at his side.

Harold addressed the whole force, thanking them for their support, which raised a cheer. He told them that Edmund would lead them as he had the experience. They all moved off to meet Leicester.

Chapter 34

Edmund led them to a ridge that overlooked Leicester's camp. He positioned all the armoured men behind the ridge out of site of the enemy. He sent the archers to each flank and told them to move into position quietly. Edmund rode onto the crest of the ridge, flanked by Harold, John, Assad and Arthur. They could see below them in the valley the camp of Leicester where men were being formed up in ragged lines. Two riders advanced to the base of the ridge and waited for Edmund and Assad to ride down towards them. Edmund had instructed the others to remain.

Leicester's knight spoke to them as they drew near. 'We are here to claim the lands to the eastern sea. Throw down your arms and your men will be spared.'

Edmund looked at him and said, 'I am Sir Edmund Ivanson of the Norfolk shire. It is customary and polite to announce yourself.'

'Sir Guy Trouville, if you must know. What is your answer before we attack?'

'My answer sir, is to tell you to remove your men from our lands immediately or face death. We give you half of the hour to be gone.'

Trouville laughed and asked where his army was as he could see no troops.

Assad blew on a horn, within minutes the ridge was covered by a line of men with the sun glinting off their armour.

'Will you now go, sir?'

Trouville and his companion turned and rode back to their lines. When Edmund reached Harold and explained what hd been said the Earl asked what was Edmund's next move. Assad blew on the horn again and the archers moved up on each flank. There was another blast and the day darkened as the air was filled with arrows arching into the sky and falling on the men below. Pandemonium broke out in the enemies ranks as men fell and died. Edmund signalled for his troops to move forward. Trouville was trying to get his troops into some sort of order as Edmund came down the hill. The knights formed a defensive ring around him as Edmund signalled his cavalry to charge. They hit Trouville's knights hard, Edmund fought his way to Trouville and met him with Talio hot in his hand. Trouville tried to defend himself but Talio was fast and found a gap under his arm, entered and pierced his heart. The rest of the enemy knights cried for quarter as Edmund's force started to round up the remainder of those who had not fled. John looked at Arthur and spoke to Assad. 'It must be magic, a man of his age could not wield a broad sword that fast.'

Edmund looked at the prisoners. 'The knights will be imprisoned and ransomed. Escort the others off our lands. They can take Leicester's body with them. Let this be a message to all who think they can invade our lands.'

Harold could not stop praising Edmund on the ride home. Edmund told him they had been lucky that the enemy were not a trained army and the result could have been different if they had to face a large trained army. Edmund was determined to get together a large well equipped and trained fighting force to hold in readiness to fight any more attacks.

They parted at the gates of Wymondham, Edmund carried on to Dunston with Assad and Arthur. Edmund instructed his captain to start the training in the morning. That night as he went to his bed his bones ached and he was thankful that Talio could still be so quick in his hands.

There was great activity in the castle as he woke. The captain was making an early start with the training and Edmund could hear steel on steel down in the training yard. Assad was waiting for him as he went to break his fast.

'The farm workers have returned to their individual tenants, it would be better if we did not have to rely on them when we have to fight.'

'I agree, my friend, but to employ that number to just be guards is not economical.' Edmund smiled as he said this as he knew that Assad was referring to the gold. A servant interrupted them to say that a group of armed horsemen were approaching the castle. Edmund and Assad ran to the battlements where they could see a group not far from the gate. Edmund soon recognised his own men escorting two ladies. He rushed down to the bailey to be there as they entered.

The party had already dismounted when he arrived, which disappointed him.

'Welcome to my home,' said Edmund as went towards Margaret'

'Thank you, and thank you for the escort. Fortunately it was an uneventful journey, though rather long.'

Edmund ushered them in and called for wine as he led them to the hall. Margaret looked around and said she had never been in a castle before.

'It can be a little draughty at times, there are fires in your rooms, let me know if you feel the cold.

'This is my friend who will help me while I am here.' Margaret introduced a pretty young girl named Joan. 'I have asked Arthur to join us at our evening meal, he is busy with the guards at the moment.'

Margaret smiled and said she was looking forward to meeting her son. She asked how was it that he was visiting the castle at this time. Edmund told her that during a training patrol they had stopped at Dunston and he had asked Arthur if he would like to stay and he was now one of his guards. Margaret was quite surprised and wanted to see her son. Edmund said that he would be here when he had finished his duties.

'This girl,' said Edmund, bringing forward a young girl, the daughter of one of his carpenters. 'Will take you to your rooms and I look forward to you joining us at table this evening.'

After they had gone Edmund thought to himself that he had been too formal, too much the 'Lord of the Manor'. He found himself walking up to the battlements as though guided by someone else. The sun was beginning to dip towards the forest and there was a pleasant glow on the stone walls. Edmund began to relax and looked forward to the evening.

'I hope I am not disturbing you.'

A voice came from behind Edmund and he spun round to find Margaret standing there. He stammered a greeting and said he was pleased she had found his favourite part of the Castle.

'My father always came here when he wanted to think. You can see quite a lot of the countryside from here, This time of day I find it most beautiful. See the sun highlighting the colour of those deer.'

Margaret came to stand beside him, she looked where Edmund was pointing and could see deer feeding at the edge of the forest.

'They look contented.'

'They do, and they also taste well when my cook has prepared them.'

Margaret laughed and could see that Edmund was also smiling, it was a comfortable moment.

'Arthur is a fine lad and will do well. I shall put him in charge of formati and hobilers. I do not think it will take him long to prove himself to be my squire.'

Margaret looked up at him and asked him. 'Why are you doing this? You do not know us. You have plenty of young men as capable as him.'

'But not with such an attractive mother.'

Margaret blushed and turned away. She made as if to leave, Edmund put his hand on her arm and she flinched.

'I am sorry, I did not mean to blurt that out. Excuse me if I am being impertinent, I do find you to be a beautiful woman and I mean to play court to you. If I have offended you I am sorry.' Edmund stood looking at her, he dropped his hand from her arm.

'This is a little sudden for me. After my husband was killed I did not think that I would meet anyone else. I do have some feelings for you but you must give me time.' Margaret dropped her head then left the battlements. Edmund watched her go and cursed himself for saying too much, she did say she had some feelings for him that must be a good sign.

Chapter 35

The meal that night was quite a grand affair, Edmund asked Margaret to sit by his side. She had spent the hour before with Arthur and was in a happy mood.

Assad smiled at Edmund when he saw Margaret by his side and winked his eye. Edmund felt his face flush and he turned to Arthur and Edward to welcome them.

Margaret complimented him on the silver saltcellar designed in the image of a swan and his beautiful gold platters. Edmund explained they came from his father. The dinner was a success, most of the knights behaved themselves until the ladies left, then the serious drinking started. Edmund soon left and went to his bed reminding Arthur that his mother would be watching him in the morning at the training ground.

Edmund lay in his bed and thought about Margaret, did he like her enough to take her as his wife, did he love her? He certainly liked being with her, she was a bright companion and had a good sense of humour but did he love her? He drifted off to sleep with the question on his mind.

He woke early and it was no surprise that he went to the battlements to think. He must build up his military strength and start grooming Arthur to be his squire. Going down to the training yard he saw Arthur busy drilling the new recruits with spears. Edmond watched for a moment and then called Arthur to him.

'I am visiting some tenants in the south of the shire. Organise a guard of twenty mounted men, I leave you to decide who you want. I will be ready to leave at noon. We shall overnight at a farm on the way.'

Arthur bowed and went off to arrange the men. Edmund found Margaret and informed her of his plans.

'Arthur will have a rest day when we return so you may do what you want. Please treat the castle as yours, Assad will be here to deal with any problems or questions you might have.'

Margaret thanked him and said that she hoped his journey would be uneventful. Edmund smiled to himself and thought that it was fortunate that she did not know his plans.

The bell in the tower sounded noon and Edmund came out to the bailey, he was dressed in light armour with Talio and a mace. Mounting Medianoche he surveyed the assembled troops. Arthur had selected half formati and half hobilers, surprisingly there was no sign of Edward. They moved off to the South as Margaret came to the door and saw her son riding proudly beside Edmund. They headed south east and stayed the first night in the village of Loddon. They set off early the next day and had not gone far when Edmund called a halt.

'I think something I had at that Inn last night has not agreed with me. Leave me one of the men and I will rest here for a while. Carry on with our plan, Arthur, as I want you to catch the tenant who is stealing our wool.'

Arthur called the men together and moved off towards the farm where they had proof from Yarmouth that wool was being shipped to Flanders under another name. When the troop was out of sight Edmund made a remarkable recovery. Telling the astonished formati to mount as he swung himself up onto Medianoche they moved off after the troop.

'Keep well back.' Edmund told his companion. 'I wish to watch out of sight.'

They neared the farm and Edmund noticed that Arthur kept the hobilers back while the rest rode towards the house. The tenant was known to Harold as being defiant of the rules and had an armed force and he had warned Edmund.

Edmund watched as Arthur reach the farm buildings where they were met by a group of men with pikes. Arthur called for the tenant farmer to show himself and explain what was going on here. A rough looking man stepped forward and told Arthur to clear off. Edmund could not hear Arthurs response however he noticed that the hobilers had moved around to the rear of a large barn which would bring them up behind the tenant and his men. Arthur sent two men to arrest the tenant and the rest of the farm hands lowered their weapons. Edmund spurred Medianoche forward and came to Arthurs side.

'Take your prisoner back to Dunston and I will deal with him later. Leave six men here to keep control. I wish to look around the barns before we depart. Well done.' Edmund rode up to the main house and dismounted, the front door flew open and a young boy came rushing out trying to wield a large broad sword. Edmund had Talio in his hand immediately and as the lad swung at him he neatly sent his sword flying through the air. The farmer was shouting out, pleading with Edmund not to hurt the boy. Edmund grasped the neck of the lad and led him over to where Arthur was holding the prisoners. He threw the boy in with the rest and said to Arthur to be on his way.

'I will meet you at the castle, don't lose any prisoners.' Edmund urged Medianoche on and the great horse moved off at a gallop.

Edmund kept his horse at a mile eating canter which did not tire him and arrived back at Dunston as dawn was breaking. A stable boy led a steaming Medianoche away to cool off. Edmund made his way to his room to get rid of his armour and dress more comfortably. When he went down to the hall. Margaret was there and anxiously asked him as to Arthurs whereabouts.

'He is safe and bring a prisoner here, he was very good and took charge of the situation well. You have a fine son who should go far.'

Margaret was overjoyed to know that Arthur had not received any injuries. She finished her meal and went to the battlements so as to see Arthur at the earliest moment. Edmund smiled to himself, mothers were all the same, worrying about their offsprings when there was no need. He retired to his room to study the finances of the fiefdom as he needed more men in arms. An hour went by as he puzzled his head on how to get what he wanted, he thought Harold would do this much easier. He closed the ledger, rose, stretched and walked up to the battlements. The family spot for thinking. The weather was fine, a sun breaking through the clouds. There was a chill in the air and he beat his arms across his chest then noticed he was not alone. Margret turned as she heard him approach.

'No sign of them yet.' She meant no sign of Arthur. 'I expect they are much slower with more men.'

'They will appear soon,' said Edmund. 'I am glad of that as it keeps the men alert. Who are these two with pack horses, I hope they are not trying to sell us something.' He quickly went down to the bailey just as the two men rode in. Edmund was surprised to see Alphonso and Antonio. Edmund offered refreshment and while they sat they explained that Alphonso's father had written asking him to return home as there was trouble in Castile.

'I have learnt much in our travels,' said Alphonso. 'While I have been in Wymondham I have also learned from your brother the method of farming you have here. I am sure I could make it work on our lands. I thank you for all you have done for me. We shall journey to Portsmouth where there is a ship going to Spain taking our ambassador home.' Edmund wished them a safe voyage and as they left he felt a little pull of the life that he had enjoyed in Spain.

As they left the castle a horn sounded outside which signalled the return of Arthur and his troop. Arthur dismounted and came straight to Edmund. Edmund greeted him and told him to take the prisoner to the tower. Margaret greeted her son who acknowledged her but carried on with his duties.

Edmund asked Margaret to walk with him in the gardens, she commented that it was not very warm so they retired to Edmunds room where there was a fire.

Edmund sat watching Margaret as she chatted to him. Even in middle years she was an attractive woman. He felt a warm glow and a stirring in his loins that he had not felt since Maria. The occasional romp with a girl from an Inn did not make him feel like this. Margaret stopped talking and smiled at him and suggested they prepared for the evening.

Chapter 36

Several days later Edmund said that he was making a trip to Wymondham to see his brother and invited Margaret to accompany him. Arthur was to lead the guards who would protect them on the journey. Edmund's intention was to introduce Margaret to Harold and explain that he was going to make her his wife.

It was a bright sunny day when they departed for Wymondham. Edmund was in high spirits and started to sing. There were some muffled remarks from the guards which reached his ears and brought his warbling to a stop. Margaret was smiling and remarked what a strong voice he had. Edmund took the hint and started talking about the countryside that they were travelling through.

Harold greeted them warmly at Wymondham. He called John to show Arthur where to stable the horses and led Edmund and Margaret into the hall. Elizabeth was there and after being introduced she whisked Margaret off to refresh herself after the journey.

'I have brought Margaret over to see you as I intend to make her my wife, if she will have me.' said Edmund.

'Does she know this? asked Harold.

'I have told her my intentions I am sure of a positive answer when I ask her. I also intend to make Arthur my squire and train him for knighthood.'

'I wish you well, Edmund, on first impressions I like her. I had hoped you might take John as your squire,' commented Harold.

'I am his uncle and close family, not a good idea. What would he feel to being a squire to Assad, it's time he had one that he could train. Assad has been a good friend and companion for a long time now and I trust him implicitly. What do you think?'

Harold thought for a moment, looked at Edmund and smiled.

'I think it is an excellent idea, you could not have a better man. I will tell John of our decision.'

Edmund was in high spirits the next morning. He called for John and invited him to join him on a ride to exercise the horses. As they rode Edmund explained the reason for placing him under the care of Assad. John replied that he was quite happy as he had liked Assad when he first met him.

'When we return to Dunston you will accompany us and start your training. No doubt some of that training will be together with Arthur.'

That evening Edmund and Harold sat talking in the hall after everyone else had gone to bed. Harold asked if Edmund would now settle down? He pointed out that Dunston needed some stability and good leadership, just like the Country.

'I do not intend to go roaming about chasing moonbeams, I intend to try and fulfil my duties as Lord of Dunston.'

'I am pleased to hear it,' said Harold. 'With Margaret by your side you will make a good team.'

They spent another day at Wymondham and then said their farewells. The only thing that marred their journey home was the shower of rain when they were half way. They pushed on quickening their pace as the rain eased off. Reaching Dunston the party were soon inside and drying themselves.

Edmund was sitting in his room deciding when to propose to Margaret. The sooner the better he thought, he would take the plunge tonight. After dinner everyone retired early leaving Edmund and Margaret alone. Edmund poured another glass of wine for them and stood looking at Margaret. He coughed and cleared his throat.

'Margaret,' he shuffled his feet and looked at her. 'You must know that I have very strong feelings for you.' He coughed again and walked over to the fire.

'Yes.' The voice came from Margaret as she smiled at Edmund and stood up to join him at the fire. 'Yes?' Harold asked with a puzzled expression. 'What do you mean?

'Yes, I will marry you, if that is what you are trying to ask me.' She moved closer to him, smiling up at him.

Edmund reached for her and kissed her to which she responded willingly. They broke apart and stood grinning at each other. Margaret took his hand and led him up the stairs. When they arrived at her room Edmund's heart began to quicken even more. She led him in, turned and faced him.

'I have been waiting for this day ever since I met you. Before you finally commit yourself you had better find out a little more about me.' With that she drew off her dress and then her under garments and stood before him naked. Edmund stood shocked for a moment and then saw before him a woman he yearned for. He rapidly threw off his clothes and drew her to him. Their kiss was passionate and he moved to the bed. They lay together while their hands explored each others body and finally they joined together. Their lovemaking was tender and when they were exhausted they lay looking at each other.

'I love you Margaret, and I want you to be my wife as soon as possible.'

'I am willing but you must give me time to prepare myself.' Edmund smiled and said that they had better inform Arthur.

The following morning Edmund sent word for Arthur to meet him on the battlements. The young man arrived and stood nervously looking at Edmund.

'You may have noticed that I have an affection for your mother,' started Edmund. 'I have made my feelings known to her and have asked her to be my wife. What are your thoughts on this?'

'My mother told me this might happen and I said at the time that if she is happy then so am I.'

'Good, we hope to have a simple ceremony soon in our church.' Edmund grasped Arthur's arm. 'I cannot replace your father and do not intend to, but I hope I will be your friend whenever you need one.' Arthur stood back, looked at Edmund and said,'I know you will take care of us and I will do my best to become a knight like you.' With that speech he bowed to Edmund, turned and walked away.

The ceremony in the little church in the woods was simple and enveloped the family in a warm glow. Elizabeth said she had never been to such a moving service. Back at the castle everything was 'moving' as there were acrobats and jugglers, singers and dancers. Edmund was sorry there was no Spanish flamenco. Margaret was keen to know why the flamenco was so interesting to him!

Life in the castle settled down to a routine that was comfortable to Edmund. He did go to the battlements and dream of his days in Spain, then he was called away to solve a problem with one of his tenants. On his return, Godwin Longstaff, the castle steward, met him with a letter from London. The letter informed him that the king had died. Edmund thought back to last year when the Black Prince had died and named his son Richard to be king. 'Now there will be trouble,' said Edmund, to nobody in particular. 'I am summoned to London with my brother.'

Edmund joined Harold at Wymondham and the party set off for the capital. They had arranged to stay at the London house. 'It is a good job we kept the house in our name,' said Edmund to Arthur, who was travelling as his squire. 'Make sure our men are ready for any event when we arrive. I don't expect trouble but we must be prepared.'

Harold was nervous as they entered the city, he remarked that the people seemed sullen. 'They are just wondering who is going to rule them as Richard is only 10 years old. I have the same concerns except I have a good idea who it will be.' Edmund said this as they turned into the gateway of their London house.

Edmund thought it was good to be in the house and away from the draughty castle. Maybe he should spend more time here but the thought of being involved in the politics at the court soon changed his mind. Elizabeth and Margaret would be arriving in one or two days time as they were taking a more leisurely journey. Edmund calculated that with their escort he would have a sizeable number of trained men at his disposal. Elizabeth and Margaret duly arrived and started organising the house. Edmund was please that the two women had become friends so quickly and worked well together.

Chapter 37

Four days later Edmund and Harold were summoned to court. They journeyed to Westminster by boat and then made their way to the Kings chambers. In the anteroom there were many knights all wondering what was going to happen.

'Richard is the successor,' said Harold, quietly to Edmund. 'As he is only ten years old there must be regent or someone to rule for him.' A door opened and a herald came in and asked for silence, when the room had quietened down John of Gaunt strode in followed by the Duke of Gloucester.

'Bend your knee to your king, Richard the second,' said Gaunt. The next person to enter was a young boy and someone said 'Long live the King.' The cry was taken up by the rest of the nobles there. John of Gaunt then preceded to tell them that it had been decided that there would be no Regent but until the King was old enough the matters of state would be decided by a council. There was a general murmur of agreement to this. There came the announcement that the coronation would be on 16th of July. Harold circulated for a short time talking to other nobles with large fiefdoms and the signalled to Edmund that they would leave.

Back at the house Harold said that it would not be practical to return to Wymondham and that they should stay in London until the coronation. Edmund wanted to return to Dunston but agreed it would be better to stay where they were as the coronation was only six days away. Elizabeth and Margaret were in a fuss as they needed new clothes and every one would be wanting to buy cloth. Harold called Feathers, the steward, and asked where was the best place to purchase cloth for the ladies. Feathers said he would consult his wife and also hire seamstress to make the clothes.

Came the day of the coronation and they all proceeded to Westminster Abbey. The nobility were there in all their finery, although some had come in black. Edmund and Harold were glad to return to their house although the wives wanted to stay and see the festivities. Harold explained that they needed to return to Wymondham as he expected changes coming and he needed to be prepared. Edmund agreed as he had already been approached by Gaunt to have his men ready to fight the French. Harold said that some landowners were worried about unrest among the peasants. They packed up and left the following morning, the ladies were not amused as they wanted to spend time in London.

Edmund headed straight to Dunston, he wanted to find out if there had been any unrest with his tenants. He needed to gather his fighting men and prepare them for what ever might occur. Assed greeted him and said all was quiet, he had heard rumours of unrest further south. Edmund said he would visit his tenants, especially the ones in the south.

The next day Edmund accompanied by Arthur and a large band of his fighting men set out to the south of the fiefdom. Their first stop was at the Saxlingham farm where they had experienced trouble before. The only problem the tenant encountered, was that he too many men wanting to work for him on account of the scheme they had. As they journeyed on they found similar stories of the farmers having to turn workers away who were coming in from adjacent areas.

'I will leave some men here to keep an eye on things and report any activity against us,' said Edmund. 'I don't want to be surprised by anybody causing trouble. I will do the same along the coast in case the French start getting ambitious.' They moved onto Lowestoft and Yarmouth and alerted both mayors.

Arriving back at Dunston there was a message from Harold for him to go over to Wymondham. When he arrived at Harold's castle he found his brother in a state of anxiety. 'A French fleet is heading for the south coast,' said Harold. 'You had better get your men ready to defend us.'

Edmund smiled and looked at his brother. 'They will not be here that quick, we need more information as to what strength they have. My men are always ready and a fight would do them good. I will try to find out what exactly has happened.' He called Arthur and told him to send a fast messenger south and find out what was going on. 'Until we have more information just be careful and admit no strangers. I must get home to prepare in case we need to fight. If the French have landed it is strange we have heard nothing from London to call us to arms. What I did learn when we were in London is that the Scots are becoming a nuisance again and are starting to gather near their border. I will wait until our messenger returns and we have more news.'

On his return to Dunston, Edmund set about organising his men and started a rota to bring farm workers into the castle to be trained. In the middle of this, a rider arrived with a message from London instructing him to quickly march south to Winchester and assist the town should the French arrive. He asked Assad to carry on looking after the castle in his absence. He said fond farewells to Margaret that night and at the crack of dawn the next day they moved out southwards. After several days march they neared the coast and met many people fleeing inland. Edmund stopped a man and asked what had happened.

'They've set Hastings afire sir, and are killing everyone.' 'Who are they?' asked Edmund.

'It's the French sir, there's too many of them.' This was his parting shot as he ran off.

Edmund looked at Arthur. 'Looks as though we might be too late. We will go on to Winchelsea and see if we can help there.' They moved off heading towards the coastal town. When the castle came in sight they could see that it was being attacked. Edmund positioned his bowmen and prepared his cavalry for a charge.

'Fire ten flights at them and then we will go in,' said Edmund. As soon as the archers had delivered their deadly fire Edmund gave the signal to charge. They hit the French with full force and the killing began. The ring was so hot on Edmund's finger and no wonder as he was in a frenzy of thrusting and slicing. No opponent could stand against him. The French fled and Edmund called a halt and not to chase them. He rode to the castle and was met by a monk who escorted him to the Abbot.

'That was a fine attack sir, who are you?'

'Sir Edmund Ivanson of Dunston,' replied Edmund. 'I was summoned to bring my men south and we saw the French attacking you.'

'Your arrival was most timely Sir. I am Hamo of Offington, Abbot of Battle. We occupied this castle as it appeared to be the best to defend. We also overlook the French fleet. They will be worried now as they will think you will attack their vessels and they will not be able to get away.'

From their vantage point Edmund could see men boarding the ships and sails being made ready. The ships began to move off and Edmund could stand his men down and relax a little. He found the Abbot to be interested in his plans and had a good understanding of military tactics, he had been in command of troops before. Edmund looked down at the shore again and could see the French ships leaving.

"I will take my men down to the shore and find out if they have left any stragglers.' They headed along the coast and found towns burning where the French had beaten the defenders and then pillage the town before setting it alight. There were a few small bands of French who had not made it back to their ships, these Edmunds band soon finished them off without mercy having the burning towns in their mind. The Dunston men returned to Winchelsea where Edmund stayed for some days to make sure the villagers were returning and beginning to rebuild. Edmund said his farewells to the Abbot and they set off to journey back to Dunston.

Chapter 38

It was an uneventful journey back to Dunston, everyone was pleased to be back with their families. Margaret greeted her husband warmly and said how much she had missed him.

'I do not like it when you go off to fight. You are not getting younger and you think you are still in your twenties.' Edmund looked down at her. 'You will find out how young I am later tonight.' Margaret covered her face and said he should not embarrass her in front of his men. 'They are not listening to me they have exactly the same thoughts and are wanting to get home. Come, wife, have me fed and watered for I am tired after my journey.' Margaret smiled and took his arm as they went into the castle.

Edmund questioned everyone regarding the state of his lands and his tenants. When he was fully satisfied he rode to Wymondham to meet Harold. He found his brother worrying about unrest in the shire. There was unrest in the south with the peasants, this was spreading and a few malcontents were trying to stir up trouble. Harold was preparing to tour the shire with a strong contingent of soldiers to put down any unrest he found. Edmund argued that this could cause more trouble, they needed to know which knights and barons were not operating the cooperative farming system their father had instigated. Edmunds information was that this was the root of the rebellion. Harold eventually agreed to take this investigation but would still go with a strong force. Arthur asked if they would be accompanying Harold but Edmund shook his head and said there were other problems that needed attending to.

Arthur had been studying the books that Edmund had advised him to do. He felt that he knew most of what was required of him to be a knight and was eager to take the next step. He was beginning to fear that Edmund had forgotten him, he wondered if he should ask his mother to give Edmund a reminder but on second thoughts he realised this would bring down Edmunds wrath. He listened to try to find out what these "other problems" were. Edmund announced that they were to return to Dunston and sent Arthur to ready the men.

Margaret was pleased to see them home and started to ask Arthur about his trip, Edmund interrupted and sent him to look after the troops.

'If Arthur is to become a knight he must learn what his priorities are,' said Edmund. 'Perhaps it would be better if he stayed at Wymondham for a while.'

'I'm sorry Edmund, I wont let it happen again. I know he desperately wants to achieve his spurs, and I promise not to interfere. There is a message for you in your room, a rider delivered it about an hour ago.'

'Where is he? I may have to send a reply,' asked Edmund.

'I sent him to the kitchen to have something to drink and eat.'

Edmund moved off to his room with a parting instruction to send the man to him. He picked the letter up from his table and noted it had the seal of the council. The message instructed him to proceed to Berwick and put down an uprising of the Scots who had taken the town again. Edmund was not pleased. Having just returned from the south he wanted to look after his own affairs. He would send a reply stating that he would comply as soon as his men had rested and had been rearmed from the fighting in Winchester and surrounds. He was just finished writing when there was a knock at his door and the messenger arrived. Sealing his letter Edmund gave it to the man to deliver to the council. Edmund called for Arthur and told him to start preparing the men, he would speak to them in the morning.

Edmund received a sullen response when he told his men that they were to head North. They had great respect for their Lord so they started the preparations for their journey. Margaret was also not very pleased and kept out of his way that day. Arthur encouraged the men saying he was sure that they would soon sort out the problems with the Scots and be on their way home before the snows came. That night when a tired Edmund climbed into bed he found a cold back facing his way.

'What would you have me do. Margaret? Disobey the kings command? I have no more wish to march to fight the Scots than to jump in our river at Christmas. As the king gets older I shall remind him of my loyalty. This trip will also keep the men fighting fit as I fear we will soon have trouble at home with the peasants.'

Margaret turned and reached for him. 'I do understand, Edmund, it is that I need you here with me.' The snuggled into each others arms to join together before sleep came.

Three days later the small army set off north. They marched for several days causing angry looks from the peasants of villages and towns that they journeyed through. When they reached York they were joined by a large number of fighting men and knights sent by the Earl. This was Yorks contribution although there was no noblemen with them. Edmund remarked to Arthur that trouble was brewing. Edmund now had a large army including several groups who had joined them looking for spoils from the fight. Halting to camp one evening, just five miles from Berwick, Edmund split his forces.

'Arthur, I want you to take some of our force, make it more archers than foot. March to Coldstream where you will find an old bridge over the river. Cross over and make your way to Berwick coming in on the west side. We should be attacking, if not wait until we are. I hope this flanking move will give them a surprise.'

Early in the morning as the mist was still on the ground, Arthur moved out with his band of soldiers. Edmund, with majority of the army, gave instructions for the battle order. The Scots were just waking up as Edmunds force reached the bridge over the river.

Sending in his cavalry fast he planned to strike the guards around and on the bridge, hard which they did and broke through. The fighting on the bridge was severe, Edmund and his horsemen pushed their huge destriers against the guards who were on foot. Suddenly they were through and making for the main gate. A hail of arrows met them, men and horses went down but the main body made it to the walls. Edmund's archers began picking off the enemy archers on the towers and battlements. The months of training and practice was paying off as one after another the enemy archers fell. Suddenly Edmund heard fighting from inside the walls. The gates were flung open and a triumphant Arthur stood up in his stirrups and waved his sword for Edmund's force to enter the town. Once inside the town The English pushed the Scots to the southern end where they suddenly found there was nowhere to go. This seemed to increase their ferocity and men were dying on both sides. Edmund could see no obvious leader to call to surrender. He abruptly lost his stirrup as a Scot cut it through. Edmund hit the ground heavily but was soon on his feet and Talio went into action. The killing was horrendous, the ring was burning and he was killing men one after another until Arthur grabbed his arm and was yelling for him to atop as the Scots had now laid down their arms. Edmund stood, panting, sweating and scarcely able to stand. Men stood in awe and fear, a lone piper started to play a lament and Arthur led Edmund away. He returned to find a leader of the remaining Scots.

'Take your men back to your homes and remember this day,' said Arthur. 'We will not tolerate invasion of our towns and we will defeat you if you try it again.'

Edmund sat in a chair looking out of the window of the town hall watching the departing Scots. He was still feeling shaky from the furious onslaught he had made. He looked at the sword and felt the ring, which was now cool. He read the inscription that his father had engraved on the blade, part of it read "With Gods Help".

He thought to himself that he was sure God would not have wanted him to reek the carnage that he had. There again he had named the sword "Talio" which meant "Retribution" and that is what he had served out to the Scots. Rising from the chair he went to find Arthur.

He found the young man organising patrols around the town. He had camped the rest of their army outside the walls and imposed a strict curfew to try and stop looting and womanising. Edmund was impressed at the way the he had taken over and the army appeared to respond to him.

'Once you have secured the town I want you to send out patrols to the surrounding towns and villages and find out if there is more unrest there. I want to get this town back to normal, or as normal as it can be. Emund said this crossing his fingers. He would have to find any leaders that were left and see if there was a militia.

Edmund found that most of the militia had been killed as had the mayor and most of the town council. He brought together all of the educated men he could find and told them to form a council and select a mayor. During this organising Arthur returned. He reported that some villages were returning to normal but that some had been raised to the ground.

'We will stay for a short time and try to settle the region and keep an eye out for any further attacks.'

Edmund installed strong men, both in body and character, in each village and town to to defend their property from marauding Scots. He also recruited and trained a force to be stationed in Berwick who could respond to cries for help from the boarder towns. When he was satisfied that he had done the best that he could the time came to return home.

Chapter 39

The mens spirits rose the nearer they got to Dunston. Edmund had left mainly the York men to protect Berwick, the rest broke off as they came near to that city. The Dunston men began to relax on the homeward march until Arthur clamped down on too much 'relaxing'. Edmund received word that there was trouble at home with the peasants. Harold had sent messages that fighting had broken out due to militant farm workers that had come into the shire. Some of our own men had, misguidedly, joined them. This news he kept to himself and Arthur and made sure that his men were still fighting fit.

When they were near Wymondham, Edmund said he would go to meet Harold and find out what had been going on. 'You take the men home, Arthur, and I will be there soon after.' He turned to his small army and spoke to them. 'Men of Dunston, you have fought well and are coming home victorious. Remember we won because we were together in mind as well as body. Those of you who go back to farms let us work for a good harvest that we can all enjoy.' The men burst into a cheer.

Harold was in quite a state when Edmund walked in.

'There has been a big battle on our lands! Some of our men have been killed and I am not sure which side did it. We didn't have many fighting men here because you had taken them. Bishop Le Dispenser arrived in the nick of time and stopped those damn peasants at North

Walsham. They have raised havoc with our men, fortunately most of them have been loyal and stayed on their farms.'

Edmund listened to his brother then said, 'Where is the good bishop now?' 'He is here. He came to inform me of what had occurred.'

The door opened and in strode the man in question. The bishop smiled at them both and greeted Edmund.

'Was your trip to the north successful? Those Scotsmen are certainly persistent.'

'We drove them back to their homes although there were less returning than came. We have given the border towns more strength and hopefully they will think of this defeat before trying again. I understand from my brother that you had success against this peasant mob.'

'We defeated the mob, as you call it, though they fought well. We have their leader, a man called Geoffrey Lister, and he will be tried in Norwich. I trust you and your brother will attend.'

'My brother, being the Earl of this shire, will certainly attend, as will I.'

The bishop smiled at the inference that Harold was the senior civil authority in the shire. The bishop was a fighting man and had been on the crusades but was not liked in parliament.

'Now you have returned with your trained army and "magic" sword We will stand down but be ready should we be needed again.'

'The sword is not magic, your grace, it is just wielded by an exceptional swordsman. Our grandfather made it so that it has balance and strength, just as the man who fights with it.' Harold looked at the bishop with disdain and fortunately at that moment Elisabeth entered the room and asked if they would retire to the next room where refreshment had been prepared. Edmund said he could eat a horse, as long as it was not his own. The atmosphere eased and the Bishop and Edmund started discussing military tactics.

Edmund excused himself after sampling the food and wine. He invited the bishop to visit Dunston where they could continue the conversation. The bishop accepted and said once he had organised himself back at the Abbey he would be pleased to take up the offer. As Edmund left he quietly said to Harold that they would have to watch this man closely.

Margaret greeted him warmly when he arrived back at Dunston and said that they had not ben troubled by the peasants or the Abbot's men. Arthur reported that the men had been settled down and those who had farms to attend to had gone home.

'I want you to summon all the tenants here in a weeks time. We will also plan to visit some of the outlying ones. I want to know that our lands are secure.'

Arthur said he would arrange it. When he had gone Edmund said to Margaret, 'he is becoming indispensable as I get older. The time has come for me to do something about it.'

That evening Edmund called Arthur to his room. 'Have you read the books I recommended to you?' Edmund asked the young man. 'What did you learn from them?'

Arthur looked nervously at him and said, 'I have read most of them, they are mainly about chivalry and how to conduct yourself as a knight. I found the one that dealt mostly with military strategy most interesting. Being in battles with you, sir, also showed me that you have to think about strategy when you are actually there, it is not something you can learn from a book, only the basics.'

'Good.' said Edmund 'You are ready for your investiture. You will go to Wymondham Abbey where my brother will tell you more. Be ready to go after the tenants meeting.'

Arthur left to find his mother and tell her the news. Margaret was overjoyed that her son would soon be a knight, she thought to herself that this was the first rung in the ladder for Arthur to hopefully succeed Edmund. The Tennants began to arrive the following day. Many had brought members of their families as they were worried that there was still some unruly elements wondering the countryside. The tenant from North Walsham was particularly nervous as the main battle had taken place near to his home. Unfortunately his wife and son had perished, and he was not sure who to blame, the rebels or the Abbot's army. He had brought his daughter with him and Margaret soon had her under her wing.

Edmund learnt from the meeting that several of his tenants had been affected by the battle and the subsequent defeat of the peasants. Many of his own farm workers were accused of being in league with the dissidents. Edmund realised that he would have to help those who had suffered most. There was a lot of discussion relating to the co-operative farming system that Edmund's father had initiated. Two of the tenants proposed that they go back to feudal days and keep the serfs in their place. This was disagreed with by everyone else as they were reaping the benefits of a happy and hardworking workers. Edmund noted who the men were who had raised the subject and decided to visit them as early as possible. One man who strongly supported Edmund was Alfred Walsh, the tenant from North Walsham. He had suffered the most as the battle had been fought on his land. He explained to the group how his men had rallied round getting things back in some sought of order, without being told, because it was in their interest to get the land back and the sheep herded together. Many sheep had died and they were buried in a large pit. 'They took care of me and my daughter when my wife perished. They were true Norfolk men and I wont have a word said against them.' After that tirade Walsh sat down. Applause and banging on the table signified the agreement from all but two of the tenants.

Edmund noticed Assad was not at the meeting and went to his room where he found his friend ill in bed. Edmund sent for the doctor and after the man had examined Assad he took Edmund out of the room to talk to him. 'I am afraid your friend is very ill. I will try all the skills I have but I have seen this type of illness before and it has only one outcome.'

'Get what ever you need. We have been together a long time, I know this country does not agree with him. There must be something you can do.'

The doctor shook his head and Edmund went back to sit with his friend. They remembered the many events that had happened in the past until Assad fell asleep. Margaret tried to comfort Edmund and said she would nurse Assad.

All the tenants left except Alfred Walsh, Edmund had asked him to stay and discuss what help he would need to get his farm back in order. Edmund left him discussing plans with Godfrey Lackland, his new reeve. He decided to get some fresh air and went to his favourite place, the battlements. Someone else had also chosen the quiet spot, as Edmund found Arthur there with Walsh's daughter Elspeth.

'I was showing Elspeth the view from up here,' said Arthur, as his cheeks began to turn red. The sun had set and Edmund thought she would not see much in this light. The girl was quite attractive, with blond hair and blue eyes. Edmund could see Arthur was smitten.

'Take Miss Walsh to the stables and show her the fine animals we have, perhaps you would like to ride in the morning. It will also be warmer there.'

When the couple had gone Edmund smiled and thought back to his youth and the time he met the gypsy women. He stayed staring into the night calling to mind what he and Assad had been through together.

Early the next morning Margaret came to tell him that Assad had passed away during the night. Edmund hurried to see his friend and found him laying peacefully in the bed. The doctor informed him that he would prepare Assad for burial and ask the castle carpenter to make a coffin.

The funeral took place two days later. Arthur said he would collect Assad's belongings together. Edmund told him that Assad had no family so leave everything in his room and he would see to it later.

Chapter 40

After Walsh and his daughter had returned to their home Edmund called Arthur to him. 'We ride to Wymondham tomorrow. I have made arrangements with my brother that we stay at the castle and the Abbot has been notified to expect us. I will make final arrangements when we get there. I expect your mother will want to be there, go and tell her the arrangements. There will be a carriage for her and her women.' Wearing a wide grin, Arthur went quickly in search of Margaret.

They all departed the following morning, it was quite a cavalcade, a carriage for the ladies, a cart for their equipment, eight mounted guards and a young man whom Arthur had not seen before. The mood was sombre as they still grieved over Assad. Edmund recalled the good and bad times they had had together, he would miss him. Edmund introduced the young man as Edwin Blackthorn, the son of a friend of his from Cambridgeshire who would be his new squire. Arthur felt a small pang of disappointment but immediately understood that he was giving up that position.

Harold was pleased to see them and said that the Abbot had everything prepared. When they assembled for the evening meal Arthur was introduced to two visitors, Sir Mark Fallowfield and Sir Luke Trebourne. These knights would be with him tomorrow night in the Abbey. Arthur was a little nervous and tongue tied but the knights soon put him at his ease. The meal was a jolly affair with everyone in good humour. Arthur was told to get a good nights sleep as he would have none the next night.

The following evening Arthur was taken to the Abbey and the Abbot heard his confession, after giving him absolution Arthur was dressed in a single white robe and taken before the high alter. The two knights were already there and together they knelt whilst the Abbot gave benediction. Then the vigil started with prayers and intonations. Edmund, Harold and all the family were already seated in the Abbey. After the evening mass they all left and Arthur with his two guardians started the Vigil.

The families and many townspeople came to early mass the following morning, and found Arthur spreadeagled in front of the high alter. His two companions helped him to his feet and they retired to the sacristy. When they reappeared Arthur was resplendent in his armour, carrying his helm. The Abbot gave him his blessing and Arthur, flanked by his two companions walked through the Abbey to applause from the congregation.

Back at the castle a feast had been prepared with many guests coming from surrounding estates. A fine day meant the townspeople could picnic around the castle and take part in the celebrations. Edmund thought that he didn't get so much fuss when he was knighted but was pleased the Arthur had reached this milestone with his help. Margaret was overjoyed with her son's s achievement. She knew it was what Edmund wanted too as he regarded Arthur as his son. They stayed that night with Harold and on the morrow returned to Dunston. The two visiting knights returned to their estates and life began to get back to normal.

Edmund sent Arthur to visit Yarmouth and Lowestoft in case more irregularities were occurring in the export of their wool. Winter was approaching and Edmund was beginning to feel his old wounds aching. Margaret was pleased to have Edmund home but Edmund soon became restless and bad tempered. He could not wait for Arthur to return with his news.

Two weeks later Arthur returned and reported that there were still irregularities in the wool shipments at Yarmouth. He had left a guard there to keep watch and would return within the month. Edmund said that that was too long, they would leave for the Fen lands in two days time.

As they rode East with a company of guards, Edmund explained why he had overruled Arthur. 'The people who are involved with this crime will not expect us so soon. I have had intelligence from France that we can expect raids along our coast. Maybe the French are involved in this smuggling. I want to alert Alwin as he is closer to the coast and patrols that area regularly. I was also a little frustrated at being cooped up.' Arthur said nothing and they rode on in silence for a while.

Darkness covered the land as they approached Alwin's camp. They were challenged by the guard who recognised Edmund and passed them through. Alwin greeted them warmly and invited them to eat with him. During the meal Edmund explained why they were there. Alwin said he had not found any French up to date but he had heard the rumours too. Edmund was glad to get to his bed, it had been a fast and long ride and he knew by his aches and pains that he was not a young man any more.

The sun rose over the Fens bathing the land in a golden glow. Edmund stretched as he stood and absorbed the beauty of this land. Waterbirds were calling and there was a general rising of noise as both animals and humans rose to their work.

'We will approach Yarmouth from the north, which is not the normal way we would come. It will also give us a chance to inspect the coast route and see if there has been any landings.'Edmund picked up a stick and drew in the soil to show Arthur the way he intended to go. 'I will organise scouts to go ahead of us. I will also organise two men to ride out on our flanks.'

After they had all broken their fast the party moved off Alwin accompanied them with men of his own. He said he would stay out of Yarmouth and stop anyone trying to escape. Alwin had certainly taken charge, he was his fathers son through and through. Dark clouds appeared to threaten the bright morning. 'I fear rain will come soon,' said Alwin. 'The waters are already high so keep to the paths or you may find yourself out of your depth.' Carefully they followed the paths behind Alwin. They reached the shore and looked for signs of boats landing. One of the scout came back to report he had seen evidence of boats landing on the beach. Edmund called a halt and gathered his men together.

'By looking at the signs I calculate that several boats have landed and that means there is a large force of French in this area. We must find them and show them that it is not wise to land on our land. Rest now while trackers search for them, make yourselves ready for a fight.'

Arthur came to Edmund and helped him with his armour. He went round and made sure all the men had helmets and breast plates.

Two of the trackers returned to report that the French had moved into the Fens. Edmund said that he suspected they were trying to get into Yarmouth without being seen. 'We will catch up with them as quietly as we can then we shall be in their rear. Wrap cloths around anything that could rattle and keep quiet.' They all prepared themselves and moved off towards the Fens.

Arthur moved up close to Edmund and said, quietly, 'the report from the scouts indicated that the French outnumber us.' Edmund looked at him. 'I know but we will have the advantage of surprise and we know the terrain. We will force them into the Fens, they will be unaware of the streams and bogs. Make sure our men remember where the paths are.'

They began to see the silhouettes of the French in the gloom of the persistent rain. Edmund called for his archers and told them to loose three quick flights as soon as they were in range. Arthur was ready to charge as soon as the last flight had been loosed.

'Now!' shouted Edmund and as the rear Frenchmen turned to see who had called they were met by the English arrows. The second flight caused panic in their ranks and as their officers tried to organise the men the third flight downed more of their soldiers. Arthur and Edmund led the charge making as much noise as possible.

The French turned and tried to form a defensive line as Arthur's men fell on them with sword and spear. Edmund had fallen a little behind the charge but was soon into battle with Talio. The ring was hot on his finger and the sword struck with the speed of a serpent. Many of the French tried to escape by making for the tall rushes and found themselves waist deep in water and sinking in the mud. One of the French knights called out that they surrendered and to lay down their arms. Edmund lowered Talio just as a Frenchman struck him in the neck. Arthur, who was nearby, sprang at the Frenchman. Fury gave strength to his arm and his sword stroke neatly removed the man's head. Edmund sank to his knees and Arthur moved to help him as the French knight came up. 'I am sorry monsieur, how badly is he hurt? If you will permit I have someone who maybe can help, if you will let her.'

Let HER? Thought Arthur. What is a woman doing on a battle field. He looked up from tending Edmund to see someone in light armour. 'I have some knowledge, monsieur. Let me see the wound.' She bent down and looked at the wound in Edmund's neck. 'He needs to be taken somewhere warm and dry so that the wound can be cleaned.' They brought up Edmund's horse and while the French prisoners were rounded up. They made for the mayors house in Yarmouth.

The mayor and his wife fussed around but the young woman took charge and Edmund was soon in a bed. She cleaned the wound and stopped the flow of blood. Edmund had not said much and Arthur asked if there was damage to his throat. The woman said, 'Not as far as I can see but the shock has stunned him.' 'Not as shocked as finding a woman in a battle,' said a croaky voice from the bed. A fussy little man arrived and announced he was the doctor. The French woman stood back and Arthur was quick to stand by her and see she was no threat to Edmund.

The French knight, after surrendering his men and being locked up with them in a barn, came to the mayors house. He stood by Edmund's bed and introduced himself as Count Pier de Coutoux. 'We were part of a plan to seize your ports and were making our way to Yarmouth. This is my daughter, Coralie, who has tended your wound until the doctor arrived. I have no son, Coralie has filled that gap in many ways. She is good with a sword and bow.' Now she had removed her armour to tend to Edmund, Arthur thought to himself that she looked good too.

The mayor, Alfred Trader, found rooms for the count and his daughter. He gave his word to remain Edmund's prisoner and assumed that he, with his daughter, would be ransomed.

Chapter 41

Edmund lay in his bed getting restless. His wound was healing and his speech had returned. They were all aware of this from the orders he gave and his grumpiness at being confined to his bed. Coralie visited him from time to time to check on his wound. Arthur made sure he was there as protection, he found the more time he spent with her the more attractive she became.

Edmund was anxious to get back to Dunston and after a week, confined in Yarmouth, he declared they would leave.

'Leave a detachment of guards here, as soon as we reach Dunston send a similar number to Lowestoft. We must warn the tenants near the coast to be on their guard and report any activity by the French. Arthur, inform the Count and that girl of his that he will be coming with us until the ransom is paid.' Early in the morning they left for home.

Margaret was worried when she saw Edmund's wound and thanked Coralie for the help she had given. When Edmund was at last resting in his room, Margaret told him that the knight who governed his area from Holt had died and Harold had asked her if his wife and daughter could stay with them until new accommodation was found for them. The knight, Harold had now installed there, did not want the widow around.

'Lady Oxbourn is most pleasant and I like her. She is a good companion for me, her daughter is a lovely young woman and is devoted to her mother, you will like them when you see them at our evening meal.'

Edmund replied that this was a small castle and there was not enough room to house waifs and strays. He then called Godfrey to him to bring him up to date on the tenants in spite of Margaret's entreaties to leave it until the morning.

The evening meal turned out to be more pleasant than Edmund expected. The count and Coralie had been asked to join them he found Lady Oxbourn and Rachel, her daughter, good conversationalists. Arthur was enjoying himself having two attractive women of his age at the table. He had a smile on his face as he turned from one to the other.

The new day was nearing noon when Harold rode into the castle accompanied by his sons John and William. He had ridden from Wymondham to see how Edmund was recovering and to find out what was happening at the coast. While Edmund brought his brother up to date Arthur took John and William into the castle gardens where two young ladies were taking a stroll. When the introductions had been done Arthur and John joined the ladies in their stroll.

After Harold had heard all Edmund's news he asked him what his plans were. Edmund said they must increase the coastal patrols and notify all the tenants to be alert. He also planned to visit as many of the ports as possible.

'Send Arthur,' said Harold. 'John could accompany him, it will do him good to get out and see what this fiefdom is. He will take over one day and he needs exposure to the problems that will bring.' Edmund agreed and said he would make the arrangements. Harold asked what he was going to do about Count de Coutoux? 'I have send ransom demands to his family and his men have been sent back to France as I do not want to feed them. I don't have room for him here, as you have the space you can take him with you when you go.' Harold said he would do as he wished as long as was not long before the ransom arrived.

The two young men enjoyed their journey around the Shire. There were many discussions about the two women they had left behind in Dunston. 'Who do you prefer?' asked Arthur. 'They are quite different.' John thought for a moment. 'I think I would be more interested in Rachel, Coralie would be too competitive with her fighting skills. I like to be the warrior and Rachel would be nice to come home to after a battle.'

'I can see what you mean, though Coralie has a soft side. I think she would be fun to be with.' Their discussions continued throughout their patrol.

Three weeks passed before the patrol returned to Dunston. They were welcomed home by Edmund, now recovered, as Harold had returned to Wymondham and taken Count de Coutoux with him. Rachel had stayed with Coralie and would return to Wymondham with John and William.

After Arthur and John had rested for a few days, John said they should return home. Rachel did not want to leave Coralie but she knew she had to join her father. Edmund instructed a number of guards to accompany them, he did not expect trouble but it best to be safe. They left on a bright sunny morning in good spirits. John led the off with Rachel at his side and William bringing up the rear with the guards. They rode at an easy pace and John pointed out some places of interest. They stopped in a woodland glade at noon ate the food that Lady Margaret had packed for them.

John suddenly held up his hand. 'Quiet, do you hear that noise?' He had no sooner said this when a band of ruffians came out of the trees threatening them with bows and swords. 'Do you know who I am?' said John.

'If anything happens to us, my father the Earl, will hunt you down.' One of the band stepped forward and said, 'If you are an Earls son then you will have money on you. Let's see what they've got boys.' He walked towards John who had spied one of the guards approaching through the trees. The man had just been to relieve himself and stopped short when he saw the scene in front of him. John called out and the leader turned to see who was coming giving

John the opportunity to draw his sword. All hell broke out as the guards swung into action with William at their head. John made for their leader who tried to defend himself but John had been well trained and easily drove a killing thrust to his chest. The fighting was fierce and it was not long before the bandits began to give in, those that were still standing that is. Rachel kept back with a lady who was accompanying her. John was moving to protect her from an attack when a guard drove his sword through the man. His eyes met hers as she smiled at him. John called to William to find out how many they had lost, dead or wounded. William reported that there were no deaths and only four guards wounded. The bandits had least five dead and eight seriously wounded. They reached Wymondham and John told his father of the fight.

Arthur was walking with Coralie in the castle gardens when they heard a man pull his horse to a stop in front of the main door. 'He sounds in a hurry,' commented Arthur. 'I hope John and Rachel reached Wymondham all right.' They went back into the castle looking for Edmund. They found him in the great hall reading a letter.

'What news father? You look worried.'

'The Black Prince is calling on me to take my men to him in France to help him in this everlasting war we have with the French.' Edmund turned to Arthur as he said this and the young man could see the anger in Edmund's eyes.

'It is time this war ended and fighting finished. We need the men returned home so that we can get them back to work here.'

'Will you go Sir?'

'I will sleep on it. Come let us eat and say nothing to your mother.' Edmund strode out of the hall with Arthur following.

That night Arthur lay in his bed thinking about the demand from the Prince. If Edmund decided to go to war then he would have to go too. Perhaps he should go instead of Edmund, after all he was not a young man any more. Perhaps he would let him take Talio. With that thought in his mind he drifted off to sleep.

The sky was dark with rain clouds when Arthur awoke. This did not help his mood as he went to break his fast. His mother met him and asked what was the matter as he looked so glum. He replied that as he had to practice with the men today and he would have preferred dry weather. On his way to the practice yard he met Edmund.

'Well met, Arthur, I have decided that we will both answer the Prince's call. Assemble all the men and I will address them.'

When the men were all together, Edmund announced that they would all be marching to France to join the Black Prince's army. There was a 'Hurrah' from the men who were thinking of the spoils of war that could be had. 'We leave in three days time so say your farewells and be ready to leave. Arthur you are without a squire, make sure you have one before we leave. You will need him to look after your armour and weapons.'

Coralie was upset when Arthur told her, they had become quite close over the past few days. 'I don't think we will be away long,' said Arthur. 'I expect John and the men from Wymondham will be going too. Rachel could come over and stay with you.'

Two days later John arrived with a large contingent of men from Wymondham. Harold would stay behind to look after the estates. The next day saw them leave, a large body of men numbering over 3000. They marched to Lowestoft to board ship for France.

Chapter 42

The army camped outside the town while Edmund and Arthur rode to the port, leaving John in command. The port was very busy with ships unloading and many ships waiting in the channel for space at the quayside. Edmund made for the mayors house where he expected a message had been left regarding what ships were to take them to France. The mayor welcomed them and produced two bulky packages. The mayor offered the use of his parlour so they could study the packages in private.

'Judging by their size there must be much information here,' said Edmund as they sat down. He unwrapped one of the packages and found several scrolls, he studied them intently. He looked up at Arthur. 'We shall be on land a little longer as we are not going to France.'

'What are we going to do then, has the war in France ended?' Edmund laughed and struck his fist on the table. 'No, that war will never end, it just uses up money and men. We are needed elsewhere, so it says. The Spanish navy are causing havoc with our shipping routes. We are to journey to Spain and meet the Prince there, so we march to Portsmouth and ships will be ready for us. Ride on and tell John to assemble the men they will find it warmer in Spain.'

Edmund thanked the mayor and told him that they were going to return to their homes. One of the letters instructed him not to make his journey destination public. He arrived back at the camp to find all the men assembled and speculating to what was going on. Arthur had not said anything to John apart from Edmund wanted the men assembled. Edmund told the men that they would be marching south and the final destination would be told to them on route.

They skirted round London and reached Portsmouth after several days heavy marching. As they camped in the woods above the town Edmund spoke to them about their destination. 'I lived in Spain for many years and you will find the weather warmer than here.'

Edmund called John to him and set off for Portsmouth leaving Arthur in command. They made for the docks and were met by a well dressed man who introduced himself as the procurement office for the journey to the Prince. Several ships were ready to accept their small army. Edmund sent John back to tell the men to come to the docks. Edmund thought of the problem he would have when it came to embarking as many men had smuggled 'wives' into their ranks. Some genuine but there was a number who had been picked up on the way. Wives were not encouraged to travel abroad and Edmund was not in favour, however, it did stop the men molesting girls on the march. Once the ships were loaded they set sail for the northern coast of Spain. Edmund had noticed that the two young men were beginning to compete with each other as to who should be in command. John tended to deal with the men as a lord and master whereas Arthur was closer to the men and they respected him more. Edmund stood on the deck of the lead ship and pondered on the problem hoping it would not develop into enmity between them. He missed the battlements of his castle where he would walk and think, just as his father had done.

The ship made a turn to starboard and slid along the coast to the port of Caruna. Once all the ships had docked and discharged all the men and their baggage Edmund called John and Arthur to him.

'Round them up and make for the east of the town, there is an open space in front of some woods and we will assemble there. I will try and find someone in charge of all this mayhem in the town. I am assuming we will march to Castile.'Eventually Edmund located a man who told him to report to a Count Escargot, which brought a smile to Edmund's face. After many enquiries Edmund found the count, a large potbellied man who lived up to his name as there was very little going on in the way of organisation. The count informed him that in due time someone would find him outside of town.

When Edmund returned to his camp he found the men setting up for their evening meal, fires were being lit and animals slaughtered.

'Arthur, where did these animals come from?'

'We purchased them from a local farmer. He was expecting us as he had them gathered together. His price was cheap and the men needed something solid in their bellies after the sea crossing.'

A man came galloping up to them and announced he had a message from the count. 'I see you have been given the bulls for your food. The count had arranged that all the troops would have a good meal when they arrived. The count invites you to a council of war tomorrow morning at nine hours.' He turned his horse and rode off. Edmund looked at Arthur, who had turned red in the face, and told him to find the farmer and retrieve their money. The next day, after the "council of war,' they moved out to find the Princes army.

The start of the march took them through part of the Pyrenees and brought back memories of Edmund's time with the gypsies. He smiled to himself as he remembered the nights when he was taught the art of lovemaking. He wondered if Milosh was still alive. Riding along he thought of the vineyard and how Gareth was faring. Had the war touched them or any of the friends he had left behind.

Leaving the foothills behind they came to the Province of La Rioja and continued on to meet the Prince at Navarrese. Edmund was called to a council of war where the Duke of Lancaster placed him with a group of mercenary who were mainly archers. Edmund told his archers to tend to their bows and make sure there were plenty of arrows available. The English long bowmen were feared by the French and the Duke was banking that the Spanish were equally fearful of them. Their plan was to encircle the French and Spanish army and cause chaos in their ranks.

Dawn was breaking as they formed up on the top of a small hill. Th archers were in a long line, two deep. Before them they could see, and hear, the two opposing forces joining battle. From where he stood Edmund could see the Black Prince being forced back. Edmund gave the order for his archers to fire and their arrows soon found their marks.

A section of Castilian light cavalry started to charge towards them but were cut down by the accurate and rapid fire of the archers. Edmund was shouting encouragement to the archers and he could see that the Gascon mercenaries were forcing Henry's army back who where fleeing from the battle. A large force of cavalry chased them as they ran towards the bridge over the river. There was no mercy and most of them were killed as they tried to get over the narrow bridge.

Edmund gathered his men together, they had suffered no losses and the only injured were one man who had shot himself in the foot in his excitement, several strained shoulders and one man who had suffered an injury in his behind where his friend, who was standing behind him, loosed his arrow too soon. Edmund went to find the Black Prince who was with a group of nobles and waving at the town of Najera.

'That's where we will find them. Go in and raise it to the ground, it will give the men something for winning the battle.'

Edmund stopped and and was appalled at what he had heard, he turned and rode back to his men. Calling them together he said, 'go back to our camp and load all our belongings, we are departing for home tonight.' There were some of his men who wanted to go to the town and take part in the looting and killing. Edmund told them all that to do that would mean becoming a traitor to him and the punishment for that was death. When night fell Arthur and John started quietly out towards the coast, Edmund rode in silence and the two young men realised there was something on his mind.

They stopped for a rest and to feed the men. Edmund called the two young men to him. 'I have decided that while I am in Spain I will go and visit the Vineyard. I want to see old friends and see if they are prospering as I have not heard from them for sometime. John, I want you to take the men home, it will be good experience for when you are lord of the shire. We will take half a dozen men leaving John with the remainder to take back home.'

Chapter 43

They set off southwards disguised as Spanish gypsies as there were still survivors of the battle in the vicinity. Edmund recalled his Spanish that he learned whilst with the Gitanos, two of his men also spoke Spanish. They called to each other in loud voices hoping their dialect was not too far out. Camping under the stars that night, Edmund was surprised to hear a guitar, Edwin was quite accomplished which added to the deception.

They journeyed further south, keeping to the byways away from villages and the main routes. One morning, as they topped a small hill, they saw in the distance a castle. There was no flag or banner flying from the turrets. Edmund sent two riders ahead to scout the area and discover who resided there.'We will make dry camp here and rest ourselves. No fires and keep the noise down.'

The riders returned to report that the castle was in a poor state of repair and no one was living there. There was a small village nearby where there was a forge and a tavern. Edmund asked if there was cover in the castle? The two scouts said there were rooms that they could shelter in. 'We will move quietly to the castle, keeping clear of the village. There are clouds gathering which could mean rain so shelter will be most welcome.' After this announcement Edmund mounted his horse, the rest of the men following suit.

When they reached the castle they could see that it had not been occupied for several years. Edmund and Arthur inspected the rooms that were still intact, some still had dusty and grubby furniture. One of the men came to report they had found the kitchens in the basement, although they were dirty everything was still there, even cooking pots. Edmund called one of the men to him. 'We will go into the village and make some enquiries at the Inn. We ask if the owners are still in the area as we would shelter there for the night.'

They settled themselves into various rooms and Arthur sent half of the men down to the kitchen to clean it as best they could. Two of them said they could cook so started cleaning pans. They built a quick burning fire that would produce little smoke and produced a hot stew that cheered the men up. Edmund, Edwin and Arthur rode out to the village. They entered the Inn and everyone went quiet. Strangers were uncommon in this area and Edmund noticed hands going nearer to knives and swords.

'We bid you good evening,' said Edmund in his rough Spanish. 'We are gypsies travelling south and we enquire who owns the castle so that we may ask him to allow us to shelter there for the night.'

The atmosphere eased and the man who stood by the inner door spoke. 'It belongs to a Temple Knight who has not been near it these many a year. We shelter cattle in there sometimes but some say it is an evil place and strange spirits are there. If you'm not afeared of ghosties then make the best of it.' Edmund smiled and asked, 'What happened to the Temple Knight, did he belong to a local temple? Has nobody lived there since?'

The Inn keeper, for that is who he was, said that many knights and soldiers came and captured the castle. They had never seen the knight, or any of the servants and guards again. The villagers believed the place was haunted and nobody would go there at night. Edmund sat down to hear more of the tales about the castle. The village and castle was well away from the normal routes and Edmund guessed that no one had bothered them. Buying a pig from one of the farmers there they slaughtered and gutted it to take back with them. Finishing their drinks they made their way back to the castle.

'My guess is that the castle once belonged to the Knight Templars. This would be one of their outposts until the King of France outlawed them.' Edmund continued to tell Arthur the history of the Templars, as he knew it, but was careful not to tell him of the previous castle he had found or the gold that was in it.

When they returned, Edmund arranged a roster of guards and made his way to the room where he and Arthur were to sleep. Edwin organised the men to hang the pig for a meal on the morrow. Edmund spent some time examining the walls and floor of the room they were to use, Arthur wanted to know what he was doing. 'Looking for bugs, scorpions and snakes,' said Edmund, which kept Arthur nervously awake for some time.

In the morning Arthur found Edmund examining the other rooms. 'Have you found any of the pests?' he asked him. 'No, it is interesting how solidly they built their castles.' Edmund wondered how he was going to search the building without raising the curiosity of the group, he could also use some help. 'There are stories that they used to hide articles of a religious nature, valuables and weapons in hidden wall cavities. You could help me look, if you would like to. It would be wise not to tell the others as they could end up tearing the place down. This is only a small castle and off the main routes so I doubt there was anything of importance here.'

'It sounds like fun,' said Arthur. 'We could arrange a foraging expedition and have a good look whilst they are away. I will summon Martin to organise it.' As soon as the men had gone Edmund and Arthur went to work examining all the walls. They found several cavities and places where something had been stored but all were empty. Edmund decided that they should finish the search before the men returned.

Chapter 44

That evening, as the men were drinking after their meal, Edmund went outside the castle. He stood looking up at the starlit sky thinking of home and Margaret. Was it worth going any further south? The country had changed since he had roamed the land in his youth. The provinces were all at war with one another and the French adding to the fighting. Walking around the outside of the castle he stumbled across a small building.

'Edwin, fetch a torch,' called Edmund. Edwin and Arthur hurried over bearing a torch. 'What have you found?' Arthur asked. 'This building, I don't know why we've not noticed it before. I can't imagine what it was used for. Come on, let's go and find out.' 'Wait, I will get another torch in case this one burns out,' called Arthur. Rejoining Edmund they forced open an old door that had been covered with brambles and bushes. Inside it was obvious that it had not been used for many years. They brushed away cobwebs and branches that had fallen through the roof.

'Not much here,' commented Arthur, 'I wonder what it was used for? It is not big enough for much.'

Edmund walked across the floor and he felt the flagstone he was standing on move. "I think this is loose. Help me to lift it.' They set to to loosen the stone more and with much heaving lifted it and uncovered a hole with steps leading down.

'Could be a way of escape.' said Edwin as he peered into the dark hole. Arthur started to descend the steps, Edmund said to be careful. At the bottom of the steps they found themselves in a chamber with a tunnel leading off towards the castle. Their torch began to flicker, Edmund said there was not much air so proboblsy the tunnel was blocked at the other end. In the dimming light they went into the tunnel and went as far as the light would let them. 'We need to come back with more torches.' Edwin said he would go back and prepare them. They returned to the entrance, as Arthur moved towards the castle Edmund stopped him. 'We will leave this for tomorrow, say nothing to the men.'

Arthur was troubled by what Edmund had said. If they did find anything he thought that it should be shared among the men. He would talk to Edmund and tell him how he felt. Edmund listened to Arthur and agreed that he had been selfish, his men deserved better and if they found anything of value he would share it. He asked Arthur to organise a party to go into the tunnel with more light and he would try to find the other entrance. Edmund searched the area where he calculated that the tunnel should be. He knocked on the wall with the hilt of his dagger and started to pull back the wall panels. He found where bricks had been placed to conceal a doorway. He went to find hammers to break open the doorway.

Edmund was swinging a large hammer at the wall when Arthur appeared. 'You have found the other entrance,' he said excitedly.

'I don't know,' said Edmund. 'These bricks are newer than the rest so I think they are concealing a door. I have calculated that it must be in line with the tunnel.' Bricks started to fall out as he spoke and Arthur grabbed another hammer and they soon had a large opening in the wall. The door way led into another small room. They could hear hammering from the opposite wall.

Edmund said that this was the other end of the tunnel. They were puzzle as to why there was a room there if it was just for escaping. Suddenly a gap appeared in the opposite wall and the rest of the men gave a cheer as they climbed through. The room was not large and Edmund was puzzled as to what its purpose was, and why block up the door if it was an escape route. They all began to search the walls for any form of hideaway. Arthur was the one who found another sealed doorway. With heavy swings on their hammers they soon disclosed a large cupboard, stacked inside were several boxes. The first one they opened disclosed a box full of candles.

'Perhaps they had parties in here,' said Edwin.

'More likely they are for illuminating the passage. Let's see what the others reveal.' Edmund answered. The next box was full of weapons, swords, daggers, several maces and a curious long tube fixed to what looked like, a crossbow. They dragged the next box out and found this one full of clothes. There were lots of tunics with large white crosses and several helmets. They were all getting a little disappointed at not finding anything of value when Arthur called for help to move a box from the corner. When they opened it there were gasps as they could see the box was full of gold coins. Edmund quickly told them to stand back. 'Before you start filling your pockets I will examine these to see what they are and what value they have. I will count them and we will share the find among us. In the meantime you are to say nothing about this to anyone.' He could see the gleam in the mens eyes and knew he would have to be careful how he handled the situation before greed caused trouble. The cleared the cupboard but found nothing more of value. Edmund ordered them to take the boxes up to a room in the tower that was still secure. There was an old table and chair and he sat down to examine their find.

Most of the coins were florins, which made sense if this was a Templar's bank. There were some Spanish doblas and French elus. Arthur came in with a cup of wine and stared at the piles of coins. 'We will have to mount a guard on this room, I will take first watch.' Edmund laughed, 'Who is going to guard you?' 'You know you can trust me,' said the young man and Edmund agreed with a smile. After securing the door as best as they could Edmund joined the rest of the men for a meal. They were excited and wanted to know how much there was and what would each of them receive.

'Most of it is in Spanish money some Italian and a little French. You will need to change it into English florins or it will raise suspicions as to where you got it from. My bank, in London, can do this for us if you can trust me.' There was silence for a moment then Peter, one of the group spoke, 'we are all soldiers from your castle, lord, we know you will treat us fairly. I say we wait until we reach home.' The rest agreed.

When everyone had settled down for the night Edmund decided to have another look in the secret room. Taking a torch he stood looking around the walls. In the cupboard he noticed a brick near the floor was out of line. He kicked with his foot and the brick moved, bending down he removed the brick and found, hidden behind it, a bundle of cloth. When he unwrapped it there, glinting in the light from the torch, were religious items. A beautiful crucifix, candle sticks, a golden chalice and other small items. He wrapped them in the cloth, pushed the brick back, picked up the bundle and returned to his bed.

They rose early to break their fast then load up and start the homeward journey. All the men were in good spirits, no doubt thinking of the money they would receive when they reached home, it was noticeable that they did not move far from Edmund, like a personal guard. Leaving the village behind they made for the coast. Edmund thought that it must be providence that he had found Templars' gold twice, perhaps if he stayed in this area and searched for old castles he would find more.

They journeyed on heading north. Sometimes posing as gypsies others as pilgrims heading towards Santiago. The group always were vigilant and protective of Edmund and Arthur who were carrying the money. When they reached the mountains they headed to a small town named Cuddillero. There was a deep water harbour here and they hoped to find a ship.

Chapter 45

Home in Norfolk there had been changes. Harold had succumbed to an illness, said to be the plague, although England had been relatively clear of it for some time. John was now the Earl and had married Rachel. The union had produced a fine son. John followed his fathers method of farming and the shire was flourishing.

Margaret had taken control at Dunston even though she missed Edmund and her son. She was proving to be an exceptional manager and the tenants responded by improving the yield of wool and cattle. The contacts in Flanders were happy and she planed to invite them to Dunston Castle. Coralie helped her and pined for Arthur's return. Everyone was waiting for Edmund's homecoming, the few letters he had written had not all reached Dunston. John, although he was the Earl by right, was nervous of Edmund's return, would he take it as his right to inherit the Earldom? He might try and take Wymondham by force. He knew that was possible, or would he respect his brothers son? John had brought all the men home, except for those who had gone with Edmund. John was well aware that Edmund could raise an army from his guards and tenants, who were loyal to him and Margaret.

The months went by as Edmund and his band journeyed home. They could not find a suitable ship in Cuddillero. After waiting for two months they decided to move on to Corruna. They had to negotiate the mountains that were inhabited by bands of bandits. Early one morning as they set off on a narrow mountain pass, Edmund told them to keep a sharp lookout. They were confronted by a group of men blocking their path. They stopped as they could see two more men on the hillside with crossbows.

The leader, a tall man built like a bull, called to them. 'Get down and send your horses to us, all of them. If your goods are worth having we might let you through.' On one side was the hill with the archers and on the other was a steep drop from the path into a ravine. Edmund signalled with his hand to Arthur to keep to the edge. He called to the leader. 'If you fire you will kill the horses and take them over the edge. All our goods will be gone and so will your booty.' Edmund had positioned his best archers at the rear of their column. While the discussion between Edmund and the bandit was taking place the bandits on the hillside were distracted giving Edmund's archers the opportunity to notch arrows and kill them. The bandit leader gave a roar and charged at Edmund who drew Talio and a fierce fight started. There was little room on the path and the fighting was close, Talio sang in Edmund's hand and the bandit leader was soon dispatched. With Arthur at his side he pushed forward and the rest of the bandits turned to flee. One of their horses, not used to fighting, reared up and cannoned into Edmund's horse who lost its footing on the loose rocks at the edge of the path. Before anyone could save him Edmund and his horse disappeared over the edge and fell down into the ravine. Edwin quickly dismounted and rushed to the edge. All he could see was a large dust cloud as Edmund and his horse dropped to the valley floor.

Arthur called the men together and sent them searching for a path down to the bottom. He tried to pinpoint where Edmund had finished up but could see no sign of him. The men returned saying that they had found no way down, they would have to go further on to find a way. Arthur gathered all the rope they had but it was not long enough to even get halfway down. He mounted and set off to find a way with the rest following.

Edmund lay amongst boulders and broken tree branches. He could see a hazy light that appeared between bouts of darkness. His body hurt and there was no feeling in his legs. As his vision began to clear he could see the body of his horse, it was not moving and had obviously been killed in the fall. Something glinted between him and the horse, it was Talio. He tried to reach out to it but the pain drove darkness back into his brain. After resting for a few moments he tried again, after several attempts he managed to hold the sword in his hand. Where was Arthur? Would he be able to find him? Edmund tried to call out but all he could manage was a dull croak. He knew he must try and find some shelter, he would consider that when he had had a rest.

Arthur and the rest of the men had ridden at least three or four miles and found no way down, in fact the valley had got deeper.

'We will have to go further,' said Arthur. 'There must, eventually, be a way into that valley. We should come across a village soon and we may be able to buy enough rope to climb down.'

Night decended to the little band, so did gloom and despondency. Everyone rode in silence as they continued their search.

Edmund was trying to drag himself to the cliff side to find shelter. The pain was agonising, a darkness kept descending on him as he drifted in and out of conscienceless. After a couple of hours he made it to a small cave where he collapsed and passed out. When he came to he found he had Talio in his hand. He must have managed to crawl over to reach it. He looked around the cave, it was very small, he placed Talio between himself and the wall. Lying there he thought of home and Margaret, Arthur would find him and they would soon be on their way. Cold began to creep over him as he lay. He tried to move nearer to the back of the cave but there was little room. Using Talio he tried to enlarge his space all he succeeded in doing was to bury the sword under bits of rock from the roof.

Arthur could see lights ahead, spurring their horses on they arrived in the centre of a small village. A church stood at the end of the square, Arthur banged on the front door which was opened by an old priest.

'What is so urgent my son,' said the old man.

Arthur quickly explained and said that he needed to get to the floor of the valley immediately so that they could search for Edmund. The old Priest turned back into the church and rang a bell. Several men appeared hurrying from their homes to the church. Arthur explained their situation and the urgency to find Edmund. Torches were lit and they followed the men to a narrow path that led to the floor of the ravine. They moved as quickly as they could through the rock strewn ground looking for where they thought Edmund had fallen over the edge. Arthur looked up to see the dim outline of Edwin, who had stayed at the spot where Edmund had gone over. He was still calling to him. They soon found Edmunds horse and started searching for Edmund, one of the men shouted that he had found the tracks where Edmund had dragged himself to the cave.

'Is he alive?' asked Arthur. 'Be careful, let me see him. EDMUND CAN YOU HEAR ME?' There was no response. 'Let's get him out of this hole so we can see him better.'

The movement caused the pain to send the darkness away from Edmund's mind, momentarily, and he blinked. 'He's alive,' said Arthur. 'Bring a torch closer so that I can see his wounds. His legs are broken and one arm. The worst damage is this branch in his side. We must shorten it so that he can be moved. Make a litter so that we can carry him back to the Village. Have you a doctor?' 'The Priest is good at that sort of thing,' said one of the villagers. They gathered some branches and using the harness from the horse they fashioned a litter. One of the men brought Talio to Arthur which he placed on Edmund, he was surprised when Edmund grasped the pommel with both hands. Lifting the litter they set off back to the village.

When Edmund felt Talio return to him he knew he must keep it, whatever happens, he gripped it with all the strength he could muster. The blackness kept returning and he felt a great deal of pain. When the blackness was at its darkest the pain went away. He prayed that the darkness would deepen and the pain stop. The party reached the village and made strait for the church. The old Priest went to work but, as he told them, his skill was limited. Edmund's clothes were cut away and they could see the branch had penetrated deeply.

'I cannot remove the branch,' said the Priest. 'We will have to wait to see if he can recover a little of his strength before we attempt that.' They laid the litter on a table in front of the alter and the Priest began to pray. They all knelt.

The darkness receded and the pain came back. He could faintly hear a droning sound and then the darkness decended again. The darkness grew denser the pain lessened. I like the dark, he thought, it's peaceful, don't let it go away. Suddenly a brilliant white light ripped the darkness away and a warm golden glow soothed his mind. He was floating in space, then, nothing.

The Priest rose and went to Edmund. He felt his neck for the beat of his heart and looked at the men kneeling there. 'He is with the Lord now.'

Arthur stood and moved to Edmund, clasped the sword to remove it but found Edmund's grasp was so tight that Talio could not be moved.

'Leave him, my son, he may relax later. Go and rest with your men and we will prepare your knight. Will you take him with you?' The Priest explained that he could be buried in the church if they wished. As a knight he would have a special tomb in the crypt of the church, or the body could be fastened into a strong casket for them to bear back to his home. There would be herbs placed around the body for a long journey, but the smell from the body would soon be obvious. Arthur said he would give a decision after he had spoken with the men. Villagers offered lodgings for the tired travellers, Arthur said they would meet early in the morning to decide what to do next.

The sun was rising as Arthur awoke. Had the previous night been a dream? He dressed and decended to the kitchen where a woman was stoking a fire under a large pot of water. He went outside and sluiced himself down from a barrel of rainwater. No, it had not been a dream, he could still visualise the branch sticking out from Edmund's side. He rounded up the men, he needed to discuss with them the nest step.

'I would like to take him home,' he started to say. 'Practically it is not a good idea. Getting a passage towards home will be made more difficult. Knowing how superstitious sailors are I am not sure we would get a ship at all. This is a remote village and very secure. Should the family wish to journey here in the future we will have his name engraved on the tomb.' There were lots of heads nodding in agreement. 'Edgar, go and find our baggage and clean his armour, we will dress him properly for burial.' Edwin, who had been very upset, had stayed with Edmunds body all night spoke. 'I will remain here with him. I have no family now in England, he was my family. I will find work and here I will stay.'

Arthur understood his feelings but said he would find it very difficult in a foreign land. The priest said he would take care of him until he felt it was time to leave. Arthur thanked the old priest. 'Father, we will leave him here. We accept your offer to entomb Edmund here. This is a beautiful church where he will be at peace. Maybe someone will come to find his resting place in the future.'

'Thank you, my son. We will prepare a tomb for your knight. I need to know his full name and title. We have a man who can engrave and he will be honoured to practice his skill. He does not get the chance very often in the area.'

'What is the name of this village, and this church too? I will have to give all the details to his wife, my mother. It is a long way from our home, in more peaceful times the family will probably like to visit.'

'This is the village of Saint Llorenc de la Muga and this is the church of Saint Llorenc,' answered the priest. 'I am father Paul and have been here for forty years. Your knight will be safe here. I will arrange a requiem mass for him in three days time.' Arthur thanked him and returned to the tavern where his men had gathered.

The following morning Arthur, Edwin and Edgar went to the church and dressed Edmund in his armour. They found it difficult to remove Talio from his grip and had to break two fingers. Arthur looked at the sword and was tempted to take it as he was sure Edmund would have wanted him to have it. In the end he placed it back in Edmunds hands, he made sure the inscription showing on the blade was "ALIS AQUILAE" (On Eagles Wings). Edmund had told him the story of how it was given to John, by his father, Edmund's grandfather, who was a village blacksmith. Was there magic in it? Who would know. He made sure the ring was on his finger and covered by his gauntlet.

On the day of the funeral they all assembled in the church, there were many villagers there too. After the mass the coffin was taken into the tomb and placed inside a stone coffin. Arthur admired the effigy that had been carved on the lid. The priest explained that there were still some work to be finished on it. The lid was then sealed. They all returned to the tavern where some food had been prepared. Edwin stayed behind, standing at the foot of the tomb. They spoke of their exploits with Edmund and mourned his death. Arthur began to think of how they were to get back to England. What would Edmund have done?

Chapter 46

Margaret was pacing the battlements, how often had she seen Edmund do the same thing when he needed a quiet time to think and plan. It was not an easy task to manage the fiefdom without her lord. Looking towards the village of Dunston she saw a horseman galloping towards the castle, perhaps it was news of her husband, perhaps it would tell her he was returning home. She decended to the main hall where the rider was brought to her. He presented Margaret with four letters which she thanked him for and suggested that he might like to refresh himself and eat before journeying on.

Margaret looked at the four sealed letters resting on the table before her. Suddenly the door burst open and a breathless Coralie ran into the room.

'Is there news from Arthur?' she gasped.

'I am just deciding which to read first,' replied Margaret. 'Sit down and catch your breath, we have been waiting for news for months, it wont hurt you to be patient for a few more minutes.' Margaret smiled as she said this as she, too, was eager for news.

Margaret selected one that was sealed with Edmunds seal and opened it out on the table. It had been written after the battle and as they started their journey home. It told how they had won the battle and that he and Arthur were in good health but missing home. He explained their plans to cross the mountains to the coast and find a ship to bring them home. The next letter was from Arthur saying much the same with a separate page for Coralie who read it and blushed. There was another letter from Edmund to be sent to the families of the men who were with him, he asked Margaret to read it to those who had not learnt their letters. The final letter had obviously been written last as it was cleaner, it bore Arthur's seal. As Margaret read it she gasped and fell forward onto the table. Coralie rushed to her and realised she was weeping.

'My Lady, what ails you?'

Margaret pushed the letter to her and Coralie read the account of Edmund's death. She put her arms around Margaret trying to calm her. Margaret clung to her, sobbing as though her heart would break. Pulling herself together Margaret said that she was glad Arthur was all right and on his way home. There was a letter to Coralie from Arthur writing of what had happened and how they had entombed Edmund's body in the little village church.

'Prepare my carriage, we must go to Wymondham and tell John what has happened.' Coralie nodded and went down to the keep to arrange the journey. They left as soon as a guard had been assembled, moving off quickly they soon reached Wymondham castle. John received them in the hall where they explained what had happened. Rachel comforted Margaret as best she could. John retired to the battlements, the place where all men of the family went to think. The news sunk in and he realised that there was now no opposition to his rule as Earl. He was sad at the demise of his uncle though he did not know him well as he had been away from Dunston many times. What should he do about the Dunston estates, he would think about that problem later. There were many people to inform of Edmund's death and he would have to arrange a memorial service in place of a funeral. He returned to Margaret, calmer and ready to comfort and support her.

On her return to Dunston, Margaret quickly summoned her tenants to the castle. Five days later they had all arrived and were assembled in the great hall. There was a hubbub of noise as they discussed among themselves as to the reason they had been summoned. Some had heard of the death of Sir Edmund and were speculating as to what would happen. A hush decended on the assembly as Margaret entered the hall. She was dressed in black with a jewelled neckless that Edmund had given to her on their wedding day.

'You have all, no doubt, heard of your lord's death in foreign lands.' Margaret stood in front of them all with her head held high and fixed them with her eyes. She turned and sat in the large chair that Edmund always used in the hall.

'Be seated,' she said, in a commanding voice. 'Sir Edmund has been absent from us fighting for our king and country many times, and we have survived. We shall continue to survive, and prosper, if we continue in the same way. My son, on his return, will be at my side and assist me in the work of the estate. You have enjoyed the method of farming that was laid down by Sir Edmund's father and I see no reason to change that. I rely on your support during this sad time. There will be a memorial service at Wymondham Abbey and a service here for all to attend.' Margaret started to rise when the tenant from Saxlingham called out. 'Lady Margaret, we offer our sympathies for your, and our, loss. You have our support.' There was a general murmur of agreement and Margaret raised a handkerchief to her face as she left the room.

Arthur gazed at the approaching dock of Portsmouth as their ship concluded it's voyage from the north of Spain. After several weeks at sea he was used to the roll and surge of a ship journeying home. They had put in at island of Jersey so as to avoid landing in France. His men joined him at the prow of the ship and he could feel their excitement as England came nearer. Arthur had shared out the gold that morning and instructed the men to keep quiet so as not arouse suspicion amongst the crew.

After they had docked and Arthur had paid the captain they went searching for horses to purchase for the final journey home. The town was still recovering from the disastrous fire started by the French forcing them to go out to local farms for the animals. No one wanted to delay so they set off at once, Arthur had gleaned as much information as he could from the men on the docks. That night they camped outside Winchester. On the morrow they headed north to avoid London, then east for Norfolk and home.

As they journeyed through the land Arthur had the feeling that all was not well in the country. They camped outside the villages and only ventured in to buy food. Bypassing Newbury they headed north east, as the flatter lands of east Anglia came nearer, they quickened their pace. On the last day of their travels, Arthur reminded them to say nothing of where the gold had come from, save that they had earned it fighting for various nobles whilst in the foreign lands. When, at last, they sighted the tower of Dunston castle, they raised a cheer.

It was late evening when they approached the castle. Arthur blew on his horn as they could see that the drawbridge was up. A guard appeared at the battlements and demanded to know who they were.

'Arthur Ivanson, lord of Dunston. Lower the drawbridge and go and tell Lady Margaret that her son has returned.'

The guard quickly disappeared and they could hear him running down to the gate. The drawbridge was lowered and Arthur's party rode into the keep. Dismounting they heard the shouts as a young lady came running to them, she made straight for Arthur who caught her in his arms. Red faced, Arthur turned to his men and said 'I hope you all are greeted by your families as enthusiastically as this.' Amid lots of laughter and ribald comments, they began to sought out their belongings from the pack horses and bidding farewell to Arthur, departed for their homes.

Holding Coralie at arms length, Arthur looked at her. 'Have you missed me as much as I have missed you?'

'She certainly has.' Arthur spun round to the new voice and found Margaret coming to great him. 'We will wait until you have recovered from your travel. After a meal you can tell us all that has happened, especially what happened to Edmund.'

Arthur recounted most of what had happened on their journey. Margaret was naturally upset at how Edmund met his death. Arthur assured her that everything had been done to try and save him and gave the reasons as to why they had left his body in Saint Llorene de la Muga. Margaret wanted to organise a return trip to recover Edmund's body, Arthur explained that it was safe and properly interned where it was and with the current situation in Europe it was not possible to attempt this. They were all going to be needed at home and he was going to start immediately in building up their military strength. The meal finished and they all retired to their rooms.

Arthur paced up and down in his room, he had gazed at Coralie during dinner and felt strong feelings come over him. Was it just that she was a beautiful women or were there deeper feelings? What ever it was he could not get her out of his mind. She had obviously thought about him and was pleased to see him home again. Her looks at him during dinner spoke volumes. The more he thought about her he could feel himself getting more and more aroused. Should he go to her room? He went to his door and opened it to find Coralie standing there.

'Did you really miss me?' He asked.

'Yes, I have. Can't you tell?' replied Coralie as she stepped into his arms. Their lips met and as they passionately embraced, Arthur drew her into the room and kicked the door shut.

As dawn broke the next morning, Arthur looked at the women laying next to him and thought about the passion that had entwined then. Coralie stirred and looked at him with a smile spreading over her face. He kissed her and she pulled him close. The warmth and softness of her body made him forget everything as they lost themselves in frantic coupling.

Chapter 47

John came down from the battlements where he had been pondering what to do. He decided that he would take over Dunston and add it to his fief so that he was truly lord of all his lands, after all Arthur was only an adopted son of his uncle and didn't have a real claim on Dunston. This would mean added income to his depleting funds. John did not manage the land as well as his father had and he had frittered away the gold that Arthur had given him on expensive horses, also refurnishing the castle. He went to find the lieutenant of his troops to arrange a visit to Dunston.

John looked at his assembled guards, would 300 be enough? He was about to mount his horse when Rachel came to him holding letters in her hand.

'I have a letter from William, he is staying in Italy and he has found a girl to marry. He would like us to go out to him for the wedding.'

'I will discuss it when I return. I don't know if I could leave the estate for that long,' replied John. He mounted his horse and led his men out of the castle leaving Rachel to worry about what he intended. She knew Arthur was not a man to be intimidated.

When they came in sight of Dunston castle, John's determination began to wane. He looked round at his men and wondered if it came to a fight would they support him? Too late now, he wanted, no, needed Dunston. They approached the drawbridge and gave a signal with a horn. The gate was opened and they rode into the keep.

Arthur was standing on the steps leading to the castle's main door. 'Welcome, John, where are you off to with such a large guard? Has there been an increase in outlaws that I have not heard about?'

'With unrest in the country it is wise to travel with guards.' replied John. 'Come in, mother will want news of Wymondham and your family.'

John climbed from his horse and ordered his guard to dismount and rest. Once they were in the castle John said that he wanted to talk to Arthur privately first. Arthur pointed out that his mother was in fact, the owner of the estate and should be present at all discussions. They went into the hall where Margaret and Coralie were sitting attended by maids and guards.

'How nice to see you John, you do not visit enough.'

John ignored the greeting and feeling very nervous he plunged into the reason for his visit.

'I have come to inform you that as Edmund is now dead I shall be governing the Dunston lands as the lord of the shire.' This speech was met by a stunned silence. Margaret recovered herself and stood up.

'A bold statement, John. Is this why you brought so many armed men? Edmund left me in sole charge of the castle and estates when he left to fight for the Prince. I shall not dishonour his name by handing over the estates to you, or anyone else. If you think you can take it by force then you do not know my son. Leave now while you can.'

John turned a bright red and his hand went to his sword but did not draw it as he felt the sharp point of Arthur's weapon as it pricked his neck.

'If I do not return to my men in the quarter of the hour, they will take the castle by force.' John flinched as he said this as the point of Arthur's sword pressed a little harder.

'Walk to the window,' said Arthur, pressing his sword a little more and a small trickle of blood ran down John's neck. John looked down from the window to see his men standing with their weapons at their feet and surrounded by archers, on the ground and on the battlements.

They went down to the keep where Arthur's men were collecting up the weapons from the ground. John's men were standing in a large group and offering no resistance. One archer, hidden at the back of the group, still had his bow hidden. He thought he would make a name for himself and be in a position for a good reward, he notched an arrow and took aim at Arthur. The moment he released, John turned to Arthur and opened his mouth to speak but all that came out was a gurgle as the released arrow struck his back and entered his heart. John fell to the floor, Arthur knelt down to him but John was dead.

There was a scuffle in the guards from Wymondham as two of the men had the archer down on the ground. One of them pulled out a dagger and sunk it into the man before Arthur's guards could get to them. Arthur stood as Margaret came to the door and said. 'Bring John in, lay him in a bedroom. I have sent for our apothecary.'

'I am afraid it is too late for that,' Arthur explained as he summoned the men to carry the body into the castle. 'Take the rest of these men to the kitchen and see that they are fed. I will come and talk to them in a while.' He escorted Margaret back into the castle and then went to the hall where they had laid John's body.

'Make a carriage ready to transport Sir John's body back to Wymondham. Tell the sergeant at arms to form an honour guard to escort the coach.' Arthur then left to go to his mother. He found her in her sitting room, being comforted by Coralie. Arthur told her what he had prepared and asked if she was fit to travel with them with Coralie. They would be better at comforting Rachel and explaining what had happened. Margaret agreed and went with Coralie to prepare for the journey.

They all assembled in the keep, the carriage with John's body, another carriage for the ladies, a mounted escort and two of the Wymondham guards as prisoners. They moved off towards Wymondham castle at a steady pace, Arthur pondered on how he was going to explain what had happened, if only John had not been so headstrong. They reached Wymondham as night was falling. Margaret and Coralie quickly went into the castle to find Rachel leaving Arthur organising John's body being taken to the hall to lay in state, as befitted the Earl.

The next day Arthur was walking the battlements of Wymondham Castle thinking about the events of the past day. The events had all happened so fast.

Why had John been so demanding, Arthur had only just returned from Spain. Was it the fact that Edmund had died and he thought that he should take the opportunity to take control of all of the shire? This did not give the reason to come to Dunston with the intention to take the castle by force. He made his decision and left the battlements to find his mother and Rachel.

He found Margaret sitting on her own in one of the side rooms, Rachel and Coralie had gone to the hall to pray beside the body of John.

'Mother, I have decided to take the position of Earl. I believe I have the right and I shall journey to Westminster as soon as possible to lay my claim before the Chancellor and the King. Someone has to take charge now and it must be one of the family so that we can continue the work that John, the first Earl, set up. Our Shire is unique and we must not let it fade away. While I am away in London I leave our interests in your hands. Use the men who are leaders such as, the Captain of the guards and the senior stewards. I shall return as quickly as I can, with good news I hope.'

Margaret replied that she had managed at Dunston while Edmund was away and she would adopt the same methods here at Wymondham.

John's funeral was arranged with the Abbot and would be held as soon as possible at the Abbey. Immediately after funeral Arthur was to leave for London with, after much pleading, Coralie to accompany him.

Chapter 48

Arthur stretched as he looked out of the window of their room. He had booked into a large Inn in the centre of the city as John had sold their London house when the Wymondham finances started to dwindle. He wondered what had happened to the money that Edmund had given him? Coralie stirred and Arthur turned and his thought was to return to her arms but he must not be late for his visit to the chancellor. He told her to rouse her maid and be ready in an hour.

Arthur explained the reason for his visit and waited outside Lord Langham's study. Eventually, after three hours, a clerk came to inform him that the chancellor had sent his request to the king and he was to go to Westminster where the king would rule on his position. Another four hours past until a page brought Arthur in front of Edward.'

'So, you want the Earldom of Norfolk I see. How do you expect me to grant this when you are not the eldest son?' Arthur explained the situation and how it had come about. He reminded Edward how he had fought for him and how he felt loyalty to him as well as his adopted father, Sir Edmund Ivanson. He had taken the name of Ivanson so that the family line could be continued. He also reminded the king, as he had Langham, of the taxes that were collected from the success of their method of farming in the shire. Edward dismissed him telling him to return in the morning for his decision.

Arthur and Coralie returned to the Inn to await the summons, this came sooner than expected when a courier came bearing a letter to attend a function at the palace, with his lady, that night. Coralie said that she had nothing to wear that was fitting and departed with her maid to find suitable attire.

The function turned out to be a grand dinner, with musicians and entertainers. Chancellor Langham had arranged to be seated next to Coralie and captured her attention for most of the evening. When they returned to the Inn Arthur wanted to know what they had been talking about.

'He wanted to know all about Dunston, how it was organised and was it the same at Wymondham. He also wanted to know when were we to marry. I told him that arrangements were to be made for the beginning of the coming month.' Coralie blushed as she looked at Arthur 'Was I right or have you other plans?' Arthur swept her into is arms and told her that he was going to ask this very night but his plan was not for next month but for next week.

Arthur was awakened early the next day by a persistent knock on their door. A messenger had arrived summoning him to Westminster at once. When he arrived he was taken to the Lord Chancellor who asked him to be seated. 'I have spoken to the king this very morning and he has agreed that your position of the Earl of Norfolk will will be confirmed at a ceremony four weeks from this date. We have taken into consideration that your blood line is not Ivanson but your loyalty to Sir Edmund was enough for the king to make this decision. I, personally, am very interested in your methods of running your estates.' (And the revenue it creates for the crown, thought Arthur.) Arthur was in high spirits as he hurried back to the Inn. They hastily packed and were soon on their way back to Wymondham.

Arthur was thoughtful on the way home: was there a hidden reason to the king making him Earl? Was Langham after more taxes? He must make the rounds of all the estates and make sure all landowners and tenants were farming as they should. Coralie noticed his thoughtfulness and wondered if it had anything to do with their forthcoming marriage. Arriving back at Wymondham Arthur set about organising the estates and meeting all the landlords and tenants. Four weeks later, true to his word, the Lord Chancellor sent papers to Arthur confirming his position as Earl.

Arthur sent letters to all the landlords and tenants inviting them to his marriage to Coralie. The castle became a hive of activity with preparations for the event. Margaret was in her element, rushing hither and thither organising everyone. When the great day came Arthur was busy greeting all the landlords and tenants who had accepted his invitation. There were some absentees and Arthur made a note to visit them as soon as possible.

The sun shone and the Abbot was at his best, he took the opportunity after the wedding service to anoint Arthur as Earl. As the couple left the Abbey the crowds of well wishers cheered them and threw flowers. Arriving back at the castle they sat down to a wedding feast where there was much toasting of the couple, and many soar heads the next morning.

Arthur woke and realised he was now a married man and was expected to raise a son and heir. He thought the time was right to make a start and pulled Coralie to him.

Three months went by in a whirl, Arthur trying to arrange matters of the shire and dealing with complaints from landlords and tenants, he decided to go to Norwich and hold court. He informed the Abbot of Norwich of his plan also the sheriff to prepare the castle for his visit, also to notify all landlords that were required to come to the castle whilst he was in residence. Arthur recalled when Edmund had done the same thing, riding into Norwich with full pomp and display. He decided to follow his adopted father's example and set about organising his military to have fresh surcoats so that he would create the right impression as the lord of the shire.

His arrival in Norwich was received with enthusiasm from the crowds that lined the streets. On his arrival at the castle he was informed that three of the landlords from the north coast did not agree to his appointment and were not attending. Arthur had expected as much and knew he would have to visit these estates as soon as possible. The Abbot was waiting in the grand hall and welcomed him most profusely. Arthur produced the parchment with the king's seal confirming his appointment. The Abbot read it and passed it to the sheriff who handed it back to Arthur. The new Earl sat on the seat that had been placed on a small diaz. 'Thank you all for attending today, I hope to meet all of you during my visit here. Some of you may think I am not fit for this title, too young and not of the family. Let me assure you that the experiences that I have had in these last few years would have taken most of you a lifetime. Sir Ivanson was more of a father to me than if he had sired me himself, proved by his handing me the family name to carry on. I intend to do just that and my first task will be to ensure that the farming methods that were started by Sir John are still being adhered to.' There was a general murmuring at this. 'I shall be visiting you all in due corse and am determined to see the shire flourish.' There was a burst of applause at this statement as Arthur rose and stepped down to meet the gathered throng.

Arthur stayed for five days which culminated in a high mass at the Abbey. He processed out of the city as he had entered with an even larger throng lining the streets. Arthur thought to himself that they might be cheering to see him go. As he rode homeward he thought over some of the comments that had been made, there was definitely a lot to do and would appear that John had done very little after his father had died. He looked forward to the challenging future and with Coralie at his side he felt that all things were possible.

Arthur's future was indeed challenging as England entered into a turbulent time., but that's another story.

The End

Lightning Source UK Ltd.
Milton Keynes UK
UKHW011030290720
367350UK00001B/8

9 781664 112186